Expect the unexpected...

First published 2012 by Walker Books Ltd
87 Vauxhall Walk, London SE11 5HJ

2 4 6 8 10 9 7 5 3 1

Text © 2012 Peter Cocks
Cover design by Walker Books Ltd
Image of figure © 2012 Getty Images, Inc.
Image of palm tree © 2012 Fotosearch / Getty Images, Inc.
Image of yacht © 2012 iStockphoto

This book has been typeset in Palatino and Pahuenga Cass

Printed and bound in Great Britain by Clays Ltd, St Ives plc

British Library Cataloguing in Publication Data:
a catalogue record for this book is available from the British Library

ISBN 978-1-4063-2728-1

www.walker.co.uk

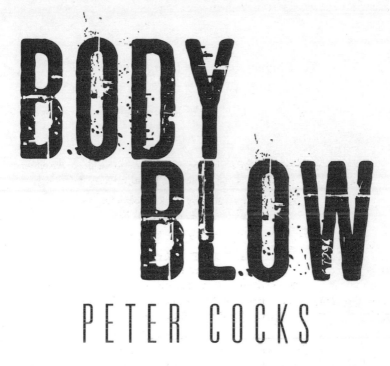

BODY BLOW

PETER COCKS

**WALKER
BOOKS**

For Davina, Rusty and George, with love

PROLOGUE

Donnie blew out a thin stream of smoke; a grey slipstream against the blue of the sky. He'd started to smoke cigars since he'd been down here. The fags were not much cheaper than at home, what with the euro and everything, whereas the la-di-das were cheap as chips. And here he had the time to sit back and enjoy a leisurely smoke on his sunbed.

It was hot.

The temperature averaged around twenty degrees all year, so it never got cold, but today it was pushing up into the thirties. Donnie stretched out his aching legs and fanned himself with a yellowing copy of yesterday's Sun, then took the last swig from his warming bottle of San Miguel. The beer wasn't cheap any more either. Donnie remembered when he had come out here years before and a handful of pesetas would buy a round. Now he had to be a little more careful and supplemented his beer drinking with Spanish brandy, which wasn't expensive and had plenty of kick, but could give you a very angry headache in the afternoon heat.

Cigars and brandy. Sun. Life could be worse, he thought.

He knew the day would come, once the heat was off, when he would be asked to get back to work. But for the moment, although it wasn't exactly what he'd had in mind, it was sweet.

Donnie had always imagined a whitewashed villa in the hills, with a pool and a stream of young birds in bikinis or less. The villa turned out to be as imaginary as the pay-off he had thought he might get. It wasn't a villa so much as a one-bedroom apartment in a block that had been built to separate retirement couples from their life savings. Most of the couples had long since gone, driven away by disco music, Germans and package hooligans on the piss; the last of them paid a third of the value to naff off back to Blighty and their gas fires. Paid by the family firm that now owned the whole block; the firm Donnie worked for. It was the kind of firm you never left. Once you were in, it was for life, or until they retired you in a wooden box.

The apartment wasn't that bad. It was clean and tidy, and Donnie had no possessions to clutter it up. If he poked his head over the balcony and cranked it ninety degrees to the left, he could just about see the sea. His bedroom had a ceiling fan, which he would watch on the nights he couldn't sleep because of the heat or the pounding house music, or if he hadn't had quite enough brandy to send him off. There was a shared swimming pool and Donnie would sometimes attempt a couple of early-morning lengths and a wallow, once the vomit of the previous night's revelries had been skimmed off and a hefty dose of chlorine had been added by the concierge.

The complex had a bar, where he would have his morning coffee, full English and first brandy of the day – and his last, near enough to manage the stagger back upstairs to the fourth floor. His favourite bar was the one behind him now on the scruffy end of the beach, a flyblown place with a faded palm roof and no bongo-bongo music to spoil his P&Q. They did a nice plate of sardines or squid rings for lunch, with chips.

The rough, black cigar was beginning to taste harsh and he stubbed it into the sand at his side, next to the dry corpses of others. He squirted a gobbet of white sunscreen over his reddening expanse of belly and rubbed it in, matting the forest of hair, which, he noticed, was beginning to turn white.

Donnie blinked the sweat from his eyes and squinted to his left, where his lady was lying on her back on the sunbed next to him.

She hadn't been quite what he had imagined either, with a few more miles on the clock and more upholstery than he had fantasized. He guessed mid-forties, built for comfort not for speed, but not bad-looking at all.

She was Spanish, Valerie. He'd met her in a bar where she was serving. She had laughed at the way he said her name, explained that in her part of Spain they pronounced "V" as "B".

He had told her his name was Vic, Victor Value, and she'd repeated it: "Bictor Balue". He'd told her he was a builder.

Donnie had thought she was cute, with her accent and lively black eyes, and he had laughed for the first time in a while. She seemed completely comfortable with him, treated him like a cuddly old bear. She'd said her ex had been a heroin addict, some skinny little rat of a junkie long since banged up just outside Málaga. She had said she liked a strong man.

A big man.

Bic and Balerie. He chuckled to himself and sat up. Thought he might have a rare splash in the sea to cool the stirrings of lust in his black Speedos.

Then sat down again, any desire suddenly extinguished.

He recognized the man walking up the beach, even with the sun behind him; knew his silhouette – the wide shoulders and muscular physique – although the round gut sticking out from his unbuttoned Hawaiian shirt like a watermelon was new. Donnie also recognized the hair, the blond, wavy mullet that hadn't changed since they'd first met back in the Eighties.

Donnie looked at the sulky-looking brass who held the mullet's hand, long enough to think tit-job. *He looked at the two heavies, one black, one white; who walked a couple of paces behind them on the shoreline. The brass and the muscle would change on a monthly basis, Donnie knew. But the mullet was still the same: leopards never change their spots.*

Donnie fanned out his copy of The Sun *and covered his face and chest with it, like a holidaymaker having an afternoon nap. He breathed in the smell of hot newsprint, the scandalous news stories of economic despair, sex and crime from back home.*

And as Donnie hid, waiting for the man to pass, he knew that his temporary retirement would soon be at an end.

I

Novillada

Novilladas *are bullfights that use bulls of three to four years old. The bullfighters are amateurs who have not yet taken part in the "alternativa", the rites-of-passage fight at which they will become matadors.*

ONE

It was raining again.

Rain, rain and more rain. And when it didn't rain, it went back to being grey and cold.

It had been more than six months since I had been shot in the stomach by Donnie Mulvaney and left for dead. Four months since his boss, Tommy Kelly, had been given three life sentences. Every time it rained, the scars on my stomach seemed to ache and I would instinctively put my hand inside my shirt to touch the puckered skin around the entry wound.

I looked out across the wet streets and beyond, to where the stubby, red-brick bodies of disused pottery kilns were dotted across the landscape like a beaten terracotta army.

I drew the curtains and climbed back into my warm bed. I checked my watch: ten-thirty. With any luck I might be able to sleep till lunchtime.

Sleep off the boredom of half the day.

I had been up here for a while, staying at my mum's in an anonymous street in a suburb of Stoke-on-Trent. It had been judged the safest place for me to cool my heels.

I had almost forgotten the name Eddie Savage. Had put it behind me, wanting to move on. My criminal intelligence service bosses had told me that, to all intents and purposes, Eddie Savage was dead. Dead to the few friends I had made on the case, dead to the Kelly crime family; alive simply as a code name on an intelligence file.

My mother called me by my real name sometimes, but mostly just called me "love". Protective. She had good cause.

I had spent eight weeks in hospital in London. The bullet hole in my stomach had healed relatively quickly, and all that remained was a thumbprint-sized scar, still thick and red with a few holes where it had been stitched up. It looked like a second belly button.

The lung had been more complicated.

It had collapsed, which was agony, and then it had become infected, which was more painful still. The fluid they were draining off it turned from pink, through yellow, to pale green. I was on morphine and running a high temperature, hallucinating about people being sliced up, shot to bits, burnt and thrown off bridges into vats of wet cement. These horrifying visions were closer to the reality than most people could have imagined, and disturbingly they became confused with memories of Tommy Kelly's daughter, Sophie, my desire for her warped by violent nightmares.

At one point my temperature went through the roof and I had a seizure. My busted ribs refused to heal and kept me on my back and in constant pain. It was a nightmarish daily cycle of pain, painkillers, fever, vomiting, more pain, more morphine, sweats, visions, broken sleep and back to pain.

Hell.

My weight went down to forty-five kilos and the faces that looked over my bed every day had started to appear worried. My mentor, Tony Morris, had come in to see me one afternoon and the look in his eyes made me wonder if I didn't have long left to live. And you know what? I didn't care. Slipping under the morphine blanket would have been a merciful release from what I was going through, and part of me would have liked to have seen the guilt on Tony's face if I had croaked.

After all, Tony had got me into this mess in the first place.

Finally, somehow I turned a corner and found myself up and shuffling around the ward, pushing along a trolley that held my saline drip and lung drain. Then I went into therapy.

Post-traumatic stress disorder, she had said. PTSD.

Dr Reeta Patel was my shrink. A specialist, trained in intelligence, who would know and understand what I had been through. She was young; brisk and efficient in her white coat, but there was warmth and kindness in her dark brown eyes.

Every rattle or door slam made me flinch, every noise a potential fear-inducing explosion. A car alarm could reduce me to tears. I told Reeta and she said it was normal to feel like this after the kind of events I'd been through. She had treated a lot of shell-shocked soldiers and didn't think my case was too bad – compared with having my legs blown off by an Afghan mine. She said it was because I was beginning to deal with things, that they were starting to come to the surface.

"I don't want to think about those things," I told her. "But my mind keeps playing them over and over again."

"Again, quite normal," Reeta said. "You've been mentally scarred by them. They're imprinted on your mind."

She said it was also common to forget the nice stuff, as if my brain had rejected the memory of all the good things that had ever happened to me. My sense of safety and trust had been shattered, she explained, but the way forward was not to avoid the trauma that had brought me this far, but to relive it. I needed to go through the feelings; identify my emotions, put them into perspective.

So I agreed to her sessions. Cognitive therapy, she called it.

They made me feel a little better. I felt flattered, just talking about myself – and my experiences seemed to interest her.

I told Reeta how I'd pulled Sophie Kelly, the best-looking girl I had ever seen. How I had fallen in love with her, but how those emotions were now mixed up with the bad feelings about her old man. How I had used Sophie to get close to Tommy Kelly, her dad, who ran the largest, slickest, most violent crime organization in South London. I felt guilty about her, but weirdly also about him. Guilty that I'd gained their trust, and love, to gather intelligence against them for Tony's organization.

"Tommy took me under his wing," I explained. "He treated me like a son."

"Does he have a son?" Reeta asked.

"Yes," I said. "That was the trouble. Jason, his son, was – is – a psycho. He was up to his neck in drink and drugs, porn, dog fights … the lot."

"He sounds charming." Reeta smiled.

I gave half a laugh. "Oh, he is," I said. "He'll be right at home where he is now, in Belmarsh. He'll have plenty of mates."

"Did you get on?"

"He hated me," I said. "He hated the fact that his family liked me, that his dad liked me."

"Do you think his dad preferred you?" Reeta asked. "Were you the son he would have liked?"

"Yeah," I admitted. "Probably." Again, images flashed through my mind: in the car with Tommy, sailing in Croatia, looking at paintings.

Like father and son. I had no father to speak of, and the idea of a father figure had appealed to me.

"So do you feel betrayed by Tommy Kelly?"

I thought about it for a moment.

"No," I said finally. "He did the right thing in the end. He looked after his own. Blood's thicker than water and all that. Even though he knew it would shaft him, his priority was to look out for Jason, love him or hate him, his own son. If anything, I betrayed Tommy."

"You sound as if you admire him," Reeta said.

"I suppose I do in a way." Despite the ruthlessness of the gang he ran and the violence he approved, I did have

15

a sneaking admiration for Tommy Kelly. I felt sick when I thought back to fighting him out on the marshes, when I remembered smashing my fist into his face.

Despite knowing that the bloke was an arch-villain, in my heart of hearts it had felt wrong.

"Do you feel betrayed by *anyone*, Eddie?" Reeta held me in her gaze.

I thought about the bloke who had been around all through my childhood. The uncle figure who had been a support for me, my mum and my brother but who had ultimately recruited my brother and me into intelligence work.

"Yes," I said. "Tony Morris."

TWO

I'd thought a lot about Tony Morris. Especially while I'd been stuck in that shithole of a hospital with so much time to think. Like I said, Tony was responsible for getting me into this mess. He had been the old trusted family friend – a copper, I'd thought. But after my brother Steve's death I'd soon discovered that he was involved in the darker and more sinister world of intelligence too.

Intelligence. From where I was sitting it seemed more like stupidity. *My* stupidity.

I felt like Tony had taken advantage of me. I'd totally trusted him, yet he'd capitalized on my grief for my brother and manipulated me to work for him and his organization. They needed someone like me, and Tony knew I'd do it when I found out it could help me discover exactly how Steve had been killed.

Now, the best part of a year later, I'd changed my identity, come close to death on several occasions, been beaten up, cut and shot twice, yet as far as I could work out, Tony had never even been in danger of spoiling his

Eighties haircut or scuffing his leather jacket.

In another session, Reeta asked me about Steve, murdered by the Kelly gang.

"I think I'm past grieving," I said truthfully. Although understanding Steve's secret life had been my main reason for accepting Tony's offer to work in intelligence, I hadn't really thought about him for a while.

"Really?" Reeta asked. "Don't you think that the way you're feeling now is partly due to his death?"

I shrugged. Maybe.

"Steve was my hero when I was growing up," I said. To my surprise, I felt tingling in my nose and my nostrils flared involuntarily. Fat tears sprung to my eyes, and before I knew it I was crying, talking between sobs and wiping away tears and snot with the back of my hand.

Reeta handed me a box of tissues.

"I wanted to be like him," I cried. "I worshipped the ground he walked on."

"So what happened to change that?" Reeta asked.

"He changed," I said. "He was using…"

"Drugs?"

"Dope, cocaine, ketamine, E, the lot… He lost the plot."

Reeta held my hand as my tears began to subside. "It's hard to find out that our heroes have feet of clay," she said. "Steve was only human."

I blew my nose and looked into her kind brown eyes, realizing that I already felt a little better.

"Thanks, Reeta," I said.

*   *   *

I felt a *lot* better when I saw Reeta again a couple of days later. After the last session I had been thinking about her. I had become dependent on her. I found myself looking forward to my therapy so I could see her.

She made me feel safe.

"You look better, Eddie," she said as I walked in. It was a bright morning and the sun streaked in through the vertical hospital blinds. It was true. I did look better, and I felt better than I had for months. On a day like this I could almost feel cheerful, like spring was in the air.

"So, how do you feel?" she asked, swinging round in her desk chair and looking me over. She smiled, showing straight teeth, white against her brown skin.

"Not bad," I said. "Not so many dreams. I've been outside quite a bit."

I had not even stepped out of the hospital doors for the first six weeks, but since my last session I'd ventured into the grounds. There were daffodils dotted around the grass and a positive vibe in the air. My mum had visited and was relieved to see me looking better. One day I had sat on a bench in the sun and started reading a book from the library called *The Catcher in the Rye*. It was about an American kid in the 1950s; about him getting expelled from school, being depressed and confused and ending up in a mental home. It probably wasn't the kind of thing I should have been reading, but it made me laugh out loud.

"Apparently they're nearly ready to discharge you," Reeta said.

My positive feelings shrank in my gut. I suddenly felt scared, not ready.

"How do you feel about that?"

"Not sure," I admitted. "A bit scared, if I'm honest."

"You need to take the first step. But I'm going to recommend that you go to group therapy once a week, just so you can meet other people who have been through similar experiences."

I pulled a face. Sitting in a group talking about myself wasn't really my thing. Not to mention that there wasn't much I *could* talk about. Most of my memories were classified.

Reeta laughed at my reaction. "It'll be a safety net," she said. "And I'll always be at the end of a phone."

"Will you?" I found myself staring at her bare knees, smooth beneath her white coat. She was wearing strappy sandals and I noticed her toenails had been painted dark purple. For a second I thought about touching her knee, then checked myself.

Reeta seemed to clock it. She gave me a bit of a schoolmarm look and adjusted her skirt across her legs. "I think you're feeling a lot better," she commented.

"Will I still be able to see you?" I asked, suddenly panicky. I realized that I was beginning to sound needy. That I had thought about little else but Reeta for days. "I just ... really like you," I blurted out.

"It's quite usual for patients to ... well, bond with their therapists," Reeta said kindly. "I make you feel better, but that's because you *are* feeling better. You're just associating those feelings with me."

I could have been forgiven for being confused. She looked great that morning.

"I think you're substituting me for someone you really love," Reeta added. "Don't you?"

She was right. I was searching for something, or someone, that might fill the yawning gap Sophie Kelly had left in my life. I had not seen her since Tommy had been collared.

"Maybe," I admitted.

Reeta got up and brushed herself down. I stood up too. She held out her hand and I shook it. "Good luck," she said.

"Thanks for helping me," I said. "So, I suppose a date is out of the question?"

She laughed, hugged me briskly and kissed my cheek. "Let me know how you get on."

"I will," I said, amazed at my brass neck and lack of inhibition – me, an eighteen-year-old, trying it on with a doctor in her thirties.

I guessed I must have been feeling a great deal better. Or maybe I had just lost all sense of what was appropriate. Maybe my experiences had skewed my behaviour.

Maybe I'd become a loose cannon.

THREE

It didn't take long for Stoke-on-Trent to bring me back down to earth again.

I left the Royal London Hospital on a sunny morning. Tony Morris had turned up to see if I wanted driving to my mum's in Stoke. I declined his offer, said I was happy to take the train. He seemed disappointed. I think he wanted to talk, get something off his chest, but I wasn't in the mood to let him feel any better about himself. As far as I knew, he'd got what he wanted with half the Kelly family banged up in Belmarsh and I was the one still suffering for it.

I was feeling the loss of Sophie more strongly than ever. The thought of not seeing her ever again left a sick-feeling emotional hole in my stomach. I would have killed to see her again.

"I'll give you a lift up to Euston then," Tony said. He opened the door of his bashed-up silver Beemer for me.

I thought it would be childish to turn down a lift across town, plus I had a heavy bag I didn't fancy dragging on and off the Tube.

"OK," I muttered. "Thanks."

We drove in silence as far as London Bridge. Tony put on Heart FM to dilute the atmosphere. I looked across at the reclaimed power station on the South Bank.

"Tate Modern," I said, for lack of anything else to say. Maybe I was trying to show Tony how cultured I was. How much I had learned under the wing of Tommy Kelly.

"Full of shit, isn't it?" Tony laughed. "Haven't they got a load of bricks they spent a million quid on or something? And an unmade bed? A kid could do most of the stuff in there."

I remembered the museum's Rothko room, which I had visited with Tommy, and the pictures he had collected – OK, nicked. How it had been the villain who had helped me see the point of modern art, to see things on a bigger, more abstract scale.

Tommy Kelly had broadened my world view; Tony Morris's idea of culture was Barbra Streisand at The O2.

We drove along the Embankment. Everywhere we passed brought back memories of nights out with Sophie, or places I had visited with her or her dad. Everything reminded me of them; they felt like the good times. Tony turned up towards Euston.

"Let me know if you need anything, mate, won't you?" he said.

"Yeah," I grunted. He pulled into a parking bay in a street near the station and took a brown envelope from his jacket.

"Oh no," I said. What was he trying to get me to do now?

He handed me the envelope. "You've got a new set of IDs there."

I drew out a passport, driving licence and bank card, all with a new name on them: Daniel Reeves. The name looked odd and unfamiliar. My real name had almost been forgotten. I felt as if I was building up layers of personality, like the skins of an onion.

"Danny Reeves," Tony said. "Just to keep you safe. You're still Eddie Savage to us, but Danny to everyone else, OK?"

"I'm not working…" I began to panic again.

"No," he assured me. "It's nothing to do with … you know, work. It's for your security."

I pulled out a smaller envelope full of cash. "What's this for then?" I asked bitterly. "Blood money?"

"It's just some wedge, mate. A bit extra to tide you over."

I looked inside the envelope. There must have been a grand or three in twenties.

"Treat your mum to something nice," he suggested.

"Cheers," I said. I made to get out of the car, but Tony grabbed my elbow and held me back for a moment.

"Eddie," he said. "I'm sorry. We let you down. You were never meant to end up in that mess. Something went wrong."

"Yeah, too right," I said. "I got shot."

"No, mate," he said. "I know that, but something else went tits up. We had you tracked all the way, but we think someone else inside the gang stitched Tommy up."

"*What?*" Tony had my attention now.

24

"We heard they were heading for Long Reach before we got your tip-off. Someone else wanted them out of the way."

What did that mean? That all my efforts had been a waste of time? I felt enough of a patsy already: worked, manipulated and turned over without knowing the whole truth.

"Does Tommy know?"

"Hard to say," Tony answered. "You beat him half to death, which he probably took as a sign that you weren't exactly batting for his team. I'm not sure *he'll* be looking for another suspect."

"Whatever," I said. I realized I didn't actually care. My part of that job was over. All I wanted to do was forget about it and live a normal life.

Tony was about to say something else, but the look on my face made him think again.

"I wouldn't hurt you for all the tea in China, mate," he said finally.

Tea's cheap, I thought.

"Go back to your mum's. Have a good rest. Clear your mind."

"Sure, Tony," I said. I shook his hand and got out of the car, lugging my bag towards the 1.00 p.m. Manchester train.

"Take care," he said. I glanced back at him. Could have sworn he mouthed "Love ya" as I slammed the car door.

The train pulled in to Stoke-on-Trent an hour and forty later. The adverts for art exhibitions and expensive underwear, featuring glossy girls with heart-breaking figures, had disappeared on the outskirts of London. All the station at Stoke had to proclaim, apart from its name, was an advert for Wright's Pies. At least I won't starve, I thought.

I got a mini cab outside the station. It was hot and smelt of sickly air freshener, and the driver had the heat whacked up. He asked me if I'd seen the football, his strong Midlands accent foreign to my ears. I said I hadn't and the conversation soon ground to a halt, which suited me. We drove under Victorian railway bridges and around a grey, anonymous tangle of ring roads. The names on the road signs looked strange and almost biblical to me: Etruria, Alsager, Burslem. Others just plain "oop north" stupid: Tittensor, Knutsford, Sneyd.

We headed into Burslem, past a football stadium.

"Port Vale," the cabbie said, as if the world was navigated around football grounds. A factoid popped into my mind: Robbie Williams was their famous fan.

My mum's house was in a long, red-bricked terrace, every house the same as its neighbour except for individual door knockers and wacky house numbers or names.

The sun was still shining; it was a nice day. But to me the overall impression was as dull as ditchwater. Like the titles of "Coronation Street".

I decided "EastEnders" was more my thing.

Some net curtains twitched as we slowed to 5 mph, peered at the numbers, then stopped. The house appeared well looked after, and after another twitch of the curtains, Mum opened the door and ran into the street. She threw her arms around me and hugged me so hard I couldn't breathe. I'd seen her only a week before but I thought she might break my neck, or at the very least chew a lump out of my cheek.

I paid the driver with a twenty and didn't ask for change. He looked like his lottery numbers had come up. I didn't have any idea of the value of money any more. I had been in a different world. I was like someone who had just come back from the South Pole.

"Come on in," Mum said. "The kettle's on."

FOUR

Within seconds I had a steaming mug of tea in one hand and a bacon sandwich in the other.

"You're not eating properly," my ma tutted. "You're too thin." She was standing over me, looking at me the way only mothers can – as if the eating of a bacon sarnie was an act of genius.

Mum's sister Cath was grinning at us from her position on the sofa. She'd been living with mum for a couple of months while I'd been in hospital.

Cath is about ten years younger than the old girl. She spent a long time travelling and came back from India last year. She looks a bit like mum might have looked had she not had a violent, alcoholic husband, a dead eldest son and a shot-up younger one. Cath is skinny and tanned with scraped-back, blondish hair, wears faded denims and has a snake tattoo on her forearm. She smokes roll-ups, likes a beer and is more of a laugh than Mum, apart from when she's had a glass of wine or two and starts spouting about star signs, spirits and all that New Age stuff.

The three of us sat and chatted all through that first afternoon. Of course I couldn't tell them much about what had gone on, as most of it was classified. I was vague with the details. Said that I'd been caught in the crossfire but it was all behind me now. Mum looked relieved. She had never wanted me to follow in Steve's footsteps, she said, and was glad I had seen sense. I assured her that I had; that all I wanted was a new start, a quiet life, and Mum believed me.

At the time, I believed it myself.

We had a balti that night and a few drinks. "This is nothing like the real thing," Cath told us. "The vegetarian stuff in the South is fantastic. Light and delicious. Bhel puris, masala dosas..." She licked her lips at the memory and looked back at her plate with something like disappointment. "Baltis don't even exist in India, they were invented in Birmingham."

"And we all know Brummies have no taste," I chipped in. It was an easy joke.

In truth, I was enjoying the balti. I just wished I could talk about some of the things I'd seen, places I'd been, stuff that had happened. But my training kicked in and I managed to keep it locked up in a box in my mind. It would have done nobody any good, particularly Mum, to know exactly what I'd been through.

They asked me if I had any plans. I said I wanted to start over. I didn't want to go back to college or anything like that. I just wanted to get a job. For some reason I had my mind set on working in a big DIY store. I'd got an interview at the job centre the following day. Mum and

Cath looked at each other and shrugged, a bit surprised, but then if it was what I wanted to do… I knew I just needed a structure, somewhere safe, not too demanding, somewhere I could just concentrate on practical things.

From now on, I was going to live an ordinary life.

The interview pulled me up sharpish.

My naive vision of what an ordinary life might be like revolved around a simple idea of routine and security. It left out the uncomfortable details of eight hours a day stacking shelves, humping compost around and drinking instant coffee out of cracked mugs while assembling this season's barbecue offers. All for a fiver an hour.

"You didn't last long," Cath said, smiling as I returned home from the job centre. Mum put the kettle on for yet another cup of tea.

"It wasn't me," I told them.

"Course it wasn't, kid," Cath said. She kissed my cheek and ruffled my hair. "Wouldn't do for me, neither." She looked into the kitchen at Mum, fussing with teacups and toast. "How about we take the boy down The Greyhound for a pint later?" Cath suggested. "Get fish and chips on the way back?"

There was a slight urgency in her voice, as if she would do anything rather than stay in with the two of us and the sense of things unsaid in the air.

Mum brightened. "Why not?" she said.

Mum looked better once she was in the pub. She'd put on a bit of lippy and was laughing with me and Cath over a gin and tonic. We were talking about how the two of them had become a pair of batty old sisters and should maybe adopt a tribe of feral cats or, Cath suggested, a pair of eighteen-year-old Filipino boys.

On impulse, Mum grabbed my hand across the table and smiled at me. I pulled away instinctively, not wanting the little boy treatment. Then I gave in and squeezed back.

"I've got my hands full with this eighteen-year-old," she said.

Mum went and got some more drinks and started chatting to a neighbour at the bar. While she was away, Cath gave me some of the benefit of her experience.

"Don't look back," she said. "Try and live in the moment. If there's one thing I've learned, it's to live in the moment. The here and now. This is a great night, here with my sister and my nephew, having a drink." She took another pull on her lager. "That's it. Don't dwell on the past, and tomorrow's another day."

I looked around the friendly local pub, the laughing faces, the twinkling fruit machine and the easy-listening records on the jukebox. It could be worse, I thought.

But something was still chewing away at me. I thought of my mum, of Cath and her string of failed relationships, her travels to India, Thailand and Australia in search of … well, whatever she was searching for. Peace of mind, maybe. She clearly hadn't found it, and neither had I.

What I felt was like an itch, somewhere in my middle. One that needed scratching.

Cath started talking about karma; putting good stuff in so it will come back around. She'd had a couple by this time, and I could detect a whiff of grass. I guessed she'd had a spliff before we'd left home and maybe another puff out in the pub garden. She was on a roll with the New Age stuff.

"Sow goodness and you will reap goodness," she said, like some cut-price guru. "Sow bad stuff and you'll only reap evil."

I tried to think about what I'd been sowing. For anyone's money, it didn't look like I'd been spreading joy.

FIVE

My life settled into a dull routine, watching daytime telly and old DVDs back to back. I couldn't handle action movies: they made me jumpy. I'd have a toasted sandwich for lunch, then maybe a walk round the grey, drizzly park, chatting with retired dog walkers or avoiding truant kids who smoked weed and carved their names into the skate park. In the evening, Mum would cook spag bol, or one of her few variations on the theme of mince, and Cath would come back from her part-time job and pour herself a glass of red. We'd chat for a bit, the details of dull days. Then Cath would nip out the back for a fag and come back smelling of grass and start the New Age chat again.

Of the almost non-existent family I had, I probably got on with Cath best. She was easy-going, not as buttoned up as her sister, and with her being that bit younger, we saw eye to eye on quite a few things. It was just her reliance on astrology to guide her life, her conspiracy theories and what she called her "submission to destiny" that sometimes got on my tits.

She was a bright woman and I was pretty sure destiny hadn't decreed that she worked as a classroom assistant or that I worked in DIY. In my view you shape your own destiny, but I felt I was losing a grip on mine.

After the fourth day of waking up feeling like a sack of shit and going back to bed until mid-afternoon, I decided I had to do something. I put the SIM in my disused mobile and dialled.

"Dr Reeta Patel…" a voice said.

"Reeta, it's Eddie." She brightened on the other end of the line. I tried to as well, but I knew my voice sounded dull and flat.

"How are you getting on?" she asked.

"I was doing OK," I said, "but I seem to have slipped into a black hole."

"You're feeling depressed?" she asked.

"No, I think it's called Stoke-on-Trent," I joked and she laughed. "Really, I don't feel good. I feel like I'm sliding back to where I was a couple of months ago."

"It's pretty normal," she assured me. "Most people will have a relapse at some point, panic attacks or depression. It will pass. Would you like me to prescribe you something?"

"I don't want to become even more of a zombie than I am already," I said. "Can I come and see you?"

She paused. "I don't think that would be helpful, Eddie."

"Let me come and see you." I saw an opening and was trying, unsuccessfully, to hide the desperation in my voice.

"I think you should try some group therapy, as I suggested," she said, the brisk professionalism returning to her voice. "It would be a backwards step if you came to see me now. You need to socialize. Let me give you a number."

I waited, disappointed, while she read out a phone number and I wrote it down.

SIX

I clocked Gav Taylor as an ex-serviceman before he even opened his mouth. His jeans were pressed and his trainers were too clean, like they were ready for inspection. I could read people from a few signals like this. He wore a surfer thong round his neck that didn't seem to belong to him. His hair was growing out from a shorter cut that didn't look like it fit his head.

The real giveaway, though, was the twisted red scar that ran from his forehead, through his hairline and appeared again behind his ear. Whatever had hit him must have taken a big chunk out of the side of his head. He limped, too.

There were about six of us in the group. We were in a big room in a health centre attached to the local hospital. It had plastic chairs and a shiny laminate floor, colourful posters on the wall and small flyers proclaiming the nasty effects of drugs, fags and unprotected sex. Jeremy Kyle ranted silently from a flat-screen TV high on the wall. The room smelt of the stale cake and instant coffee we were offered. I was the youngest, a few years younger than Gav. Then there were three women and one other bloke, who chewed his fingernails and looked around nervously. One of the women smiled at me in a sickly way, her mouth downturned at the corners. The other two looked at the floor.

It wasn't a cheery group.

The therapist came in and smiled at everyone in a practised way. She had shortish, dyed red hair and dangly earrings. My heart dropped when she said she was going to ask us to introduce ourselves before going on to do a few warm-up exercises.

I felt like a plum as I had to say my name not only once, but then again as we threw a beanbag from one to another. To build trust, the therapist said.

"Danny ... Gav ... Sharon ... Geoff ... Pam ... Deb..."

Everyone calling their names out in dull, depressed voices made me want to run and Gav looked even more uncomfortable than me. The urge grew in me as the team leader, Kate, took off her Birkenstocks and invited us to lie on the floor to try some relaxation techniques.

I lay down next to Gav, who seemed reluctant – or unable – to lie flat. It was as if the vulnerability of the position left him open to attack. I felt the same.

Defensive.

The deep breathing was OK. It was when she put some whale song on the CD player that I began to crack.

I opened an eye, rolled my head round to the left and saw Gav Taylor, eyes wide open in fear. He looked like someone had asked him to put on high-heeled shoes and use a handbag. He caught my eye and I began to giggle.

"Fook this for a game of soldiers," he said.

I had to agree.

Half an hour later, Gav dumped two pints of lager on the table as if they were a challenge. There were a few hard-core drinkers at the bar of The Brown Jug and some office workers with halves and scampi and chips in baskets for their lunches.

"Going to take more than whale song and a couple of beanbags to sort my fookin' head out, Danny mate," he said, tapping his skull. His sentences were punctuated with "fooks" like they were commas. "A couple of fookin' pints work better. Cheers!"

I gulped down a mouthful of chilled lager. It *was* good. Better.

We talked about this and that for a few minutes, the cold beer relaxing us. I looked at the scar on his head. "What happened?"

"Roadside bomb," he said, matter-of-fact. "Helmand Province."

"Afghanistan?"

He nodded. "I was out there with the QRL," he said. "Queen's Royal Lancers. The Death or Glory Boys, they call us." He laughed drily. "Should have changed it to the Death Boys. I saw more of that than I did glory."

"Did you lose mates?"

He nodded again. "I was in Iraq before that, when they topped Saddam." Gav took a swig of his beer as his voice went croaky. "Three lads, mates from here, Stokeys like me. Adrian Turton, Ben and Ant Carter. Took a direct hit in an Armoured Recovery Vehicle. Burnt to death."

I shook my head. He emptied his beer and I bought him another.

"Thing is," he continued as I returned from the bar, "I should have been in that ARV with them. While they were out there, I was in the sickbay shitting through the eye of a needle with dysentery. Dysentery's pretty bad, but burning to death in a steel trap's worse, your skin peeling off and your bones frying in your own fat. Suppose you could call me lucky. Lost me three best mates, though."

"How old were they?"

"Eighteen, nineteen and twenty three," he said. "Ben and Ant were brothers, so their mother lost both her kids." His nostrils flexed and his eyes darted about.

"So you ended up in Afghanistan after that?" I asked.

"Yep, promoted from Trooper to Corporal Gavin Taylor, QRL, by the time I was twenty-one. Got a brag-rag for holding a position single-handed in Basra."

"A what?"

"Brag-rag ... a medal, well, a medal ribbon to stick on me battledress, to keep me keen."

"Was Afghanistan worse than Iraq?"

"I reckon," Gav said. "It's a fookin' hellhole. The Afghans are hard bastards; ruthless. You might think they're simple towel heads, but they're cunning. You lie awake, knowing you've got better forces and weapons, but you still shit your pants thinking one of them's going to creep up and slit your throat in the middle of the night."

We were into our third pint by now; the afternoon was drifting away in front of us. The pub was emptying and ex-Corporal Gav Taylor was warming to his theme, and I wasn't going anywhere now. I wanted to know more.

"The Taliban are the worst of the lot. Even though they were supposed to have been overthrown ten years ago, they rule the place and they support al-fookin'-Qaeda. Between them they train most of the world's terrorists."

"Did you have much contact with the Taliban?" I asked.

Gav laughed. "Mostly at the end of a gun barrel," he said. "But we had to go out on patrols and you'd never know where they were hiding, or what they'd planted in your path. They'd put the fear of God into us," he said. "Or Allah."

"But you must have been better kitted out…"

"They spooked us out," Gav explained. "Three of our lads went out on a patrol. One of them's a Sikh, right? Rajinder Singh Sidhu. From Leicester. So he's not even a Muslim. One of Raj's patrol steps on a mine and kills two of them instantly. Raj is knocked out cold and when he wakes up with a couple of broken ribs, he finds he's been captured by the Taliban. They've thrown him in a Transit and driven him to some wasteground, somewhere in the outskirts of Kandahar. They tell him he's not righteous, that he's a traitor and is fighting for the enemy. That he must convert to Islam or he'll die. Now Raj has been a devout Sikh since he's born. He's campaigned to wear his turban and grow his hair an' beard and all that, and he's not going to be told what to do by some ignorant twenty-year-old sect who beat women with sticks and run around like homicidal lunatics off *Indiana Jones*."

I began to visualize a heroic ending where this Sikh warrior beat off a dozen Taliban single-handed, rescued the girl and rode off on a white horse, like in the movies.

"What happened?" I asked.

Gav had gone quiet. He took a sip of his beer and swallowed hard. Stared into the space ahead of him.

"They tortured him. Stripped him and dragged him for miles, roped by his feet to the back of a jeep. Hacked his hair off with a knife, scalped him. Drove a power drill through his kneecaps ... then they sawed his head off with a bread knife."

"Shit."

"And how do I know?" he said. "Because they filmed the whole thing on his own phone then dumped it, with his body and his head, outside our camp two days later. I found him. Found his head. Found his phone. Watched it. Fookin' animals."

"I'm sorry," I said. I flashed back momentarily to my brother's body washed up in the Thames, a "K" carved into his skull by the animal Donnie Mulvaney. But compared to Gav's comrades, Steve had been treated almost humanely.

"So," he went on, "every time I'm out on patrol after that, I've got images of old Raj's nut coming off ... I hear his screams in my head. I can remember them now, crackling out of his moby. I start to wish myself dead, a clean kill, a shot to the head or a great big bang. Anything rather than be captured by them savages. Coming home

41

in a Union Jack box isn't the worst thing that can happen.

"Turns out, when I got my one, it wasn't so clean. These roadside bombs – home-made IEDs they call them, Improvised Explosive Devices – are messy bastards. The Taliban take a biscuit tin full of nuts and bolts, nails and glass and a fag-packet-sized lump of plastic explosive. They bury them in the earth at night and then wait for patrols to go out in the morning. They must've been watching us. My sergeant got his face blown off in front of me. I just copped a lump of shrapnel that ventilated my brain for a bit."

He raised his finger to the scar and touched it. Then his hand went to his ankle.

"And lost me leg, of course." He pulled up the leg of his jeans to reveal a steel rod where his shin should have been. A pink plastic foot covered in a white sock fitted snugly into his trainer. He saw my reaction and grinned. "Not bad, eh?"

"I didn't realize," I said. I'd seen he had a bit of a limp, but he walked pretty well for someone whose leg had been blown off at the knee.

"So what's your story, Danny mate?" Gav asked. "What have you been *traumatized* by?" He grinned as he said the word, as if anything less than his experiences were lame – which they were, really. By now I was feeling a bit pissed, but I was careful not to let my tongue get too loose.

"I got shot," I said.

"Unlucky," he said. "You're not forces, are you? You don't look like you are…"

"No," I said. "I got involved with some drug dealers. Stepped in the way of a bullet."

Gav studied me for a moment, summing me up. "Droogs, eh?" he said. "Child's play."

SEVEN

Donnie chopped a line out on top of the toilet cistern, rolled up a twenty euro note, put it to his nostril and flushed. The gush of water disguised the sound of him snorting the white line up his nose.

Valerie wouldn't have liked him doing it; she was dead against drugs of any kind after her ex had wasted years of her life, spending all her hard-earned cash on cocaine and heroin while she brought up their daughter virtually alone and penniless.

Donnie kept it a secret from her. The money wasn't an issue if you knew who to ask for the gear. This town was awash with cocaine, coming in by the boatload from North Africa on its voyage from South America to mainland Europe, controlled by his firm. Donnie had secured himself a couple of nice little gigs; a couple of evenings on doors of local nightclubs and the odd bit of security work, driving and escorting people whose movements needed the protection of muscle. The nose candy came as a perk on top of the cash wages.

Life was working out pretty well, all in all. He'd done three months already, and a month ago he'd met Valerie, who was now sitting on the balcony of the apartment, hair washed, smelling of perfume and sipping a Bacardi and Coke. It had been her birthday earlier in the week and they were going for a rare night out. Her daughter Juana had promised to join them.

Donnie checked his domed skull in the bathroom mirror for any stubble he might have missed with the shaver. He thought the shaved head suited him. With the Zapata moustache he'd been growing, and now that his sunburn had deepened into a brown tan, he could have been a different man. His old mum wouldn't have known him.

She'd hardly known him anyway, he thought.

He tipped out a slosh of aftershave and slapped his clean cheeks, running a hand over his smooth skull. Then he took the heavy gold chain, a new acquisition, off the glass shelf and fixed it around his bull-like neck. The cocaine was beginning to do its work, trickling down the back of his throat and spreading a feeling of well-being down the muscles of his back.

Donnie unlocked the bathroom door, checked his ear lobe for the diamond earring that Valerie had given him as a present, and stepped out onto the balcony in his underpants.

"Another drink, darling?" he asked, the term of endearment still strange on his curse-hardened tongue. He poured rum into his glass while Valerie covered the top of hers with her hand. The Spanish can't really drink like we can, he found himself thinking, not for the first time.

"We got to drive, Bic," she said.

Donnie snorted, lit a fag. "The law ain't going to pull me over just 'cos I've had a couple." He chuckled.

The law had plenty to do around here without stopping him, Donnie knew. Besides, if they did, the mention of a couple of names and a crisp fifty euro note sorted out most problems. He took a swig of Bacardi and leant over and kissed Valerie on the head. She smelt great, and the dress she had on this evening exposed inches of generous cleavage. Donnie stroked her shoulder and slid a meaty paw inside her dress. Valerie placed her hand over his without repelling him.

"Maybe later," she said. "If you're a good boy."

Donnie grinned, took the knock-back good-naturedly and went into the bedroom to finish dressing. He pulled on a pair of black slacks, struggled to put on white moccasins without socks and buttoned a black silk shirt tightly across his barrel chest.

"Your carriage awaits," he said, in an approximation of a posh accent, coming back out onto the balcony. Valerie finished the last of her drink, got up and joined him.

"Vámonos!" she said. "Let's go…" She kissed him on the mouth and linked her finger through his necklace, pulling on it, leading him towards the door.

"Tease," Donnie said.

The restaurant was in the better part of town, not that there was a best part of Benalmádena, but a couple of streets back from the harbour where the mug punters hung out. Benalmádena only really drew the second or third best of everything, the yachties and the villains who weren't up to the riches of Marbella and Puerto Banús. The town was down on its luck, with businesses closing on a weekly basis. Even many of the expats had gone back home in search of a better life than the better life they'd imagined in Spain.

The bar was English-owned. Julie and Barry had sold off the building firm in Orpington twenty years earlier and, with a little help from connected friends, had set up a restaurant,

Bodega Jubarry, in a small plaza surrounded by palm trees. The locals pronounced it Bodega Hoobarray, which made it sound quite Spanish, but every expat lag for a radius of fifty kilometres knew Jubarry's as a safe haven for retired British villains. They had a Spanish chef, Carlos, which meant that locals also ate the paella Valenciana for which it was known. Julie was rarely seen now. She was generally exiled upstairs with a bottle of cava and reruns of British soaps on Sky Plus, plugging endless Fortuna cigarettes into her sponge-bag mouth.

Barry, however, was still committed to front of house, his retirement career cemented by his ability to recognize the names and faces of those who both protected and subsidized his rent and kept his business afloat.

Barry paced the bar, set the tables and welcomed guests with a gushing style that disguised his nerves. The cocktail stick constantly chewed in the corner of his mouth, the ulcer medication and the large Bobadilla brandy and milk behind the bar gave a truer picture of his state of mind.

"Vic!" Barry gushed, shaking Donnie by the hand, fully aware of his real name. He showed them to a table at the front of the restaurant.

"Señorita." Barry kissed Valerie's hand and pulled out a cane chair for her, flourishing a napkin and laying it on her lap as she sat down at the table. "Lovely to see you both again."

"Stop blowing smoke up my arse, Baz, and get us a drink, will you?" Donnie said. Small talk wasn't Donnie's thing.

Barry smiled queasily and laughed, enjoying Donnie's joke, then Donnie looked at him and he realized it wasn't a joke at all.

"Pint of cerveza ... beer for me," Donnie said. "And a bottle of..."

"Rosado, por favor," Valerie said, smiling. She wanted a nice evening with a bottle of rosé. No aggro.

They studied the menu. Donnie's eye was drawn to the steak, but it was Valerie's night so, like her, he settled for gazpacho followed by the paella to share. In Donnie's opinion, gazpacho – cold tomato soup – was like a cup of cold sick, and paella was just hot rice and winkles. He preferred his seafood eaten standing outside a pub, sprinkled with vinegar and on a separate place from rice, which, he considered, was a pointless grain that only went with curry to soak up lager.

But keep the lady happy, he thought. Using the excuse of a piss, Donnie snorted another line in the lavabos *and his appetite for food became secondary.*

He had to admit, it was a lovely evening. The cocaine made him unusually chatty, and he managed to tell Valerie how happy he'd been since he'd met her. Away from all the shit at home. Another line in the toilets and his resistance was lowered enough to tell her he loved her.

Juana turned up a bit later and shared the rest of the paella with them. Eating here was different. You didn't just order your own nosh and neck it; Spanish people shared, like the food was just something that happened while you chatted with friends and loved ones.

And Juana was a lovely girl. Loved.

"Hola, Vic," she'd said when she'd turned up. "Qué tal?"

He had felt himself blush as she'd kissed him on both cheeks, and only managed a shy "Good. Yeah. You look lovely."

She had her mother's smooth brown skin and curves – and something else that Donnie had to admit must have come from her waster father's Gypsy genes: sharp cheekbones, glossy black hair, full lips and a length of limb that Valerie had missed out on. She drew all the male eyes in the restaurant and he felt proud, like a real stepfather.

Around midnight they were on to brandies (on the house, courtesy of Barry) and Donnie, sozzled and wired, had not noticed the white Porsche Cayenne that pulled silently into the square. Donnie didn't see the man who came up behind him and put his hand on his shoulder five minutes later. But he saw from the look on Valerie's face that the interruption wasn't a welcome one.

"Donnie?" The voice was loud but whispery; harsh as sandpaper, roughened by the bullet that had once gone clean through its voicebox.

Donnie twisted round in his chair, trying to see the man. "Got the wrong guy," he said. "Name's Vic."

"Have it your way, Vic," the voice rasped. Donnie used his bulk to shrug the hand off and turn around. He recognized Terry Gadd straight away by the mullet, as he had done on the beach weeks before. Closer to, he could see the broken Roman nose, the scarred fighter's eyebrows, the thin lips. He didn't know the two heavies – the black guy or the punter with the muscles – who loitered in the background and both stiffened as Donnie stood up.

"We need a chat ... Vic," Terry Gadd said. He looked at Valerie, whose face had hardened into a fearful scowl, a hand placed protectively in front of her daughter.

"What is this, Vic?" she asked.

"Don't worry, darling," Donnie said. "Mistaken identity. I'll sort it out."

"Don't fancy yours much, Vic," Terry Gadd wheezed. "Bit

too much meat on it for my taste. I'd give the daughter one, though. Very nice."

Donnie felt his fists tighten and his knees go. He wanted to unleash a punch that would take Terry Gadd's head off, but he knew there would be a knife in his ribs or a bullet in his skull before his fist even reached Gadd's horrible face.

"Everything all right, gentlemen?" Barry hovered, nervous, anticipating a scene at best, Armageddon at worst. "How about you all have a nice drink, on the house, talk things over…"

"You're all right, Barry," Terry Gadd said. "We're not stopping."

Donnie leant over to Valerie. "I'll just go and see what all this is about," he whispered. "Don't worry. See you later." Then added under his breath, "Luv ya."

"You soppy git," Gadd croaked as they walked across the square towards the waiting car. "Not like Donnie Mulvaney to go soft over a bird. Even a big old boiler with plenty of breakfast on it like that. Eh, Don?"

Donnie's fists twitched again at his sides, but he didn't fancy himself against Terry Gadd, whose explosive violence, inhumanity and speed with a cut-throat razor was legendary. Rumour had it that he'd once crept up on a rival in a restaurant urinal, grabbed his knob, sliced it off and flushed it down the toilet before the bloke even knew it was missing.

Terror worked at every level.

"What's all this about, Terry?" Donnie asked. Gadd was silent. "Tel?"

"Shut up and get in the car, Don," Gadd said finally. The rear door of Patsy Kelly's Porsche Cayenne swung open and Donnie got in. "Patsy wants to see you."

EIGHT

Gav Taylor was shit-hot at snooker.

I guess he should have been, as whenever he was not downing pints of lager, smoking or sleeping, he was playing it. I went to his flat in Hanley to meet him a few days after our therapy session. There was no way either of us was going back and we had kind of decided that we might, rightly or wrongly, be the best kind of therapy for each other.

Gav wasn't the sort of bloke I would normally have made friends with, not that I made friends easily. He was pretty coarse and blunt, but he always managed to see the funny side of things.

He said it as it was.

In his sing-song Stoke accent, he made everything sound like a joke or a laugh, and a lot of the time it was. Gav didn't take anything seriously, even his metal leg. Sitting in a pub, he'd say he was a crippled ex-soldier and ask someone to tie his shoelace – but he'd have unscrewed the leg so the foot would come off in their hand. Or he'd jam it in the toilet door and as someone came to help him, his leg would drop off. He thought it was a killer watching their faces.

I began to realize that our joint therapy was basically meeting up on a more and more frequent basis, playing snooker, then going to the pub. My snooker game was improving, but I was getting pissed more than I should.

The old girl had become a bit concerned about the amount of time I spent down there. I'd come home late afternoon and fall asleep on the sofa, mostly because I'd had a few at lunchtime. She was glad that I'd found a mate, but was worried about what I was getting up to with an ex-soldier.

Gav's flat was a tip; it smelt of socks, fags, bacon and unwashed beds. "Girlfriend pissed off about a year ago," Gav said glumly.

"What after you'd...?" I searched for the word but looked at his leg instead.

"I lost me leg, Danny." He laughed. "Not the crown fookin' jewels."

I flustered excuses, but he knew what I meant.

"Nah, we weren't getting on before," he said. "And months out in the Gulf or Afghanistan doesn't help a relationship that's not all that anyway."

I saw a look of hurt pass across his face for the first time. I could see that a rough, boozy, snooker-playing bloke wasn't the best deal to begin with, but with a lump out of his head and a metal leg, well, it wasn't going to be a fairy-tale romance.

I thought back to how six months before I'd had

the fittest girl you could imagine, money, clothes and a lifestyle to match – and, even when she wasn't around, another girl who'd look after me when things got shitty. More than anything I regretted losing Sophie; regretted that in doing my duty and nailing her old man, I'd put paid to ever seeing her again. But compared with Gav, my time undercover had been like a pig rolling in shit.

We were sitting in Gav's flat, drinking beer. The big flat-screen and Xbox lay dormant. He said he couldn't play *World of Warcraft* any more.

"Too much like the real thing," he said. "Without the blood, guts and fear. Still gives me flashbacks." He couldn't even watch TV.

"Snooker?" he asked. So we wandered down to the snooker club again: the dark, twilight world, focussed by the clack of balls and the contemplation of making subtle angles work; the slow pacing around the table, chalking a cue and taking time over a shot. It was as close to meditation as we got.

But I had begun to get antsy; the daily routine was beginning to stifle me. Something needed to change, and on this particular day my game wasn't at the forefront of my mind.

My Aunt Cath was.

Something had happened the night before that was weighing heavily on my conscience. We'd sat up late after Mum had turned in.

"Don't get stuck here, kidder," Cath had said. We were drinking red wine and Cath had spliffed up a couple of times out in the garden earlier, so she was in the mood for one of her pep talks. "You're too big for a town like this. You should see the world."

I'd rambled on, like you do as the second bottle empties. Banged on about how I fancied Thailand or a roadtrip across America. Stuff you think you'd like to do, but have no real idea what it would entail. Half-remembered ideas of other people's adventures and posh kids' gap-year photos on Facebook.

"Maybe, like, run a beach bar in Goa," I said drunkenly, with only a vague idea of where Goa was. All I had in my head was a picture of me in shorts and a straw hat, mixing cocktails for girls with henna tats and loose bikini tops.

"Do it," Cath said. "I'll come with you," she added, giggling. Then she massaged my shoulders, corded by anxiety and three days on the bounce hunched over a snooker table. It felt good.

"You're really tense," she said.

I relaxed as her hard fingers kneaded the tight tendons in my shoulders. Closed my eyes as a delicious wave ran down the muscles either side of my spine. I heard her exhale as she pressed into my shoulders and rotated her thumbs into my shoulder blades. My muscles began to loosen and I became aware of her warm, red-wine breath on the back of my neck. I rolled my head to the right and found her mouth there, waiting. Shit.

I kissed her.

It was nice.

The memory brought me out in a hot sweat of shame as the snooker table came back into sharp focus. I tried hard to concentrate on my shot. I had potted an easy red over the pocket and found myself in a position to go for the eight ball. I fluffed it, concentration gone.

"Roobish," Gav whispered. "You blew it."

Cath had been all right about it. Just a bit embarrassed in the cold light of day. But I'd been mortified. A mark had been overstepped. I avoided eye contact over breakfast.

I had snogged my aunt; she, her nephew. At that moment I felt we both realized that we needed to move on. I needed to get on top of these random urges that seemed to take hold of me.

There was a big wide world out there. Fish in the sea.

"I've got a mate who does up yachts," Gav said, sizing up his next colour. "Easy pink or difficult brown?" he asked, using a tired old snooker joke. He potted the pink. "Y'know, gets them out the water, scrapes the barnacles off, paints the hulls, scrubs the decks an' that. He's got more work than he can handle."

"Yeah?" I said.

He took another red and then the black, another red and the blue, putting up a break of twenty-two and racing a good thirty points ahead.

"Good life," he added. "In the sun. Service boats for rich fookers in the day. Nightime, world's your lobster."

"Lobster?" I said. "You mean oyster?"

"Prawn, whatever…" He shrugged. "Spain."

I managed to let the cue ball go down off an easy red. Lost four points. Game over.

"I've got a flight from Manchester to Málaga," Gav told me. "Next Friday. Thirty-nine quid. Fancy it?"

Leave grey Stoke-on-Trent and head for the sun? Fancy it? You bet.

"Why not?" I said.

NINE

The flight got in to Málaga about ten. As the cabin doors opened, a gust of hot air hit my face and the odour of spent aircraft fuel filled my nostrils. It was the heat and the smell of foreign places, and it was exciting. By the time we had cleared immigration and customs and got on a bus down to the coast, we were starving. The tea and bacon butty at Manchester airport at six-thirty seemed like a lifetime before, and the kind of flight we were on didn't do grub. They'd even charged us to stow our backpacks.

Benalmádena, our small-town destination on the sea, looked pretty run-down. The bus rumbled through the outskirts, where cats played on rubbish tips next to unfinished building projects.

I hauled our bags off and helped Gav down on to the hot street. Steps were still a challenge to him, and getting off a bus or climbing a ladder was the only time you ever saw him look crippled.

"*Y Viva España!*" Gav shouted in Stoke-accented

Spanish. It turned out to be the only Spanish he knew. His tactic was to shout everything else in loud English. "Harbour. Which way?" he called out to a passer-by with arm gestures to represent boats and waves. The passer-by looked disdainfully at Gav in his Stoke City football shirt, and walked on.

"Down here," I said, pointing to a street off to the left. My GCSE Spanish was minimal, but I saw a sign that read *"Puerto"* and a shop further down selling outboard motors. I was picking up clues. I began to wonder how useful Gav had been as a soldier.

Moments later the harbour opened out in front of us on the other side of a car park.

"Burger King!" Gav shouted, spotting one across the street. "Nice one."

"You can't come all this way and have a Burger King, Gav," I protested. I had been looking at a bar opposite, where a couple of Spanish men were sipping cold beers.

"Why not?" he asked. He really didn't see my objection. "Proper food, mate. I could eat a scabby dog."

"Tell you what," I said, "you get a burger, and while you're doing that I'll get us a couple of beers in." I nodded at the bar.

As Gav hobbled across to the Burger King, tired on his dodgy leg, I suddenly realized that I knew next to nothing about my travelling companion other than his experiences of warfare and his waster's ability at snooker. All we had in common was beer and a brush with post-traumatic stress disorder.

"Dos cervezas," I said to the waiter. I knew enough

Spanish to order a couple of beers. The waiter nodded. If he was grateful for my attempt at Spanish, it didn't show.

I looked round the corner into the covered yard near the kitchen. An old man in an apron speared a dead octopus on a long fork. It was the size of a large cat. He dunked it into an oil drum full of boiling liquid heated by a gas burner, then pulled it out after a few seconds and the limp, purple body had contracted to half its size, tight and pink, its tentacles curled up like a chandelier. I watched, fascinated, as he repeated the process three times before dropping it completely into the bubbling drum. The beers arrived.

"*Que es esto?*" I asked the waiter, pointing at the oil drum.

"*Pulpo a feira,*" he said. "Galician octopus." He pointed at a sign in the window advertising it as their speciality. €8.

"*Uno* for me," I said, pointing at myself. "*Por favor.*"

The man at the barrel hoiked out a steaming octopus and cut the tentacles into rings with big scissors. In a bowl he mixed it with yellow chunks of potato, seasoned it with salt, paprika and olive oil, and served it up on a wooden platter. It was the best thing I had ever tasted.

"What the fook's that?" Gav asked. He plonked his empty Burger King bag in a bin.

"Octopus," I said. "Want to try it?"

Gav wrinkled his nose in disgust and looked across at the man cooking them in the oil drum. "Don't be daft," he said. "It's like eating summat off *Star Wars.*"

I looked at the suckers and tentacles on my plate and

laughed out loud. I supposed he had a point.

With the hot sun on our faces and our bellies happy with food, we wandered across to the harbour. It was relatively small, surrounded by a strange, Arabic-looking development of apartments and a couple of bars. It looked as if it had seen better days. Gav surveyed the lines of wooden pontoons and took a scrap of paper from his pocket.

"Pontoon F," he said. "Fifth berth, on the end."

The pontoons bounced underfoot as Gav and I walked along, checking the boats. After the shallow white fishing boats, they were mostly small yachts. They didn't look like the billionaire-owned craft I'd seen in the Tommy Kelly days, but more like well-loved shabby boats owned by fairly prosperous private individuals and retired couples. They came from all over: there were a lot of German flags, Dutch and Spanish, and a few English ones. Finally we reached a boat marked *Sea Dog of Ramsgate*.

A dark-brown, well-muscled bloke with long, dark hair and wearing nothing but denim shorts was hosing the deck. He looked up at us and smiled with white teeth.

"Gavster!" he shouted. His accent was harsher than Gav's. Manchester, I guessed. He dropped the hose and jumped over the taffrail onto the pontoon. He and Gav hugged and gave each other a homeboy handshake.

"Adie," Gav said. "This is my man, Danny."

"Ey up, dood," Adie said. He clasped my hand in the same thumb-to-thumb shake. "Welcome aboard."

We helped Gav up over the gangplank and onto the deck. Adie spread his arms wide, revealing pale, untanned patches around the tufts of hair in his armpits.

"This is the life, gentlemen," he said. "Beer?"

"What you waiting for?" Gav laughed. "I feel like me throat's been cut."

TEN

Donnie was sweating like a pig.

His shirt was glued to his back with perspiration and he was fighting for breath as he hauled his ninety-eight kilos uphill towards Casa Pampas in the midday sun. The taxi had dropped him half a kilometre down the road, as Donnie didn't want the driver to see where he was going. Donnie had been told not to let the driver know where he was going. But he hadn't been offered one of the firm's drivers to pick him up either.

He knew what they were doing: trying to put him on the back foot. And it was working.

The night before, having picked him up from Jubarry's, Terry Gadd had taken him in the Cayenne up into the hills above Benalmádena. They had climbed up through the pueblo and out onto a road above the inland village.

Flanagan's Bar was not welcoming to passers-by.

With steel doors and barred windows, Flanagan's was not welcoming to anyone. Only the carefully selected guests on its list felt any degree of comfort there, and even then the atmosphere was always tense. Terry Gadd had buzzed the door open and ushered Donnie inside, pushing aside a rattling, beaded curtain. Donnie was already feeling edgy now the cocaine had worn off a little and his teeth began to ache. Inside the bar he felt the cold snap of full-blast air conditioning hit his nostrils. He could make out a few figures sitting on banquettes on either side of the room, but the light was low and he couldn't see their faces. He looked down at his feet. Even for a big, fearless gorilla like Donnie, staring was never a good idea. Eye contact could always be a cue for a drawn gun or a flashing knife.

On the wall above the bar, a wide-screen TV relayed live racing from somewhere on the globe. A red-haired man sat watching it at the bar with his back to Donnie, a white silk shirt stretched across his shoulder blades. The race finished and he slapped angrily on the counter: clearly it had been a loss. He jabbed at a remote control and the screen went off, leaving the room in silence for a second before the sour-faced woman behind the bar put on a Neil Diamond CD. The man didn't look round, and Terry Gadd nudged Donnie. Donnie walked up behind the man.

"Patsy?" he said.

"You been avoiding me, Don?" the man answered, still not turning round.

"No, Patsy," Donnie said. "Of course I ain't."

Finally, Patsy Kelly cocked his head sideways to look at Donnie. "Guinness?" he asked. He nodded at the vinegar-tits behind the bar who was already pouring Patsy Kelly's next one, complete with shamrock in the froth.

"Lovely," Donnie said. "Cushty."

"It's just I hear you've already been here for months at my expense," Patsy Kelly said. "And not had the courtesy to give me a tinkle, let me know you're about ... invite me for a drink?"

"I needed to lie low for a bit, Pats," Donnie confessed. He was aware that there was a slight whine beneath the gravelly growl of his voice. "I had a rough time, you know. I thought the apartment was on Tommy's bill."

"Tommy who?" Patsy Kelly asked. There was silence for a moment. "Didn't I used to have a brother called Tommy?" he asked the bar in general.

Donnie said nothing. Couldn't believe what he was hearing. Even from inside, surely Tommy Kelly was still pulling the strings.

"Anyone here know a Tommy?" Patsy called around the bar. There were shrugs and shakes of the head. "That's showbiz," Patsy said, turning back to Donnie, looking him right in the eye.

Donnie felt the ground shifting under his feet.

"You work for me now," Patsy Kelly said. "Turn up tomorrow."

Donnie breathed heavily as he pressed the entry buzzer on the steel gate outside Casa Pampas.

Although the white painted walls were covered with fragrant jasmine and bougainvillea, barbed wire was laced along the top of the walls and security cameras swivelled and trained on Donnie as he approached.

He heard a click and placed his face close to the intercom. His mouth felt like a train driver's sock and salty sweat poured off his shaved head, stinging his eyes.

"Donovan Mulvaney," he said hoarsely into the speaker. The door buzzed and was opened by a squat Spaniard with a face that could have been carved into an ancient Inca monument.

A face that would not have flinched as it tore someone's heart out as an offering to the sun god. Without speaking, he stepped back to allow Donnie in.

Donnie followed him through the cool, tiled house, past vast screens and white leather sofas. He could smell disinfectant, as if the place had been thoroughly scrubbed after the previous night's debauch. They went out through French windows onto a terrace and Donnie blinked in the harsh sunlight, his eyes having adjusted to the shade of the house. Terry Gadd was standing by the side of the pool, ready to greet him with a handshake and a grin that showed flattened, ground-down teeth. He was naked except for Nike flip-flops and the smallest pair of turquoise Speedo budgie smugglers, tucked under his proud belly and around his tight buttocks. Wedged into the back of the Speedos was an automatic pistol.

Apart from Gadd's beer belly, the rest of him was in good shape, Donnie thought: worked-out arms and chest. No beer tits, just a drum-tight gut, reflecting his lifestyle.

"This is the life, eh, Don?" Gadd slapped his deeply tanned paunch and took a sip from a clear drink full of ice cubes.

Brown as a turd, Donnie thought. Said: "You look well, Tel."

"Stop pulling my plonker, Don," Gadd said. "It's not your style."

Donnie followed Terry Gadd round to the far side of the pool. A couple of girls were wallowing in the shallows. Nice nips, he thought, his attention straying despite himself.

They walked past three more stretched out on sunbeds, topless, sun-oiled and wearing thongs. Donnie glanced at them, trying not to stare. They did not glance at him. A few big guys, Patsy's firm, floated in the pool, red faces slick with sweat.

Patsy Kelly lay face down on a sunbed at the end of the pool. A blonde was rubbing cream into his back and shoulders. The sweet smell of coconut oil in the air made Donnie feel sick.

"Mr Mulvaney to see you," Gadd said.

Patsy Kelly turned over. He gave the girl a playful pat on the bottom, dismissing her. Donnie saw the girl's white tanline momentarily as she giggled and wiggled off, then dived into the pool. Patsy picked up a cigar from the ashtray by the sunbed and relit it. Then he took a swig of a cold drink and Donnie felt himself swallow, his throat grating with thirst.

Patsy lifted his sunglasses off his face and rested them on his head among the red curls. He fixed Donnie with pale eyes, the bleached eyebrows and sunburn over his eyelids giving him a permanently angry expression.

"What do you want, Don?" he asked. "You look like you want something."

Donnie was only aware of the clothes stuck to his body by sweat. Of his mouth, parched as the Sahara. "I could do with a drink, Patsy," he said. "I feel like I've swallowed a sock."

Patsy Kelly nodded and gestured to Terry Gadd. "Get Don a drink, Tel, will you?"

Gadd took a used glass off a nearby table and dunked it in the pool, filling it with water. Handed it to Donnie.

Ever since last night, Donnie had been trying to get his small, wired brain around the power shift that had taken place. Now he had turned up at Casa Pampas, Donnie realized that, in Patsy's view, he had somehow fallen short. The ritual humiliation was part of his penance. He would have to swallow it, all of it, or die.

Donnie put the used glass to his lips and swallowed half a

pint of warm, chlorinated water straight down. It was wet. That was all.

"You let us down, Don," Kelly said, shaking his head. "You let Tommy go down. You dropped the ball."

"I never..." Donnie protested. They were trying to make him feel as if Tommy Kelly's downfall was all his fault.

"Saul Wynter was getting fed up with Jason," Donnie began.

Patsy Kelly cut him off. "As I understand," Patsy said, "Solly Wynter's getting a bit of P&Q in some concrete off the M20/A20 intersection. I always told Tom not to trust a front-wheel skid. They only ever care about the money."

"The kid grassed him up," Donnie said. "Sophie's boyfriend. I done him. I shot him. It's all over."

"I don't know nothing about the tossing kid," Patsy spat. "The kid was a decoy. He wasn't connected. He just gave the Micks a chance to hit us while we wasn't looking. They must love that boy, Sophie's choice."

"They all loved that boy," Donnie told him, "Tommy, Cheryl. A right old charmer, he was." He thought for a moment. "The Micks?" he repeated. He was gradually coming up to speed.

"Real IRA. All them Irish bastards at The Harp. They were determined to invade our pitch. And while Tommy's busy buying shoes in Bond Street, bidding for paintings a monkey can do down at Sotheby's and planning his daughter's wedding with the first jockey who thinks he's big enough to have a go, they stitch him up like a kipper."

Donnie remained silent. Patsy Kelly's words were beginning to make sense. After all, how could an eighteen-year-old have engineered the downfall of Tommy Kelly? Donnie knew in his heart of hearts that what Patsy said was true: Tommy Kelly had gone soppy over his daughter, and the boy Eddie who was becoming like a son to him. His protégé.

And he'd let his guard down.

Patsy watched the cogs work as Donnie processed the information; sensed his change of mood. "Get Don a proper drink," he instructed Gadd.

An ice-cold beer found its way to Donnie's grateful hand. He enjoyed the prickling sensation as half of it glugged down his throat.

"So the Paddys might have the upper hand over there right now, with Tommy-boy banged up," Patsy continued. "But they know that the Clapham Junction of all deals is right here on Spanish soil." Patsy prodded his strong, blunt finger into the ground to reinforce his point. "Forget a few lorry-loads of E and all the stuff you can make in your bedroom over there. The big gear comes through here. Argentineans fly to Morocco and the Moroccans organize the drops here by ferry. Colombians bring ships up the Atlantic coast off Casablanca and we bring it in the rest of the way. We had it sewn up before, and we'll get it back under control."

Patsy poured another clear drink from a thermal cocktail jug by his sunbed. Lit a cigarette.

"And where the Micks are, the Russians follow, then come the Albanians and the Ru-fucking-manians. They're all at it now. Ten years ago we had a ninety per cent share of the charlie going into mainland Europe. Now everyone wants a go at the trough. And they're hungry, so they don't mess about. They'll chop your head off for a couple of grams; they're terrorists. But they won't frighten me into submission. We're British, Don. The bulldog breed. We don't roll over."

Donnie felt a certain pride rise in his chest. He downed the second half of his beer and Terry Gadd replaced it with a strong rum and Coke. He felt like he was listening to Churchill on the eve of a battle. Patsy passed him a cigarette and he lit it.

"We're going to have to hit them hard, Don. Hit them where it hurts. Take out some of the key people. I need a couple doing straight off the bat."

He fixed Donnie with his pale eyes again.

"Then we whack at least one small-time dealer a week until they've got the message that we still run the show. You're a soldier, Don," he said. "Are you in?"

Galvanized by the alcohol, nicotine and relief that coursed through his system from his own stay of execution, Donnie nodded.

"I'm gathering troops," Patsy explained. "Some of the old school: Stav Georgiou, Johnny Reggae, Gypsy Tom and Georgie Nash, Billy Gorman, Jas Singh, Mehmet Engorulu, the Dentist…"

Donnie took a swig of rum and Coke, swelling as if he was up for selection for the first eleven at Eton. Patsy was listing the A-team of British hard men and hit men, guaranteed to quell a riot in Broadmoor.

Leaving no one alive.

"I'd like Donnie Mulvaney on the team," Patsy said. The stare again. "If he hasn't gone soft?"

Donnie enjoyed hearing his own name among a roll-call of hard bastards. He nodded again, definite this time. For the moment, thoughts of a quiet life and semi-retirement with a good woman were shelved.

"I need foot soldiers, lieutenants and generals," Patsy told him. "Couple of results as a soldier, you'll become a lieutenant. After that, who knows? You with me?"

Donnie nodded once again.

"Good," Patsy said. "Now let's have a proper drink, because we're going to war."

ELEVEN

I was sitting on a plank, suspended by ropes over the side of a boat. I had rubbed down the fibreglass filler, which had repaired the hole in the hull where a drunken crew had given the boat a dink on a hard mooring, and with a steady hand I was touching up the navy blue waterline. This kind of damage was par for the course down here. English or German bankers and brokers would charter boats and then go on to drink their annual bonuses as they zigzagged them across to the Balearic Islands and back, crashing them into the jetty on their return. That's where the extra money was made.

The punters didn't want to get involved in complicated insurance raps that would spoil their holiday and land them with an extra week's admin, so they'd hand over wads of fifties to repair the boats and then piss off back to their five-figure salaries in the city.

That's where us bottom feeders would come in: no income tax, no VAT, take a slice of the cash and make the boats ready for the next merchant bankers on a jolly, and so it would go on.

I say I had a steady hand, but in my first couple of weeks there was a bit of a shake some mornings. Not as bad as Gav Taylor, though. He caned it; burned the candle at both ends.

He got the lighter duties on account of his dodgy leg and he had a soldier's eye for detail: scrubbing out the galleys until you could eat your breakfast off them, hosing and bleaching the heads – toilets to you and me – doing hospital corners on the bunks, shining the metalwork and coiling the ropes until the boat looked like new. If there's one thing the army teaches you, it's how to get pissed as an arsehole at night, then be up at the crack of dawn and make everything look spick and span.

By the time I'd crawled out of my sleeping bag – or "scratcher" as Gav called it – and stumbled up on deck at 7 a.m., blinking in the sunlight, Gav was on his third strong black coffee and fag, ready to assign me my duties.

Which were the shit ones.

I felt like the cabin boy. I'd have to take the rubbish ashore, empty endless bottles into stinking bins, arrange to have all the shite pumped out of the bilge-tanks, then get myself wet unclogging the propellers in stagnant harbour water and polishing the green mould off the waterline. Then it would be unfurling coarse sails that smelt of stale washing and drying out damp ropes from the lockers, taking the skin off my constantly wet hands in the process.

It was hard graft. Despite the picturesque setting, I reckoned I'd have an easier gig digging roads.

By 7 p.m. I'd shower on whichever yacht wasn't in use, get some clothes on, and head ashore for a drink, cream-crackered. Gav and I would start at a workman's bar at the far end of the harbour, have a couple of beers there and a game of pool or table football. Or Gav might shovel euros into the fruit machine while I stood at the bar. The locals, mostly weather-beaten old sea dogs off fishing boats, were pretty friendly. They'd grin at me as they smoked, but they spoke no English. Over time my Spanish expanded a bit into greetings and short descriptions of the weather.

"*Es muy caliente.*" It's very hot.

"*Sí.*"

"*Mucho trabajo.*" Hard work.

"*Sí.*"

It was limited, but I was doing better than Gav, who was still asking for "Beer ... pint." With gestures.

Later on we'd pick up something to eat, usually a pizza, toasted sandwich or burger, but sometimes I could persuade Gav to sit down for something proper like a steak or a plate of sardines. By ten in the evening I would begin to find my second wind, and as the restaurants filled around the harbour we'd head into town to the clubs around 24-Hour Square.

Gav was on nodding terms with most of the doormen. The majority of them were English anyway, ex-servicemen or bouncers recruited from more dubious security firms in the UK. In this environment, Gav's less likeable side came out. He'd bump fists with the heavies like he was their best mate and call them "my friend", "bro" and "dood", which made him sound like a wanker. When they weren't exchanging hard-man stories about this ruck or that, or listening to Gav dishing up some gruesome tale from Iraq, they would go into a quiet huddle, leaving me standing around like a spare part.

The more Gav's stories were trotted out, the bigger and more violent they became, as did his role in them, and I started to get the sense that some of his tales were porkies. Once he'd had a few, he'd tell anyone who'd listen. We were in a bar one evening, standing next to a couple of blokes who were on a golfing holiday. Gav was spouting off as usual, describing his lucky escape from a Taliban ambush, when one of the blokes, pretty drunk himself, started quizzing him about exactly where he'd been. You can spot a forces bloke a mile off: something about the way they stand, their tidy hair, clean denims. Turns out this bloke had been in Afghanistan eighteen months before and wanted to know *exactly* where Gav had been stationed, who he'd been with, and he wouldn't let it drop, like he was trying to catch him out. The more he questioned, the more prickly Gav got.

"You calling me a fookin' liar?" he spat. He rolled up his trouser leg to show metal. "That a lie, is it?"

He started pulling the bloke's shirt, and within seconds it all kicked off. As Gav's associate, I got caught up in it, taking a right-hander from the bloke's mate. Then Gav started swinging a pool cue and a couple of Spanish guys dived in. I ended up dragging Gav out into the street and sending him away, then going back in to apologize. They were pretty reasonable about it, considering – once

I'd bought them all drinks and put fifty euros behind the bar. But I didn't want to be clearing up after Gav.

When girls started getting involved, it got more uncomfortable. There were plenty of them to go around in the clubs we hung out in. The summer season hadn't really kicked off, but there were weekend hen parties and groups of girls taking early summer holidays while the flights were cheap. 24-Hour Square was the hub of all the clubs in Benalmádena: Mango's, Kui, Los Brothers, Lineker's. As the name suggested, they were pretty busy all day and night.

This kind of nightlife was pretty new to me. Clubs and dancing aren't really my thing, but I'd be a liar if I said I didn't take advantage of what was on offer. You could get a snog and feel a girl's lumps and bumps after just a couple of drinks. At the end of the night it was like all-in wrestling. The girls were all out for a good time, drinking for England, looking for blokes. Blokes like me with a bit of cash on the hip, a deep suntan and a yacht in the harbour. The boats were a great pull: "Ey, Stace, he's got a yacht. Are you a millionaire, mate?"

Gav would rarely tell them otherwise. He was sound most of the time, happy as a pig in shit. He would sit drinking vodka on a club banquette surrounded by drunk girls hanging on his every word. His false leg just added to the attraction.

Then things started to unravel.

He'd be hitting the Es and the blow and whatever else was knocking around and go missing for a few days, leaving me to do all the work. Then he'd turn up looking yellow and sweaty, then sleep for another two days before starting again. He said he was getting the flashbacks again, panic attacks – couldn't sleep at night. I suspected it might have more to do with the amount of pills and booze he was swallowing but didn't like to mention it.

Meanwhile, my own state of mind had improved. I sent a postcard home to tell my ma that things were working out and I was fine.

The work kept me occupied, and I didn't touch the narcotics. It was all right hanging out in the clubs on 24-Hour Square, and although the girls I was meeting weren't really the kind I'd usually go for, they scratched the itch. They were fun; mostly airheads, easily distracted by flashing lights, bright colours and flaming Sambucas.

I had a bit of a fling with one or two party girls, but I had memories of better. And the more time passed, the more I yearned for what I'd had with Sophie Kelly. Impossible to go back now I'd stitched up her old man and she was God knows where, but I felt the loss like a hole, deep in my stomach.

Then one night I got back to the berth about two in the morning and heard a load of screaming and shouting. One semi-clothed girl was on Gav's back, grabbing his hair, while another yelled "Pervert!" at him as she nursed a bloody nose, pulling a shirt back on over her naked shoulders. Once I'd got the first girl off his back, I helped them both back to the pontoon as they protested that they would report him to the Guardia Civil. Never a good idea: the Guardia were pretty rough and not keen on foreigners kicking off.

When I got back to the boat, Gav was smoking, sitting looking out to sea. He dabbed at a bleeding scratch on his face with tissue. I didn't like to ask what had happened, but with two naked women, a couple of bottles of vodka and a mirror covered in cocaine below deck, I didn't imagine it was good clean fun.

"You need to calm down a bit, Gav," I said.

He didn't look around at me or smile. "What's it to you?"

"We'll get into grief with the Guardia Civil if we're not careful."

"No worries," he said. "We won't be around the next few days. We're going back, me mam's ill."

I'd never heard Gav mention his mum before. "Do I need to come with you?" I asked.

"Our tickets run out in ten days, so we may as well make use of the return flight, pick up another cheapie in the UK. We'll be back in a week."

I thought for a moment. It wouldn't be a bad idea to catch up with my mum for a couple of days. I missed her. I'd neglected her. Apart from the postcard, I'd let it all slip and I knew she would be worried about me. I felt a warmth creep over me at the thought of going home.

"Get a proper bit of English grub inside us," Gav said. "Bit of R&R and back to work week after next."

"OK," I agreed. "I'll come with you." I yawned, unprotesting, ready for my bunk.

"Pack your fookin' bag then," Gav said. "The flight leaves from Málaga in four hours. We're going 'ome."

TWELVE

Apparently the N-340 road between Benalmádena and Fuengirola had been improved in the last few years, no longer the major accident black spot of the south of Spain. The new motorway had reduced some of the traffic, but in Donnie's opinion it was still a piece of shit; too narrow for the traffic it carried and too twisty for the Spanish nutjobs that hurtled along it, sitting on Donnie's bumper and flashing their lights to overtake.

Donnie noticed he was doing a steady 100 km/h. Slow, really, but his hands were shaking on the wheel. He felt he had ring rust; out of practice. He'd been assigned a guy called Curtis Tucker as his partner, an Essex boy who had cut his teeth at the firm by blasting the head off an ambitious Southend club owner with a sawn-off somewhere on the Essex marshes. The case had drawn quite a lot of publicity; there'd been so little left of the victim's face. The forensics had had to pick teeth out of the roof of the Range Rover to identify him. The publicity had been a good thing, showing what happened when you tried to muscle in on Kelly business.

Donnie glanced across at Tucker, chewing ferociously on an

Airwaves, stinking of Armani and adrenalin, constantly checking and rechecking the gun in his hand. Donnie sighed.

It had been a crap week since he had reacquainted himself with Patsy Kelly. Valerie had caught the whiff of trouble the evening he'd gone up to the bar in the hills. She'd gone back to her own flat the same night and hadn't come over to his apartment since. Donnie had done his best: taken her to the beach, treated her to lunch once or twice, bought her flowers. He'd had a word with Barry at Bodega Jubarry and got Juana a job serving and doing some of the front-of-house stuff that Barry himself was increasingly less inclined to do.

Valerie was grateful up to a point, jobs were scarce down here since the economic slump. But, she made it clear, she didn't want herself or her daughter caught up in any of the funny business that seemed to accompany the resident Brits.

Donnie felt he was having to charm her all over again, but she was worth the effort. He liked her; liked having someone to share his lonely life with. He liked the fact that she lived for her daughter and fought like a tigress for Juana's well-being. Donnie understood that the girl was well worth fighting for. The germ of humanity that lurked in his soul would fight for her too.

Lovely girl. He had always had a soft spot for charming, gracious girls who seemed so far removed from his own ugly, brutal life. Far removed from his own daughter, Donna, now on her second kid by another bloke and spending all her benefits on scratch cards, weed and cider.

Donnie breathed deeply and let it out slowly. He had also shaken Patsy Kelly's hand and that was a bond of a different kind. He had a long-standing loyalty to the Kelly family. Women would come and women would go, but Donnie had made a promise to Patsy that you kept or you died. Simple.

The exit for Fuengirola loomed up ahead and Donnie swerved across to the inside lane, cutting up a lorry so as not to miss it. "Here we go," he said flatly to his partner.

They drove slowly through the backstreets, down towards the seafront. Donnie knew that at various points along the coast others would be doing the same. Stav Georgiou was taking Torremolinos, Georgie Nash was a few miles back in Mijas Costa, and Terry Gadd, with Billy Gorman, Gypsy Tom and a couple of others, would be doing the big number in Puerto Banús.

When Patsy Kelly had explained the plan inside Casa Pampas, with a big map and a flip chart, it had seemed masterful. A military strategy: Night of the Long Knives, he had called it, borrowing one of Hitler's phrases. They needed to put on a good show. A good, hard, coordinated whack that would let the new boys know who was in charge.

Various nationalities had taken towns as their own. The Albanians had tried to secure Torremolinos and get the bulk of the tourists, while at the other end, the Russians were trying to nail the big business around Marbella and Puerto Banús. Plus there were rumours of a Serbian gang trying to muscle in on Benalmádena.

Bottom line, it was all about trying to monopolize the sale of drugs, cocaine in particular, in those areas.

Donnie had to hand it to Patsy – while he was nothing like the smooth operator his brother Tommy had been, he worked in broad brush strokes. Tommy would have thought around the problem, dealt with it by stealth and subtle manoeuvres. Patsy had always been the wild card, lashing out left, right and centre, which had landed him out here in Spain in the first place, exiled by Tommy as too much of a risk to the UK operation. But Donnie admired the way that Patsy likened the whole thing to a boxing match: damage the body and the head will drop; then batter the head and the body will collapse.

Donnie was no stranger to fighting and knew the tactics: if you pummel away at the ribs and solar plexus, digging hooks into the kidneys and heart, the heavy body blows drain the energy from the fighter.

Then the head, the brains of the machine, will finally drop, ready for the killer punch. The big right hand that no one sees coming. The punch that will finish it all off, stunning the brain and sending the whole lot crashing to the canvas.

So now the plan was for Donnie and his cohorts to deliver the body blows: to hit the middle men who held the whole drugs business together, drawing the bosses out from the safety of their yachts and mountain hideaways and into the open, ready to be picked off.

Donnie pulled up outside La Bamba, a flashy joint near the front in Fuengirola. He took care parking the car in a proper space, something he might not have considered a few years before.

"Worried about getting a ticket?" Curtis quipped, trying to disguise his nerves.

They got out of the car and Donnie checked the automatic stuck in the waistband of his trousers in the small of his back.

The two of them stood around in front of the marble steps of the club, smoking, acting like a couple of drivers waiting for their pickup. A few gorgeous, drunk girls spilled out. One asked Donnie for a light, which he reluctantly gave, never taking his eyes from the door. Then his phone bleeped. A signal from someone inside. Donnie and Curtis stamped out their fags, and ten minutes later the target came out, a Romanian called Cezar Lupescu. With him was his sidekick, a man known as Gabor.

The Romanian gangsters had been the most recent imports to try to take hold of some of the turf. They were vicious and lawless, but disorganized. Apparently, Lupescu seemed to think that he now controlled some of the cocaine traffic in Fuengirola. He also brought Romanian girls in on the promise of a job and put them to work in the sex industry as lap dancers, strippers and whores. Patsy had made it clear that Lupescu was a nasty piece of work, and Gabor even nastier. If any of their girls played up, they were usually found in bits in wheelie bins or in black bin bags washed up on the shore.

To Patsy Kelly, Cezar Lupescu was still a relatively small operator – and on the basis of last in, first out, Patsy wanted to hit him hard and get him off the turf.

Lupescu and Gabor walked towards the kerb, past Donnie and Curtis. Donnie noticed that the neon lights reflected off their shiny jackets.

"Taxi?" Curtis Tucker asked, nudging Gabor on the elbow as he passed. The Romanian turned, furious at having been touched. He was ready for a row but too slow to react. Tucker took half a step forwards, held the silenced 8 mm Baikal IZH-79 to the man's face and blew his brains out in a single movement. Donnie simultaneously stepped up to Lupescu, but the Romanian, given a split second, brought his knee up into Donnie's crown jewels, wrong-footing him. The gun went off in Donnie's hand, but the bullet only grazed Lupescu's jaw and he attempted to run. Donnie lurched forwards and dived on him, driving Lupescu's injured face into a parked limo, leaving a bloody face print on the shiny white paintwork. Donnie raised the pistol again and shot him in the back. Lupescu slumped to the floor and Donnie stood over him, firing a third shot into the side of his skull at point-blank range. The Romanian went limp as blood spouted from his head and poured into the gutter.

Job done. But messy.

"Don!" Curtis shouted. Donnie turned to see two more Romanians running towards them from the door of the club. The first fumbled with a gun inside his jacket, but Curtis shot him before he reached the bottom step. The second ducked behind a potted palm in a huge urn, pulling a gun and letting off two shots.

Very messy.

Hearing the shooting, people began to pour out of the club, and suddenly the air was full of screams. Curtis let off a final bullet, pinning the Romanian behind the urn, before turning and running towards the car.

"Leg it!" he shouted to Donnie, who stood clasping his shoulder.

"I don't know if I can," he wheezed. "I've been hit."

THIRTEEN

I necked a small, bitter black coffee at the bar in Málaga airport. My eyes felt gritty from lack of sleep and I blinked to stay awake. Gav seemed to have a new lease of life, probably from having hoovered up what was left of the cocaine on the boat. He was smoking and chattering, drinking beer at five-thirty in the morning.

He was getting on my tits.

We checked in at 6.00 a.m. for the 7.30 flight. A dour Spanish girl with thick make-up and scraped-back hair checked our passports, looked at us and asked if we'd packed our bags ourselves. I nodded, barely paying attention, tired and bored by the usual run of questions. Gav had different ideas.

"Actually, a bloke with a big beard and a towel round his head crept into me room and packed mine," he said. The girl glowered. "Joking, love," he added.

"It's not funny," she said. She was weighing up whether or not to call security.

Gav checked himself. "Sorry, love, just a joke. I was

84

out there, you see. Iraq, Afghanistan." He pulled up the leg of his jeans, showing metal.

The girl behind the desk looked at him from behind dead eyes, as if the leg might have been a joke too – that it did not compute – but decided to move on; too early in the day for ructions. She pushed our passports and tickets back across the desk. "Gate Fourteen."

"Thanks," I said, embarrassed. She gave a tight, mirthless smile and went back to her screen.

The flight was full of families on low-budget package deals; fractious kids and depressed parents heading back to the humdrum after their couple of weeks in the sun. The cabin crew looked weary too. Most of them were starting shifts that would finish late that night, having taken them back and forth between the UK and the Costa del Sol four or five times over during the day. They had a shit job – they were like well-dressed bus conductors, dishing out drinks, food and duty-frees, duty-bound to keep the smiles on their faces through the demands of drunk passengers, badly behaved kids and bags of vomit.

I sat by the window, ignored the standard safety demo and shovelled down a block of wet scrambled egg and damp sausage before shutting my eyes. It was difficult getting to sleep next to Gav, who fizzed with nervous energy. He jiggled his knees in his seat and rustled magazines, but plugged into my iPod, I finally dozed off.

A couple of hours later, we shuffled across the tarmac into a drizzly Manchester morning. No change there then. I helped Gav with his bag as his dodgy leg had stiffened on the flight. We queued at immigration. My false passport got me a second look, but something obviously came up on the system that gave me the green light.

"I feel like a bag of shite," Gav informed me. "Me mouth tastes like the bottom of a budgie's cage and I need a shit."

"Too much information, Gav," I said.

He hobbled off to the toilets while I waited with the bags. I found myself looking forward to getting back to my mum's for a fry-up and half a day in a comfortable bed.

"Weight off me mind," Gav said as he came back from the bogs. "Made me mark on English soil. Nice to be 'ome."

He didn't look too good. He looked grey, his eyes red-rimmed; his hands were shaking and he was sweating like a pig. The excesses of his past few days were catching up with him. I felt smug. A bit of kip on the plane had done me good and I felt healthy, suntanned and clean compared with Gav Taylor.

By the time Gav had sorted himself out, most of the charter flight families had already picked up their bags at reclaim. We followed the remaining few through the customs queue. Gav made the most of his limp but then picked up the pace and started chatting to a family returning from their holiday.

"Have a good time?" he asked. "Nice sombrero. Where were you? Torremolinos? Sweet. I got some mates there. Cracking place." While Gav sailed through the customs with his adopted family, I found myself several steps behind, alone with my rucksack.

A customs officer in a white shirt stepped out from behind a desk and stood in my way. He directed me towards one of the stainless steel benches that lined the customs hall.

"Gav," I called ahead. "Hang on." But Gav had gone, limping across the airport concourse with his new friends.

I watched, helpless, as the sliding doors closed and I thought I saw him glance back, then disappear into the Manchester Airport crowds.

"Can you empty your bag for me, sir?" the customs man asked.

Huffily, I dumped my rucksack on the desk and unzipped the top. There wasn't much in there. My good shoes, a couple of shirts and trousers, some crumpled pants. I'd left most of my stuff behind on Adie's boat, fully expecting to be back in a week. The official turned out the pockets, shook out the shirts and scanned the heels of my loafers. He looked inside the bag, felt around with his hand and then turned it upside down. There was a zipped section on the bottom where I kept my wash bag – toothbrush, toothpaste, paracetamol, aftershave and stuff.

"Open this for me, please?" the officer said. I did as he asked, and he pulled out my washbag. He checked the toothpaste tube, the shampoo bottle and the pack of paracetamol and seemed satisfied. I was just getting ready to move on when he reached further into the pocket, dug around and pulled out a package wrapped in cling film, about the size of a bag of sugar.

"What's this?" he asked.

"I don't know," I said, panicked. I really didn't.

"You'll need to come through here, sir," he said, gesturing behind the screens. Two more customs officials appeared. I had no choice.

I was sitting in a white room, lit by fluorescent lights. Cold and harsh. My rucksack and washbag had been dumped at one end of the table and at the other, in front of me, lay the package. Two customs officers sat and watched, while the third opened the package with a penknife. He scooped out a sample of the white powder on the tip of his knife.

"Finest Colombian, I'm guessing," he said. "Brought in via Morocco and up through the Costa, am I right?"

I shook my head. I was beginning to sweat. "I've no idea."

"How much have you got there?" the second officer asked. "A key?"

"I honestly have no idea," I repeated. "I don't know what a key is. This stuff has been planted."

They both smirked.

"Never heard that one before," the first man said.

"A key, as if you didn't know," said the second, "is a kilo of cocaine. One thousand grams, which, at today's price of around fifty quid a wrap, is fifty grand's worth on the street. You might even double that by the time you've cut it with baby laxative and whatever other shit you use."

"Did you really think you could walk straight past us with fifty thousand pounds' worth of class A in your bag, you silly boy?" The first officer leant on the table, his face close to mine. I winced at his words and his sour breath.

"I didn't know it was in my bag," I insisted. "The guy I was travelling with must have planted it."

"Which guy?" asked the first officer. "I see no guy. Where's the guy? All I see is someone with a key of pure cocaine in his luggage."

"He's called Gav Taylor, he's ex-army. He planted it on me."

The third officer, who hadn't spoken until now, stood up. He appeared to be senior to the other two.

"OK," he said calmly. "The sooner you stop all this 'planted' business, the better we will get on."

"It's the truth…" I protested, but he held up a hand to silence me.

"Now, I'm sure a young man like yourself hasn't purchased a whole kilo on his own. Not for your personal use, is it?" He smiled like someone suffering from bad indigestion. "So perhaps you'd best start by telling us who you work for?"

"I don't work for anyone," I said. "I was just taking some time out, doing up boats for a bit of money."

"Whose boats?"

"Just charter firms, private individuals," I said.

"Smugglers?" he asked. I thought not, but perhaps I was being stupid. "So, let's try again. Who do you work for?"

I began to panic. I clenched my fists, digging my fingernails into my sweating palms, trying to keep a grip physically and mentally. They asked me the same questions over and over again, trying to catch me out, playing good cop, bad cop. They jumped on any slight hesitation or deviation in my answers. They were good at it, making my brain spin until I would have admitted to almost anything. My legs began to shake and I felt sweat trickle down my back as I realized that they didn't believe a word of my story – and that the weight of evidence wrapped up on the table in front of me was enough to send me down.

"So, who is it you work for?" the senior officer asked for the hundredth time. I pressed the heels of my hands into my closed eyes, willing myself away from this nightmare. Then a thought crossed my mind. I *had* worked for someone. Someone who could be my lifeline. My only way out of this stitch-up.

There was a pause.

"I'm travelling under a false passport," I said finally. The first two officers smiled at one another. Now they were getting somewhere. "My name isn't Daniel Reeves." I pushed the passport across to them. "I work for a man called Tony Morris."

"What kind of villain is he?" the officer asked.

"He's not – he's involved in intelligence."

The senior man looked sceptical while his fellow officers smirked at my unlikely tale.

"If you give me my phone, I'll find you his number."

The senior officer shrugged and nodded to his colleague, who slid my phone across the desk. I went into where my secure numbers were kept. I found Tony's number at the top of the list and handed the phone to the senior officer.

"Please call him," I said. "Tell him Eddie Savage is back."

II

Tercio de Varas

Tercio de varas (*"third of lances"*). *This is the first stage of the bullfight, in which the bull enters the ring and is tested by the matador and banderilleros. The matador uses this phase to observe the bull's behaviour: how it charges and its ferocity.*

FOURTEEN

I sat in the small, bleak cell somewhere behind the scenes in Manchester Airport.

Fear was still gnawing away at my insides. What if they hadn't been able to find Tony or, for intelligence reasons, he'd had to deny my existence? Then I would be really stuffed.

I'd been held there for twenty-four hours so far. I'd been interviewed thoroughly by the customs men and then by the police inspector from the drug squad, who had called by to make me go through everything yet again. I told them nothing beyond the fact that I was a victim of some kind of stitch-up, that my travelling companion had probably used me as a dumb drug mule. I even refused a solicitor: I didn't want to say anything until they had contacted Tony. Apart from anything else, I was frightened of saying a word about my undercover work. Most of what I knew was strictly classified and I didn't want to spill the beans to some customs official, the local plod or a lawyer until I knew exactly what my position was; what I could and couldn't say, and whether what I did or didn't say could get me locked up for a long time. I'd already told them I had a false identity: anything more would have sounded like a fairy story.

Naturally, I hardly slept. The narrow bunk was hard and covered in sweaty plastic and the cell light was left on all night. I lay awake, staring at the grey walls, thinking what a complete idiot I'd been getting mixed up with Gav Taylor in the first place. I couldn't believe that, after all I'd been through, I'd been taken in by a crippled squaddie who could hardly write his own name. The angrier I became, the harder it was to get off to sleep. I began to contemplate the cell I'd been in for the best part of a day and it already felt like a month. I wondered about Tommy Kelly and how, after his life of luxury, he could adjust to the idea of spending twenty years or more locked up like this. I almost felt a pang of pity for him.

My emotions were still very mixed. I knew, deep inside, that part of me did regret bringing him down. Regretted all the grief it had caused, not only to Tommy Kelly and his family, but to myself. I'd probably had all the information and means to help him escape. And if he had escaped, I might have gone with him. And been with Sophie. My unlikely fantasy continued along these lines: I saw myself hiding away somewhere lawless in a sun-drenched villa, backed by Tommy Kelly's blood money. I saw me and Sophie – we'd probably have got married – living a life on the run. It was an outlaw romance.

A pipe dream.

I knew it could never have happened, but I still longed

for her. At the time I had found it hard to forgive her acceptance of her old man's way of life, but that was his fault. He'd ruined it for us.

I brought to mind Sophie's smell, the feel of her hair, her lips against mine. I had never felt so much for anyone before, and nothing could change that: no one else would ever match up; no one came close. Unwelcome desire began to gurgle deep in my gut, rapidly quenched by the plastic mattress stuck to my legs and the harsh light overhead.

In the morning I was brought a lukewarm cup of tea from a machine and a congealed bacon roll, but I wolfed them down. I had a stand-up wash in cold water at the steel basin in the corner. Then a good couple of hours' more waiting. I didn't know what time it was as my watch had been taken away with everything else.

I heard voices outside the cell. The keys jangled, the door opened and in stepped Tony Morris.

"Hello, old son."

If he was pleased to see me, he hardly showed it His mouth was set in a grim line, like I was about to be hanged. But there was a welcome warmth in his eyes as he shook my hand.

"What a pickle," he said. Then he suddenly pulled me into a bear hug, and like a baby I burst into tears.

He sat me down on my bed and passed me a big white handkerchief. He chatted uncomfortably about his train ride up north while I recovered myself. Said he'd been up since the crack of a sparrow's fart to bail me out again, pretending he was put out about it.

"So," he said. "Start from the beginning."

I told him about my group for PTSD, lying around listening to whale song, how it hadn't suited me and I'd ended up drinking in a pub with Corporal Gav Taylor. Then I went on to explain how Gav had asked me to go to Spain with him after a few weeks and I'd jumped at the chance.

"What did you think was going on down there?" Tony asked.

"Honestly, Tony, I really thought it was just odd jobs on boats, days in the sun, a bit of nightlife. The flight was cheap. I was going nuts in Stoke."

Tony nodded. "Well, we know about your *Private* Taylor," he said. "If he got a medal, it was for doing the high jump. He was reported AWOL twice in Iraq and got blown up running away in Afghanistan."

"Not exactly a war hero then?"

"Not exactly. Three of his mates were burnt to death in an armoured vehicle. He should have been in it, but he was caught elsewhere, flogging moody fags and bootleg porn DVDs. A regular entrepreneur. We're looking into it, but we're getting reports of British soldiers doing deals with the Afghans and bringing back heroin in empty coffins."

"You think Gav was up to that?"

Tony shrugged. "Wouldn't put it past him."

"He said he had dysentery," I remembered.

"It seems he would say anything to get away from the action. If anything was kicking off, then Private Taylor was registering himself sick or unfit for service, or running in the opposite direction. And it was while running the other way that he stepped on a bomb. They tried to chuck him out in the end, but he cried foul and claimed PTSD so he'd get full benefits."

From what I knew of Gav Taylor, it all made sense.

"One thing I will say, kid," Tony observed, "is that you do have an instinctive nose for trouble. Of all the places you could have gone, the south of Spain is like a war zone at the moment. A bloodbath. And you were slap bang in the middle of it."

"I didn't see much evidence of it," I said. Sure, I'd seen a few drug deals in nightclubs, seen bouncers slap a few Herberts, but nothing worse than you'd get anywhere in South London.

"It's going on, believe me," Tony said. "In the backstreets and up in the hills, gang-on-gang warfare, trying to control the trade. The kind of trade your mate seems to have involved you in. That's if you're telling me the truth, Eddie?"

His use of my code name pulled me up short.

"Of course I am, Tony," I pleaded. If Tony thought I might be lying, there was a big possibility I might not actually get out of this. My feeling of panic returned. "I wouldn't lie to you. Haven't you pulled Gav Taylor in? Then you'll know I'm telling you the truth."

"I don't think we're going to, mate. I've put someone on him. It will be more interesting to see what he does next, where he goes, who he meets. You know the form."

"So what about me?" I asked.

Tony looked at me squarely. "It's a bit tricky," he

admitted. "The last people you want to mess with are HM Revenue and Customs. They have more power than all of us put together; if they want to make it stick, they'll make it stick."

"Can you get me out of here?" I asked. My voice came out quiet, meek. I tried hard not to sound like a whining kid.

Tony whistled between his teeth, stared at the floor. "I'm doing what I can. But I warn you, there'll have to be some kind of trade-off."

"What do you mean?"

"I mean there will be a deal, a bit of quid pro quo. There always is."

"I'm innocent, Tony," I said. I tried to keep my voice steady. "But if you can get me out, I'll agree to anything you ask."

"I'll do what I can, mate. It'll take a bit of fancy foot-work, but seeing as it's you, I'll do my best."

Tony stood up and squeezed my shoulder and, without looking back, shut my cell door behind him.

FIFTEEN

There was no one around the pool at Casa Pampas when Donnie arrived for the second time. No crumpet in sight, just a load of blokes – fully dressed in shorts, flip-flops and gaudy shirts – mooching about the house, talking in whispers. It was like a funeral.

It was a funeral.

Billy Gorman, one of the hardest nuts in the firm, had copped it in Marbella a couple of nights before. He'd died in hospital the following day when they couldn't find enough brain left to make him function.

Donnie had not gone to hospital. He'd taken a bullet in his left shoulder, but if he'd gone to A&E with a gunshot wound he'd have been in police custody within hours. So he'd had to make do with a retired, alcoholic GP on the Kelly payroll who extracted the bullet from his shoulder in Donnie's apartment. The old boy's hands had been shaking as he delved into Donnie's flesh, pulling out the slug with a pair of tweezers. Donnie had nearly fainted with the pain, but fortified by a shared bottle of brandy and a couple of novacaine jabs, he pulled through and was advised to take a few days' bed rest.

Two days was too much time out in the current climate, so Donnie had driven up into the hills this morning to report back in, his arm stiff and his shoulder throbbing.

Donnie felt paranoid as he joined the cohorts of hit men and heavies: they seemed to be looking at him as if he was the one who should be dead; Billy Gorman was the better man and he, Donnie Mulvaney, was past his prime. He'd done the job, but it wasn't a clean kill. He'd been seen.

"How's the shoulder, Don?" Terry Gadd asked as he greeted him.

"I'll live," Donnie said. Gadd looked at him as if he suspected that he wouldn't for much longer.

"Patsy wants us in the lounge," he croaked.

Donnie followed Gadd and the others through to a vast, modern room that looked out through sliding windows over the rocky valley.

Where Tommy Kelly would have had modern art and antique furniture, Patsy's taste leaned more towards smoked-glass coffee tables, white leather furniture and realistic pictures of white horses galloping through surf. Donnie spotted a big pair of Muhammad Ali's satin boxer shorts, signed and framed.

Patsy shook each of their hands as they entered the room. He shook Donnie's but failed to make eye contact.

"Morning, gents," Patsy said. "I know we're all gutted about Billy, but we've only just started and we have to carry on. Billy Gorman would have wanted that. He was one of the best and we'll miss him. That's all I'm going to say." There was a murmur of phlegmy-voiced agreement and Patsy turned to the map on the largest table. He'd stuck black spots at various points along the coast. "Billy aside, it was a pretty good result, gentlemen. We wiped out a dozen of the bottom feeders in one fell swoop, and have done damage to all the new kids in town: the Romanians, Albanians, Lithuanians and even some of the Russian chancers. Although we have to play careful with the big Russian boys, it's in our interest to keep it sweet with one or two of their key players. We already have an agreement over who does what and where, and we need to keep those channels open for business."

"How we going to do that, Pats?" Stav Georgiou asked dimly.

"We're going to be very specific, Stavros, dear boy," Patsy patronized. "We're going to stick with the towns and territories we've identified and pick the small fry off in ones and twos. Then the bigger ones will be drawn in to try and sort it out."

"What protection have we got?" Stav asked.

"We need to keep light on our toes," Terry Gadd put in. "We'll keep changing teams. If you were in Estepona this week, you'll be assigned another town next time, unfamiliar. And we'll change partnerships, disguises, whatever it takes. "

"Exactly," Patsy agreed. "But we're going to let the dust settle for a few days. It's like we've kicked a wasp's nest with a hobnail boot. The place is buzzing with angry Eastern Europeans looking for someone to sting. They'll probably start by taking it out on each other, so hopefully they'll do some of the job for us."

Stav Georgiou laughed. "Roobanians, Almanians, whatever. They'll fuckin' shoot each other for us, innit?"

The others looked at Stav and smiled indulgently. Never the brightest bulb in the firm, he was cottoning on.

"And the Spanish filth are already turning a blind one to this

101

week's row," Patsy said. "As far as they're concerned, we're doing them a favour cleaning up the Costa, so they're deliberately being a little slow with their enquiries. Besides, they owe us: we've been paying them for the best part of twenty years and there's hardly a village in the hills where the mayor hasn't been chosen and funded by us. So if there's anyone lively hiding up in the pueblos, they'll dob 'em in. The Spanish know where they are, working with us. They know the Costa del Sol belongs to the Brits."

There were pats on the back and grim chuckles, and the mood in the room improved. Terry Gadd placed a wad of photos on the table.

"These are some of our main targets," he said.

He spread them out with his hand: surveillance shots of moustachioed men in bars and on beaches; Eastern Europeans looking from car windows unawares. He pointed to one, a dark man with a moustache and slicked-back hair.

"This one in particular," Gadd said. "He's supposed to be the Serbian big cheese. Radish, he's called. Nasty piece of work."

The men caught each other's eyes, all thinking much the same: that "nasty piece of work" was rich coming from Terry Gadd.

"Have a look, memorize them. We'll give you copies," Gadd continued. "Keep your nuts down and your eyes peeled and when the wasps' nest has died down, let's have another bash. We'll be in touch."

"Everyone happy?" Patsy asked, not expecting an answer. "Now let's have a drink."

Donnie wasn't happy. His shoulder was throbbing, giving him gip. He had three swift vodka and tonics, so as not to be rude, took a stack of photos and made his excuses.

Forty minutes later he was outside Valerie's block. He hadn't seen her for days. He mopped the sweat from his face with a sleeve and got out of the car feeling light-headed.

He pressed in the entry code, walked slowly up to the second floor and pressed the buzzer outside Valerie's apartment. The chain rattled and Juana opened the door. She looked at him warily.

"Hola, Vic. Qué tal?" she said.

"Is your mum in?" Donnie asked hoarsely.

"I don't think she..." Juana began.

Valerie's voice could be heard from inside, asking who it was, and seconds later she was at the door, wiping her hands on the apron around her waist. Her face was fixed, unsmiling.

"You drunk?" she asked. Donnie shook his head. She softened a little as she saw his battered face, pale and pained.

"Valerie, love," he said. "I've had an accident. Can I come in?"

Juana stepped back inside while her mother considered a moment.

"Please," Donnie said. "I don't feel too clever."

And he collapsed in a heap on her doorstep.

SIXTEEN

Tony didn't say much in the car.

He'd sprung me from Manchester Airport a couple of hours earlier. The officers in charge seemed genuinely sorry to see me go. And it wasn't just because they had begun to warm to me over the last two days. I think the overriding feeling was that I was their "collar", and they didn't like me being taken away by another agency.

Tony Morris, or someone, had clearly done a deal higher up the food chain and allowed me to be released into Tony's custody.

"You're a lucky lad," the chief officer said to me as I left customs. "That little package would have guaranteed you a seven-year stretch."

The idea of a seven-year prison sentence seemed unimaginable. I'd have been twenty-five before I got out.

"He'll pay for it," Tony answered him. "Don't worry on that score."

I was pretty brassed off, to be frank. In my opinion, I had nothing to pay for. Apart from, perhaps, my own stupidity. Before the shooting I'd spent months living on my wits in London, hanging around some of the most dangerous criminals in the country, then ultimately had been stitched up by a one-legged scammer from Stoke.

Tony told me we were going to call in on the mother ship. He had been in touch with her. Mum had been very worried, naturally, and when she'd found out *why* I'd been pulled in, her fear had turned to anger. Apparently she'd been livid, assuming I'd got involved with something illegal. She'd already lost one son to drug-related crime. So Tony had promised he'd bring me to her before he took me off God knows where.

There were tears, of course, and once Mum had released her stranglehold on me, she hugged Tony, clearly grateful for my return.

We spent the afternoon chatting over endless cups of tea. I told them about the boats, the work and some of Gav's antics, and how he'd stitched me up at the airport. Mum said she'd never liked the sound of him from the start.

Cath had gone off again, to Marrakech this time. It was evident Mum was lonely and would've liked me to stay, but Tony made it clear that wasn't an option: I had to be with him under the terms of my release. But for one day we settled into the familiar routine that occurred whenever we were together. Tony and I had a quick one in the pub before going back to Mum's for a takeaway curry.

I wolfed down poppadoms and lime pickle, onion bhajis, stuffed paratha, sag prawn and rogan josh, aloo gobi, pilau rice. I sat back in my chair, galvanized by two cans of lager, and belched contentedly, ready for what life might throw at me next. It was like a condemned man's last meal.

The next morning was a different story. I felt sick with butterflies in my stomach and a sense of foreboding. A cup of tea and a bacon sarnie did little to settle my guts and I only managed half of it. Tony did some terminal damage to a full English while my mum watched us both, her face strained and worried.

When the time came to leave, I didn't think my mum would ever let me go – and the mood I was in, the tug of the apron strings was a powerful force. Both of us would have done anything to have kept me there.

Tony and I drove onto the endless ringroad around Stoke in silence, which I eventually broke with some quip about how overprotective my old girl was. I didn't really believe it; it was simply a bit of male bravado to cover up my feelings of insecurity.

Tony's reaction took me by surprise. He told me what a good woman my mother was, how I shouldn't under-estimate the work she'd put into bringing us up, how she wouldn't accept help or handouts from anyone. She'd had a hard time and I should respect that.

I considered myself told.

We sat in silence for a while longer until Tony slipped in a CD. I looked sideways at him as he hummed along.

"What are you thinking, Tony?" I asked. *"Coldplay?"*

"It's what young people listen to, isn't it?"

"Not this one," I said. "The only good thing about that wet fart is Gwyneth Paltrow."

Tony laughed for the first time since we'd left and the mood was broken. "OK," he said. "I'll give you Paltrow, if you go for that cool preppy thing... Top ten birds."

Tony loved a car game. It was usually general knowledge or a pop quiz, but this was a new one.

"Do they have to be Hollywood?" I asked.

"Nope. Film, telly, anything."

"Dead or alive?"

"Anyone you like," Tony said. "But alive's obviously better if you're thinking of shagging them."

"OK. Scarlett Johannson."

"Good choice," Tony said. His first choice was someone called Raquel Welch. Apparently she'd been in some caveman movie when he was a kid, and her fur bikini had had a lasting effect on him.

I followed with Penélope Cruz, Anne Hathaway, Kelly Brook and Holly Willoughby.

Tony went for Marilyn Monroe, Cheryl Cole, Christine Bleakley and, slight curve ball, Meryl Streep.

I came back with Angelina Jolie, Gemma Arterton, Jennifer Aniston and Beyoncé.

Tony winced at Beyoncé: she'd been his next choice.

"Oof," he said. "Her off 'Mad Men'..."

"The blonde wife?" I asked.

"No, the big one, redhead. Christina Hendricks. She's all woman." It was a good counter. She was definitely all woman. "Brigitte Bardot – then, not now. Julie Christie, same. Princess of Wales, God rest ... and Barbra Streisand."

"Barbra Streisand?" I laughed.

107

"Each to his own," Tony sniffed.

"People used to think Mum looked a bit like Barbra Streisand when she was younger," I said.

Tony nodded. "Yeah, she did a bit," he said. "Good game."

We wrestled over the CD choices, and after settling on a bit of Bob Marley on the M1, we hit the M25 with Queen's *Greatest Hits* and found ourselves roaring along, singing about fat-bottomed girls.

It was good to be with Tony, and for a while I felt happy again. Until we took a turning off towards Beaconsfield and I knew where we were headed next.

SEVENTEEN

Sandy Napier looked older than when I'd last seen him.

He still looked as hard as nails, like the ex-marine commander he was, but his skin appeared tighter across his features, as if he was tense and under pressure. His sandy hair was showing streaks of white at the temples. His handshake was still bone-crushingly firm, though, and he didn't appear to be angry with me. As far as I could tell.

"Eddie Savage returns?" He raised his eyebrows in question.

"Looks like it," I said. I always felt I sounded like a smartarse in front of Sandy Napier.

"Well, I'm glad to see you looking so well," he said. "For a dead man."

I laughed, a fizz of excitement growing in my gut as fear ebbed away, a thrill at going back into the fray.

"Eddie Savage" had been declared dead when I'd been shot, six months or so before, in London. The idea had been to give me time to recover; to lick my wounds and to establish a new identity ... and then to work out what to do with me.

Except that as soon as I'd been able to speak again, I'd told Tony in no uncertain terms that I didn't want to continue working for their organization. Now, six months down the line, only just over post-traumatic stress disorder, I was back in front of Napier's desk with a big black mark against my name.

It appeared I had no choice in the matter.

"Tony has filled me in on this business in Spain with the drugs and so on," Napier said, looking at a file on his desk. "From what I know of you, I've taken Tony's word that you were an innocent bystander in this situation." I nodded eagerly. "But I have to say, Eddie, you were bloody stupid to get mixed up in something so obviously suspect. Have you learned nothing since working for us?"

I had learned plenty, but my instincts had been poor about Gav Taylor, I had to admit.

"We had to work like stink to wrest you from the HMRC, and they, like everyone else, are driven by results.

"Results?" I was confused.

"Convictions." The word hung heavy in the air.

"Sorry, sir," I said. "I—"

"Given that, we also have to get those results and share them," Napier said, cutting me off. "We have to make customs feel as if it was their intel that hooked the big fish."

"But I'm not a big fish, sir."

"You're a bloody kipper, Savage. Stitched up, filleted and smelling fishy. But, that being the case, you might make useful bait."

Napier was talking in riddles. I looked helplessly at Tony for an explanation.

"We're going to send you back over there, kid," Tony said. "To satisfy the HMRC."

"What?" I couldn't believe what I was hearing.

"Listen." Tony put a hand on my shoulder. "Sandy's right. You were done up good style. Someone in Revenue and Customs had intelligence on you: they'd never have stopped you otherwise. They don't usually hang around much early morning when the low-cost punters are coming back from 'Una Paloma Blanca' or wherever."

"But Gav Taylor was the one who set me up. Why didn't they nobble *him*?"

"We think," Sandy Napier explained, "that Taylor is a runner for someone much bigger. Someone who is prepared to see a whole kilo of cocaine go to waste to divert attention from their main haul. There's a hell of a lot of cocaine getting into the UK via the Costa and we'd like you to sniff around, see what you can find out."

"We're assuming your mate had at least four times what you had on him, if not more," Tony said. "Did he ever take his jacket off? It was probably stuffed in the linings, strapped around his body, stuffed up his arse..."

"Thank you, Tony," Napier said.

I thought back to Gav, sweating like a pig as we went through security at Málaga, remembered him going through the metal detector with his padded jacket still on, his bag through the X-ray. Spending a long time in the bogs. It was all adding up.

"Why didn't it show up at security then?" I asked.

Napier rolled his eyes while Tony spoke to me patiently.

"It didn't show up because someone chose to ignore it," he said. "Nobody walks through security in a padded jacket."

"Someone was paid to ignore it," Napier added. "The technology is in place now to spot ten grams of cannabis resin in a toothpaste tube. All the errors that take place are human."

"There'll be someone, or several people, on security in Málaga who have been bought by one of the major crime firms," Tony explained. "The bent officer can turn a blind eye, distract his colleagues, all sorts of tricks. That's how the gear gets through. Tons of it."

"And unless customs have been tipped off at this end, then the stuff slips through. Ninety-nine per cent of everything that's caught is down to intel." Napier tapped his head. "And someone tipped them off about you."

"Who?" I suddenly felt paranoid.

"Whoever Taylor's working for," Tony said. "You were just the fall guy. When you go back, you might be able to find out."

"But they'll recognize me," I bleated, trying to find a way of wriggling out. Going back was the last thing I felt like doing.

"That's something we'll sort out," Tony promised. He patted me reassuringly on the shoulder. "And you'll be here for a bit first, retraining. By the time you're ready, not only will *they* have forgotten who you are, so will you."

Tony's attempt at humour didn't make me feel any better.

"Your job," Napier said, "is to go back there and put yourself right in the centre of this cocaine business. You were clearly pretty close already. We want intelligence on how and where it comes in, who controls it and who buys it. We have a few hunches, but we want hard evidence and inside information. When we eventually go in, we want to make sure we cut the head off the snake. Get it wrong and we do more harm than good. *Comprendez?*"

"*Sí, señor*," I said. I attempted a smile. I thought I knew what he meant, but whichever way, it was a big ask.

Sandy Napier stood up and held out his hand. "Good luck, Savage," he said. "Welcome back."

EIGHTEEN

Ian Baylis was no nicer to me than he'd ever been. The fact that I had been shot and effectively killed off on his watch seemed to have no bearing on how he spoke to me. No apologies, no regrets.

"Thought we'd seen the last of you," he said.

"If I'd had my way, you would have," I said. "Nice to see you, too, Ian."

He smirked and gestured for me to sit. "We're going to start some language coaching straight away," he said. "You won't need to be fluent. Your cover is that you're half Spanish: Spanish father, English mother. You've been brought up in the UK by your mother, but you've picked up a bit of the lingo visiting your relatives. Have a squizz at this." He passed me a file across the desk.

Your name is Pedro Garcia, birthplace Valencia, 1992. You moved to London aged two. Your father left when you were six. You went to a comprehensive school in Ealing and left before sixth

form to attend catering college. You dropped out
after a year and worked in several London hotels
and restaurants, including Sevilla Mia in Hanway
Street, La Rueda in Clapham High Street, then in the
upmarket Barrafina in Soho. You are keen, polite
and friendly, but a little bit slow off the mark…

"Read, absorb, remember," Baylis instructed. "We'll take you to these places so you can form a picture, get your backstory clear in your mind."

I felt myself resisting the idea of going through the whole process again. It had not been so long since I'd had to learn to be Eddie. "I don't even look Spanish," I said.

"All in good time," Baylis said. "You need to crack on with the Español before anything else."

The tutor was a nice guy. José Gonzáles, a short, bespectacled man from Seville – *Sevilla*, he said, pronouncing the *v* as a *b*.

I knew my way around bar talk already and he was pleased when I managed a brief conversation about beer and meatballs.

"*Muy bien*," he said.

We went through some basic grammar: how to address people without being too formal, how to ask a girl if she'd like a drink.

"Mistakes don't matter too much as you have been in England most of your life," José said. "Is just a case of being relaxed, trying to communicate, is charming."

He gave me a long list of vocabulary to learn, mostly

to do with restaurants and food; cooking terms. We worked from a GCSE textbook, all about finding your way to the skate park or swimming pool, football teams and *la discoteca*.

"I've seen enough Spanish clubs to last me a lifetime." I laughed.

"You like Spanish girls?" José asked. "Beautiful … *guapa*!"

He made me repeat *guapa*. When I said it, it sounded more like "whopper".

I had liked some of the Spanish girls I'd seen: beautiful, distant and dignified, walking around the port with their friends at night. They would stop for the odd *café con leche* or *chocolate caliente*, never drunk, never lairy. In truth, most of the girls I'd met in the clubs that Gav Taylor had hauled me around were English. They were of a type: poker-straight blonde hair and make-up designed to be worn in ultraviolet light. Scary in daylight. They were usually full to the brim with Smirnoff Ice and shots; hooters spilling out of lycra tops and lip-glossed mouths ready to snog at the drop of another drink.

I tried to get my mind back on the grammar.

"Is enough for today," José said. He could see that my concentration was wandering. "The most important thing … *muy importante* … is to listen and comprehend. You *must* understand. That way you will get information, but both the British and the Spanish will treat you as stupid and forget themselves when you are around. Act dumb, amigo."

* * *

I went back to Ian Baylis's office armed with textbooks, dictionaries and voice-coaching CDs.

"*Qué tal?*" Baylis asked in heavily accented Spanglish.

"*Bien, gracias,*" I answered, with a slightly better accent.

"Good. *Bien.*" Baylis sat down at his desk and flicked through my file. "You'll be glad to know that I'm no longer your case officer by the way," he said.

"Oh?" I was wary. As much as I was inwardly cheering, he was the devil I knew. Another case officer might be even worse.

"Why?" I asked politely. I thought I should show at least a glimmer of regret.

"I requested not to be." He brushed his hand across his crinkly hair and pursed his thin lips. "As you know, I was never keen on bringing you on board in the first place."

I nodded at the understatement. But the put-down hurt. I had laid my life on the line in his service. I felt bolder. "So what exactly is it you don't like about me, Ian?"

"Apart from your age?" He considered. "I think you're something of a loose cannon. I'm a bit old school. I was recruited after my degree. A first. Then the master's degree." I noticed him swell slightly with pride.

"What were your degrees in?" I acted interested.

"Politics, history and postgrad engineering," he said smugly. "Top of my year. I went straight into the service and spent my first two years analysing data at HQ." He found something to underline heavily in pen on my file. "Then another year sitting in a darkened room in

Sarajevo, listening to the conversation of lunatic politicians and warlords planning – and succeeding despite our best efforts – to wipe out whole villages of young Muslim men."

"Heavy stuff." I didn't know what else to say.

"Indeed. Tedious work, but important. Genocide: still going on in the late twentieth century, three hours from our doorstep. Most of them are dead or in prison now. That bastard Slobodan Milošević was lucky enough to have a heart attack in prison. We have Karadžić and Mladić, but there are still plenty of them about. Many will have moved on, some living in Switzerland, working as doctors, lawyers and so on. But there are others who will have taken advantage of the new freedoms in Eastern Europe – Russia, Serbia, Croatia, Romania, Albania – and used their experience, expertise and connections for organized crime. They have no national loyalty. Whoever is paying – arms dealers, terrorists, drug barons… They will be there to oil the wheels."

"So you're going back to Eastern Europe?" I wondered why he was telling me all this. Baylis swelled again and I could see it written all over his face. Promotion. It was as if he was an estate agent who had been elevated from flogging terraced houses to negotiating the sale of stately homes.

"I will be based here mostly," he said. "But don't forget, yesterday's Serbian war criminal will be today's drug baron or arms supplier. There are still some big fish out there that I am – we are – out to catch."

I nodded, trying to look suitably impressed, allowing

him the moment to be pleased with himself.

"So, you will understand, Mr Savage, given the kind of work I have done—" Baylis shuffled my file and stacked it on the desk— "why I might not be *so* enamoured of a young man who is thrown into the thick of South London crime, *living it large* and making my job difficult, with scrappy and random results?"

I was more than a little narked. They'd got their man and I'd got shot. Result.

"Different times?" I suggested. Baylis prickled.

"I'm not *that* much older than you, Savage, but fifteen years' experience makes a big difference in this game." He stood up, our meeting at an end. He held out his hand across the desk and I shook it, as limp and damp as I remembered. "I suggest you have an early night and start mugging up on that Spanish. You will meet your new case officer in the morning. I'll follow your progress with interest. Good luck."

"And good luck to you," I said. He looked at me as if he didn't need my good wishes. It was down to him to dish out the good fortune.

"Er, yes," he said. "Carry on."

NINETEEN

The hard bed in the accommodation block kept me awake half the night, but finally I'd nodded off with my iPod still in my ears, Spanish repeating over and over again and sending me to sleep. Then I woke up, panicking, wondering where I was. Once I had worked that out, I panicked more – about the situation I now found myself in.

Again.

The night went like a tape loop: a little sleep, panic. Nod off. Panic again. Shit.

At four in the morning, as the dawn was fingering its way through the institutional blinds, I got up and had a swig of water from the basin in the corner, then lay back on the bed. I drew the lumpy pillow around my neck and looked at the ceiling, seeing faces in the mottled paintwork and damp patches. I plugged the earphones in again and switched the playlist over to shuffle.

I found the heavy bass line of Public Enemy strangely inspiring so early in the morning: samples of Martin Luther King and James Brown, with Chuck D's deep voice rapping out mantras of protest and aggression. Like a call to arms, it got me out of bed, out for an hour's run and back for a shower.

By 7 a.m. I was in the canteen. It had only just opened and a few people who looked like they had come off a night shift sat around drinking tea and flicking through newspapers. I was starving after my run and browsed the selection behind the canteen glass. I went for porridge, followed by scrambled egg, tomato and beans, washed down with black coffee and grapefruit juice. Quite healthy, I thought, then returned for bacon and a sausage. I sat alone and was just reading the music review in the paper when someone sat down opposite me.

"Hello, handsome."

I looked up, my jaw dropping open mid-chew. It took me a moment to register her: the hair was a different colour, longer maybe. She had lost a little weight but still looked great.

Better than great.

The last time I'd seen Anna Moore had been just as I was losing consciousness on the floor of my flat in Deptford. At the time I had been bleeding heavily from the two bullets Donnie Mulvaney had popped into my stomach and lung. Anna had saved my life.

"I thought…" I began.

I didn't really know what I'd thought. The last time I'd seen her properly had been in Croatia while I was dicking about with Tommy Kelly, shifting champagne bottles full of cocaine and several million euros' worth of moody pictures. She'd left me instructions in a dead-letter drop in a

121

newsagent and I'd fluffed the pick-up, causing her no end of problems, no doubt.

Anna smiled at me wryly across the table. "What *did* you think?"

"I dunno," I said. "I guess I felt I'd let you down. I didn't know where you'd gone after Croatia. I was worried you'd been killed."

Anna took a bite from a piece of my toast and wiped a crumb from her lip. "I've been doing this a lot longer than you, Eddie," she said. "I know my way around."

I realized she was lifting a big lump of guilt that I had buried in the back of my mind.

"Obviously when you found me in Deptford I knew you were alive," I said. I tried to bring to mind the picture of Anna leaning over. But my life, or what remained of it at that point, was a blur of pain and morphine. It was just a bad dream now.

"Don't look so worried." She smiled. "I hopped across to Italy from Croatia, then went north and chartered a small boat to cover my tracks. I even managed a couple of days on the beach in Venice."

I must have looked taken aback.

"I'd got you tracked, of course," she explained. "I made sure I locked on to your phone when we were in Skradin. I sat on the Venice Lido watching your progress back to London, spent a couple of days in the Paris office just while you settled in, and then I was back on your case."

She was good.

"I never knew," I admitted.

"Of course you didn't. I'm very good at my job."

My hand went unconsciously to my stomach and touched the scar tissue of my bullet wounds. Anna caught the gesture.

"Although not so good that I could get there before you were shot, I'm afraid."

"Wasn't your fault," I said stoically.

"There were a lot of cock-ups that night, Eddie," she said. "But nothing that you can be blamed for." I was grateful for that. Like Tony, she seemed to be letting me off the hook.

"I'm back here though, aren't I? Whether I'm to blame or not."

Anna shrugged. "Nature of the business. Once you're in, you're in."

"At least they've taken Ian Baylis off my case."

"Yup," Anna said. "Good news for you."

"Do you know something I don't?"

Anna nodded. "Bad news for me, though." She smiled. "I'm your new case officer."

TWENTY

"So, Pedro Garcia," Anna said. "What do you think he looks like?"

We were sitting in Anna's office in the training centre a couple of hours later. I had run through my cover with her again and again, detailing my background.

"As little like me as possible," I said.

"I have a few ideas." Anna pushed some photos across the table. They were pictures of me, but they had been Photoshopped and digitally altered. They ranged from faces that looked pretty much the same as mine but with darker skin to someone with a completely different face shape and long black hair.

"How would you make me look like that?" I asked. Methodically I arranged the pictures from those with the least changes to the most extreme.

"Cosmetic surgery is an option," Anna said matter-of-factly. "A lot of war criminals and major villains will have a nose job, cheek or jaw implants or their eyelids tweaked to look a little different."

"I quite like my nose as it is," I said.

"It's a very nice nose." Anna smiled at me. "But we need to make some changes. A moustache or beard can make a big difference, or a change of hair colour."

"I don't think I can grow much of a beard," I admitted.

"Let's look at hair colour then." She held up some coloured swatches against my own dirty-blond hair. "We don't want to go too dark," she said. "Pedro has some English blood and if it's too dark, the regrowth will be too dramatic."

She pulled out a strand of chestnut brown from the hair swatch and layered it into my own. I felt her strong fingers and sharp nails against my scalp and found myself swallowing hard.

"Looks good," she said, "and your skin's already quite tanned. But you'll need to keep the colour up. Now, eyes."

Anna went to the desk and opened a small box full of tinted optical lenses. She planted herself in front of me and leant down, looking into my eyes. Hers were clear and greeny blue; wide with large pupils and full lashes. She held the coloured lenses in front of my own eyes, adding and subtracting tints. I broke away from her stare and found myself looking down the front of her shirt. It was a good view. Anna caught me at it and rolled her eyes.

"You don't change much, do you?" She laughed. She didn't seem to mind – after all, I had seen it all before. But our relationship had shifted. She was now effectively my boss.

"Sorry," I said.

"We'll have to go brown, but again, not too dark." She

selected a tint. "Contact lenses," she said. "Big difference."

For the rest of the morning I was seen by a hairdresser, an optician and a dentist. My longish hair was cut into a choppy, layered style and dyed, along with my eyebrows and lashes, the brown Anna had chosen. The hairdresser covered me with fake tan until my body was a couple of shades darker too. I was measured for contacts and the dentist took impressions of my upper teeth.

After lunch Anna took me through a rail of clothes that my alter ego might wear. None of them were what I would have chosen for myself and I grumbled a bit.

"That's the point, Eddie," Anna said. "It's not supposed to look like anything you'd have chosen. We're trying to hide you."

There were worn, sun-bleached sweats and vintage hoodies. T-shirts advertising metal bands and American bourbon. Board shorts and Levi's almost through at the knees. A pair of Camper shoes, some worn suede desert boots and a few pairs of Havaianas flip-flops.

That was about the size of Pedro Garcia's capsule wardrobe.

"You're quite scruffy. You probably wear your T-shirts a bit too long before they get washed," Anna said. "If your jeans were frayed at the bottom from dragging on the ground, it wouldn't worry you. Most days you hang out in just flip-flops and shorts."

I looked at the dark-skinned, dark-haired beach bum who stared back at me from the full-length mirror and began to feel Pedro Garcia take over. I walked around and found that the flip-flops gave me a certain splay-footed swagger. I rolled my shoulders, like I thought I was a bit hard but none too clever with it.

An hour later, the guy was back with the lenses and he showed me how to fit them. They were scratchy at first, as I'd never worn lenses before, but he told me I would soon get used to them. I would have to: I'd have them in for days on end.

Finally the dental assistant came back with a plastic box. Inside was a section of gum with three teeth attached, along with two spare sets. He sat me down and I opened my mouth. The extra teeth were wafer-thin and clipped over my own.

"Why *three* teeth?" I asked. I noticed already that the change in my mouth made me sound a little different, with a slight lisp.

"Four would look too symmetrical," Anna explained. "Most people have asymmetric faces. It's more natural."

The dental assistant held up a hand mirror to my mouth and I saw that the teeth matched my own in colour and size. The front incisors were perhaps a millimetre or so longer, but the effect just gave me a slightly more rabb-ity look. The third tooth was set at an angle and made my upper lip curl in a barely discernible way, as if I was doing a subtle Elvis impersonation.

Anna grinned and looked at me strangely, even she was convinced by the changes, despite having watched the process. I felt quite excited and ran my tongue around my mouth. I felt different. I got up and walked over to the mirror. I didn't recognize the dark-haired, brown-eyed bloke staring back at me.

Pedro Garcia.

And if I didn't recognize myself, I was pretty certain no one else would recognize me.

"*Buenas dias*," Anna said.

"*Buenas dias*," I replied. I shrugged, and noticed that even my body language had changed.

Anna picked up the phone. "Ready," she said into it. She turned to me. "There's someone here to see you."

A minute or two later, Tony Morris walked through the door. His mouth dropped open. He gave me the same strange look that Anna had, like he knew it was me but couldn't quite believe it.

"Bugger me," he said. "Pardon my French. I wouldn't recognize you in a million years. Great job, Anna. Genius."

"Thanks, Tony," she said. "Now we'd better get him trained for the job."

"What job?" I asked.

"Didn't I mention it?" Tony said. "You'll be working for a living."

TWENTY-ONE

In the days that followed, I spent my mornings training and my afternoons learning Spanish.

I was reacquainted with Jim Owen, the martial arts instructor. He put me back in the ring, sparring and shadow-boxing, then came with me on five-kilometre runs to improve my stamina. We moved on to some knife-fighting techniques and he showed me the differences between fighting with a long blade and a short one. Next to a gun, he said the knife was the weapon I was most likely to come across in southern Spain. He showed me how to parry an attack from a long knife or machete and how, if attacking with a longer knife, to get the dominant position. Very little was about chopping or stabbing: ninety per cent of it was to do with finding the right position then making a clean cut – across the eyes or to the throat.

Short-knife fighting was different, but again, like judo, was about finding the right position, using your opponent's weight and momentum against them. Then once you had your opponent where you wanted them, preferably in a headlock, you used the knife like a short, sharp punch into the thin bone of the temple or the cartilage of the windpipe. There was none of the dancing and circling you see in films; it was hard, fast and brutally effective. People didn't recover from this kind of combat. They didn't carry a brave-looking trickle of blood from a decorative nick on the cheek. These techniques left the opponent with blood pumping from the jugular vein or twitching as their brains shut down from a puncture wound to the skull. Dead as a dodo.

The next part of my training used sharp knives as well. Kitchen knives.

My evenings were to be spent training on the job. Once I'd covered everything I needed with Jim, Anna drove me to a restaurant in Clapham, Meson Iberico. She introduced me as Pedro Garcia to the patron and chef, Anibal Fonseca. He greeted me warmly in Spanish and I replied in my own halting way. Anna explained about my English origins and that I was coming to my mother tongue late in the day. He clapped me on the back and assured me that any friend of Señorita Moore was a friend of his and he would take good care of me.

Anna left me at the Iberico to work my first shift. While I was working there, the plan was for me to stay with her in her flat in Vauxhall.

"Are you sure that's a good idea?" I'd asked when she explained the plan.

"I'm cool with it if you are," Anna had said. "I need to keep an eye on you."

I wasn't sure I was *cool* exactly, Anna was still as hot as she'd ever been.

Anibal Fonseca started me on onions, keeping my fingers behind the blade and chopping them in an even dice. After I'd prepared enough for the evening's sitting he started me on tomatoes. I blanched, skinned and deseeded three crates, then chopped them into a *concassé*, the all-purpose tomato pulp used in much of Anibal's cooking.

During my first week, I learned how to make a stock from chicken carcasses and another from fish heads, bones and crab shells. My afternoons were spent stirring steaming vats of stock, full of onions, carrots, celery and parsley and seasoned with salt, black peppercorns and bay leaves. It was hot work, and in the evenings I would be running around, sweating, burning my arms on scorching pans and my fingers on hot plates.

You learn fast in a kitchen. It's a dangerous place, full of sharp instruments, scalding liquids and frayed tempers. Things are constantly going wrong: you have to think on your feet and most evenings are spent firefighting, forever keeping one step ahead of disaster.

It was good training for the kind of world I was getting involved in.

The atmosphere at the end of a busy night in the Meson Iberico was great. As the last guests rolled out, the tops were flipped off iced San Miguels and dozens of Marlboros were smoked in quick succession out by the bins. We would unwind with loud chatter and leftover plates of tapas: meatballs, calamari, *gambas* (prawns) and paella.

During my first three weeks at Iberico, I picked up

more Spanish than I had in all the previous months. I found myself relaxing into the rhythm of the language and, because we were constantly busy, I didn't have time to think too much about what I was saying. Words started to click into place.

After service, late at night, I would walk back to Anna's flat. It wasn't far, but the streets around there were rough. I found myself walking with Pedro Garcia's swagger; I felt harder than if I'd just been myself – or Eddie Savage. Pedro was quite streetwise and my recent training in hand-to-hand knife fighting made me feel that I could handle anything.

Anna's flat was on the top floor of a big Victorian house near Vauxhall Bridge. It was a week into my stay and I was just arriving back after a busy night. As I walked up the steps, I looked up. The lights were still on. I let myself in and headed up to the top floor.

The flat was spacious, with big rooms and real fireplaces, and I was impressed, complimenting Anna on having such a nice place. But, having stayed there a week, I was becoming aware that there was something missing. Most women have the trick of making places cosy and comfortable. Anna seemed to lack those skills. The place was clean and tidy, but cold, with no imprint of Anna's personality: no family photos, no pictures or ornaments.

Anna was still up when I got in. She was in her dressing gown, her hair still shower-damp, drinking a large glass of red wine and watching a late film on TV.

"Hey," she said, turning to smile at me.

"Hi," I said. I got myself a beer from the fridge. "Do

you want something to eat?" I called from the kitchen.

I decided to take her a small plate of paella, whether she liked it or not. I wanted her to try my first attempt.

"I made it," I said, going on to explain how I'd cooked it, how I'd fried the chorizo before the onions to give it depth of flavour, how I'd made the fish stock, that we only used the best saffron and Calasparra rice. Anna laughed at my enthusiasm.

"You sound like you're enjoying the job," she said. I realized that I was. "I wish I could cook," she added. "I even burn baked beans."

"I'm sure you could learn."

Anna shook her head. "No, I don't have the knack. It's not in my skill set. Besides, I like being cooked for." Anna scraped up the remaining rice with her fork and put it in her mouth. She licked her lips. "Plus I have you to cook for me now. Delicious."

I laughed but saw a look flash across her eyes. For the first time, I think I saw a chink in Anna's armour. She was lonely.

"You OK?" I asked.

"Yeah," she said. "It's been a long week, that's all. I'm tired, but my mind's racing and I can't sleep."

I felt the same, the adrenalin of a night in the restaurant still in my system. I glanced at Anna again, looked at her lovely profile as she turned back to the TV. Without make-up and with her hair tied up, she looked vulnerable and a bit girlish. Her dressing gown gaped a little and I could see the beginning of the curve of her breast. I took a gulp of my beer.

"I like cooking for you," I blurted out. Anna looked at me, puzzled. "I think you need a bit of looking after." I felt my face redden.

She smiled. "Thanks, Eddie," she said. "We'll look after each other."

I leant across and put my arm around her shoulder. She yielded slightly and I went to kiss her. Her lips met mine, close enough that I could taste a hint of red wine, but then she pulled away.

"I don't think it's a good idea, Eddie," she said. "It'll confuse things."

I didn't really care how confused things got. The more confused, the better. She stroked my face and kissed me lightly again.

"Let's just sit here together, can we?"

I pulled my legs up onto the sofa and lay my head in her lap. Anna stroked my newly dark hair.

"I'm not used to this new you yet," she said. "You're good at this, Eddie, it's like you're a different person."

"I'm the same inside," I whispered into the warm white towelling of her dressing gown. She smelt delicious; clean and fresh, a cocktail of hair conditioner, moisturiser and baby oil.

I nuzzled at her bathrobe, pushing open a gap in it. I placed my cheek against the smooth skin of her upper leg and breathed in heavily. As I breathed out, I felt her leg twitch. Her hips shifted as if she was adjusting her position. I breathed again, and placed my lips against her skin.

I felt her fingers tighten in my hair and her hips move

again. I put my hand on her knee and pushed the bathrobe away from her leg.

And when she didn't move my hand away, I thought
I might try kissing her again from this position.

TWENTY-TWO

The routine went on for a few weeks. I stayed in London and increased my shifts at Meson Iberico, and as I did, both my cooking and my Spanish improved. The whole kitchen was Spanish-speaking: from the patron, Anibal, and the sous-chef down to the Brazilian washer-up. I eventually became capable of understanding different speeds and dialects.

My repertoire of Spanish dishes also expanded. Anibal told me that an apprentice would not usually progress so fast, but I was being hothoused on Anna's instructions, plus I was a good pupil.

I learnt to make Gazpacho Andaluz – cold tomato and vegetable soup – and a Portuguese fish stew with orange peel and anise. I was shown how to cook hake in salsa verde – I'd never even heard of hake before. Anibal told me if you can cook hake, *merluza en salsa verde*, then you'll get by in a Spanish kitchen.

I learnt a rustic recipe for rabbit stew and couldn't believe how simple it was. One onion, chopped and fried in olive oil, one rabbit cut into pieces and browned in the same pan, a tablespoon of flour sprinkled over it, plus half a bottle of white wine. Throw in some carrots and herbs, cover for 45 minutes and it's done. Sprinkled with fresh parsley and with mash or rice on the side, it is *good*. *Conejo guisado al vino blanco.*

I cooked it for Anna one night and she loved it. In my opinion, she didn't eat properly if left to her own devices. Her fridge was full of half-eaten tubs of coleslaw and cottage cheese and bottles of sauvignon blanc. I started bringing back proper food, and when it was presented to her she ate like a horse. Although she was supposed to be my boss and mentor, sometimes it felt like I was treating her paternally. Making sure she was properly fed and watered.

Over a few weeks, we had slid into an odd arrangement. Some nights I would sleep in my own bed, other nights Anna would call me into hers. I began to get a growing sense of her loneliness; hungry for physical closeness one night, withdrawn and distant the next.

I knew very little about the real Anna Moore. All I'd ever seen was the confident, fast-talking, great-looking woman who seemed to take everything in her stride and could hold her own in a dangerous, violent world. I remembered how originally she'd been set up to keep me sweet and how I'd felt cheated by her. I realized now that she considered petty morals unimportant in the scheme of things.

She must have been in her early thirties but seemed to be married to the job. The only things I knew about

137

her background were that her father had been in the army and that she'd been to twenty different schools. She was pretty closed off about the rest of it. A combination of habit and training, I suppose.

In sensing Anna's loneliness, I became aware of my own. When I looked at my circumstances, I realized we were not so different. I had an absent, alcoholic father, a depressed mother and dead brother. No real home. The only girl I had ever been really close to, Sophie Kelly, had gone.

But Anna was here now, and she made me feel secure. Plastered the gap in my own life. She had already saved my life once and knew the ins and outs of the business we were both in.

I enjoyed my job, too. I was working hard and it gave me the sense of purpose I had been missing.

After six weeks, Anna told me that my basic training was nearly complete. I remember the morning, lying back on her bed with the sun streaking through the high Victorian window. I was watching her hooking up her bra and thinking, idly, how good her bum looked. She turned round and caught me in the act.

"Never seen a naked woman before?" she asked cheekily.

"Not one as good-looking as you," I said. It was only half true.

"Don't get too comfortable, will you, Eddie?" she said. "They're making noises about sending you over pretty soon."

My stomach sank. She was right. I was getting

comfortable. The job was hard work, but I enjoyed it, not to mention coming home to a beautiful older woman every night with no strings attached. What's not to like? An eighteen-year-old's dream.

I got out of bed and headed for the shower. Anna grabbed my wrist as I passed.

"Don't be spoilt, now." She must have seen the look on my face. "It's been good while it's lasted. Hasn't it?"

"Yeah," I agreed reluctantly. "It's been good." I kissed her cheek and got into the shower.

I was signed off the following week and I said good-bye – in reasonable Spanish – to my friends at Meson Iberico. They were genuinely sad to see me go, and I was sad too. It *had* been good. Anna drove and we headed across Vauxhall Bridge and up towards the A40 and Beaconsfield.

"I'll be keeping a close eye on you," Anna said. "And I'll be over to see you now and again."

"Yeah?" I asked. "How does that work?"

"I'll be your sister who's come to visit or something. You'll have an apartment."

"Sure." I was being surly and I knew it.

"Come on, lighten up, you know the way this business works."

I did, but it didn't mean I liked it.

Tony Morris was there to meet us at HQ. He laughed and gave me one of his bear hugs.

"Hola, Pedro." He chuckled. "I still can't get used to you looking like this, kid."

It was funny how quickly I had got used to being

Pedro Garcia. Under Anna's guidance, I knew how to top up the dye in my hair and did it without thinking every five days or so. I took out the contact lenses as soon as I got back to the flat every night and put them back in again automatically every morning. Eventually I just left them in. Anna and I had pretty much forgotten what I looked like before.

Tony briefed me about what to do. He gave me an address and the keys to an apartment tucked away in the backstreets of Benalmádena.

I was a bit surprised to be sent back *exactly* where I'd started and said so to Tony.

"You hit the jackpot straight off," was all he said. Then changed the subject. "You can see the sea," he remarked. "If you go up to the roof and use a periscope."

He also gave me keys to a moped to get around. I would find it underneath the apartment block. There was a floorplan that indicated a loose panel in the bathroom where I would find everything I needed, including currency, a cash card, a Spanish driving licence and two Baikal IZH-79s – a Russian pistol, the gun of choice on the Costa – plus two hundred rounds of ammunition.

"If you're found with a converted blank pistol, a Walther PPK or anything else, people will want to know where you got it," Tony explained. "If you happen to be caught with a Baikal, no one will think twice. I hope you won't need to use them."

"Thanks," I said. I'd done some firearms training with Jim Owen and I was pretty accurate, if I say it myself, although confronted with a real person rather than a cardboard cut-out with a target over his heart might be a different matter.

"There's a variety of bugs and listening devices in the apartment as well. You know the drill."

I did know the drill; I had planted plenty of them in the Kelly house in my time. I knew the fear of being caught out every time I planted a new one. Remembered how I had felt when one was discovered and I looked like the only sucker who could have planted it.

"It's mostly a looking and listening job," Tony said. "You need to keep your eyes sharp and your ear close to the ground, and once you've made some contacts, do a bit of covert surveillance. It'll take you a while to find out what's what, so don't dive in at the deep end."

"I won't," I promised. Pedro Garcia is a little slower than me, and I could imagine him taking his time, looking blank when necessary.

"We've got you a little job down there," Tony said. "Give you something to do while you keep your nut down. It's a bit of a blood bath where the drug deals are concerned, and our priority is for you to be delivering intel back to us to keep Revenue and Customs sweet."

"Gotcha," I said. "Where am I working?"

"Our contacts have got you a place working in a restaurant owned by a couple of expats," Tony said. "It's just a few streets back from the harbour. It's called Bodega Jubarry."

TWENTY-THREE

The body count was rising on the Costa, but since he had recovered from his shoulder wound, Donnie had been put on lighter duties in and around Benalmádena.

Nearly twenty middle-ranking drug dealers had either been shot or had disappeared, and the paranoia created by this was having the required effect, turning dealer against dealer, gang against gang.

And Donnie had only scored one scalp.

He knew he wasn't going to earn his stripes this way and he realized that in Patsy Kelly's eyes he had probably already failed. Not only had Tommy Kelly's downfall back in London happened on his watch, but he'd also got shot on his first job on the Costa and been seen. Plus he was getting on, forty-eight next birthday, and at this rate destined to be a foot soldier for the rest of his working life.

While Terry Gadd and the rest took out the big boys in Puerto Banús and Marbella, Donnie had been assigned to keep an eye on the clubs and the small-time pushers closer to home.

Benalmádena had been hit harder by the recession than

most of the coastal towns. It did not have a big, smart harbour to attract real money, neither did it have the architecture or scenery to be a proper holiday resort. Dozens of bars and small businesses had closed their doors in the past three years; building sites were abandoned and chained up and new developments stayed undeveloped.

Donnie had noticed the change in the Spanish youth since he'd been here. They were no longer respectable kids who avoided trouble and went home to large families; with the huge unemployment in the area, they had begun to hang around the streets, and in particular an area known as 24-hour Square. They had begun to do anything for a quick buck – spliff, trips and Es – and had started to look like the "gangstas" they modelled themselves on, wearing tattoos and baseball caps, pimp-rolling around the backstreets and port area looking like something they'd seen on MTV. They drank, too, aping the habits of the British holiday-makers who swamped the coast in the summer, and now they were dipping their toes in the drugs trade.

Bizarrely, Donnie found himself feeling a little moralistic about this change in the Spanish kids. He'd liked it here before, when everyone was pretty well behaved – apart from him and his colleagues, of course. He hated the idea that the local youth were now getting involved in the business; didn't feel it was theirs to become involved in. Like Patsy said, the drugs trade had always been controlled by Brits. Now, to Donnie's disgust, his job was like being a village policeman, mopping up these small-time Spanish dealers and giving them a slap.

Stav Georgiou had joined him. Everyone knew Stav was as thick as two short planks and had messed up on his second mission, shooting a British doorman in the face instead of the

Albanian gangster he'd gone for. So, he was assigned to the small clubs with Donnie. The only benefit of working with Stav was that his stupidity meant he didn't question anything. He simply followed orders.

He made Donnie feel like a mastermind.

The night before they'd been to a club called Kon-Tiki, a Hawaiian-themed dive near 24-Hour Square. Some young Spanish kid had made it his base for dealing and was acting like something from Goodfellas, standing at the bar, smoking; good-looking and sharp-suited. Cocky, like he was José Big-Bollocks. That was until Donnie and Stav arrived around 1 a.m.

The kid had cut up rough, telling them that it was his town and that he needed to make a living. He said his uncle was the mayor of some village. Suggested they could do business together.

Donnie said he could be the Lord Mayor of Bleedin' Madrid High Street for all the difference it made, laughing with Stav at the boy's presumption and, while they were still laughing, dragged him outside, flattened him and kicked his head around like a football before stamping on his face. He would never be quite so good-looking again.

If he lived.

Donnie and Stav had left the scene calmly, satisfied that they had given an effective warning, while the Spanish kids picked up their friend's limp body.

Donnie reached for the alarm clock. 10.30 a.m. He'd not got to bed much before five, after a few beers and the best part of a bottle of brandy. He put the clock back and looked at his fist. There were a couple of tooth marks from where he'd laid out

144

the Spanish youth. His knuckles throbbed with arthritis. He lay still for a moment, trying to identify the other aches and pains in his head and body, then reached out again, this time for a packet of fags. He pulled one out and lit it, instantly convulsing into a fit of coughing. He was still coughing when his mobile rang.

Number blocked. He looked at it for a moment, got the better of his cough and answered it.

"Arthur Sixpence…"

"Don?" the voice asked.

"Who is it?"

"Dave."

"Dave?"

"Don, it's Dave."

"Dave who?"

"Dave, Don. Dave."

"Dave Dave? Why didn't you say so?"

"I … listen, Don. I need to know what's going on."

Dave Slaughter's voice finally got through to Donnie's hung-over brain. Donnie hadn't seen or heard anything of Dave since Tommy had gone down and he'd come to Spain. In the old days Dave had been Tommy's driver and closest confidant.

"Where are you, Dave?" Donnie asked.

"Can't tell you, but I'm not over there."

"Lucky you," Donnie grunted. "It's shit."

"I know," Dave said. "That's why I'm calling you. I need to know what kind of shit. We're getting all sorts of reports back and the guv'nor doesn't like what he's hearing."

Donnie's head was beginning to clear. The guv'nor meant only one person: Tommy Kelly. And he was in Belmarsh.

"What do you know, Dave?"

"I know that Patsy thinks he's running the show; that he's started some kind of turf war down there. But Tommy doesn't trust Patsy to see the bigger picture. He's trampling over all sorts of stuff Tommy set up and he's really going to mess things up with the Russians and that. If Patsy thinks he's running anything, he's wrong… You know as well as I do that Pats couldn't run an under-age cider-drinking contest at a school fucking disco. Tommy still has a lot of clout even from where he's sitting."

Donnie suddenly felt guilty, as if he'd somehow betrayed Tommy Kelly and jumped far too quickly when Patsy had told him to jump. On the other hand, if he hadn't, he was pretty sure he wouldn't be alive now.

"What do you want me to do, Dave?" he asked. "It puts me in a difficult place."

"Who's your loyalty to, Don?" Dave asked. "The bloke who treated you right all those years, or the one who you already had to bale out ten years ago and who's about to cock it all up again?"

"The guv'nor, of course," Donnie said.

"Right," Dave continued, "what I want you to do is be my eyes and ears over there. Let me know what's occurring on a daily basis. Tell me who's next on the hit list, who's whacking who, how high up the list they've got. TK needs to square it with the big boys, otherwise the firm is going to be very unpopular worldwide."

"I've been sidelined, Dave," Donnie admitted. "I screwed up a hit; I'm a bit on the outside."

"Then get back in, Don." Dave sounded impatient. "You're

in the right place. Hang out in the right bars. Pick up what you can, get back to me."

Donnie's hangover began to pulse loud in his head. He was getting confused, couldn't work out which side his bread was buttered. All he knew was that he still wasn't a big fan of the younger Kelly brother – or his mullet-haired sidekick.

"I'll do what I can, Dave," he said.

"Yes, you will," Dave concluded. "By the way, bit of good news. They're moving Tommy."

"Moving him?" Donnie asked slowly.

"Out of the 'marsh. Be careful who you tell, Don."

Donnie tried to pull his fried brain into focus. "I will," he promised.

But Dave Slaughter had rung off.

TWENTY-FOUR

It was easy to find Bodega Jubarry.

I knew my way around the harbour area of Benalmádena, of course, and Jubarry's was a couple of streets back, overlooking a small plaza.

I went in and introduced myself to my new boss, Barry Ambrose.

"You come highly recommended, Pedro," he said.

I hadn't a clue who had recommended me, or how. Connections, I guess.

Barry's handshake was not just a little limp, but shaky, his fingers trembling into nicotine-stained points. He picked another Benson & Hedges out of the gold packet and put it to his purple lips.

"Pleased to meet you," I said. "Great to be here."

He raised his eyebrows, as if it was a surprise that anyone might be pleased to be in Benalmádena.

"Drink, Pedro?" he asked. He waggled a bottle of brandy that he picked up from the bar.

I nodded. "Just a beer, please."

Barry poured me an Estrella Damm from the pump and tipped himself a large brandy into a glass of chocolate milk.

"*La Bamba*," he said. "Chocolate and brandy. I have stomach ulcers."

I suspected that he might be better off without the brandy altogether, but he looked like his nerves needed steadying. I took a sip of my beer, ice-cold with condensation on the glass, and looked at Barry properly. His clothes were sharp; pink cardie, pressed white shirt and creased grey slacks, but his body looked malnourished and shrunken inside them. His face was drawn and red veins crackled from his nose across his cheeks. The end of his nose looked slightly blue and the whites of his eyes yellow.

On close inspection, he looked as sick as a dog.

"We're quiet in the mornings, as you can see." He waved his fag around in a vague gesture. "A few in for lunch, but Wednesdays are always calm, so it'll be an easy start. Couple of hours off in the afternoon, then we get busy proper from about nine till the cows come home."

"Fine," I said.

"Can you start straight away? I'm short-staffed."

I had come directly from Málaga and still had my bag with me, but I didn't see why not.

"No time like the present." I smiled. "I guess I can take my stuff to the apartment this afternoon." Barry looked relieved.

"Good man," he said. "I'll give you a lift up there later."

A door opened behind the bar and a woman stepped out into the shadows. I could see she had a good figure and nice hair, but when she came into the light I realized that she was made up to be seen from a distance of ten metres, in low light. At least ten years younger than Barry, she had probably been good-looking once, but her hair was dyed red and her orange foundation was thick on her face. Like Barry, she had expensive clothes and, like him, she looked like she'd shrivelled a bit since she'd bought them.

"Hello, darling," she said, looking me up and down. She tilted her head coquettishly.

"My wife, Julie," Barry said. Julie held out her hand graciously.

"Pedro," I told her. "Pedro Garcia."

"Get me a drink, Barry," she ordered. "And one for Pedro." Barry obediently put a large vodka in a tall glass, poured in some lime and filled it with soda, then poured me another beer.

"English, then?" Julia asked.

"Yeah, my dad's Spanish. Mum's a Brit."

"You've got the Spanish looks," Julie said. I guessed she might have had a drink already.

"Put the boy down, Julie." Barry laughed. "He's starting work straight away."

I drained my beer while Julie smoked. I didn't want to chat too much, remembering that I was supposed to be shy and a little slow on the uptake. Then Barry took me on a tour of the premises.

We ended up in the kitchen, where the permanent

chef, Carlos, was making soup, stirring pots and basting chickens that were slow-roasting on a grill.

"*Hola, amigo,*" he said. "*Qué tal?*"

"*Bien,*" I replied, shaking hands. He was a short, dark man, unshaven with twinkling black eyes and uneven teeth. His chef's whites were anything but, and he had a greasy little cap jammed on top of his curly black hair.

"Show Pedro the ropes, Carlos," Barry said loudly. He gestured around the kitchen in place of speaking Spanish.

"No problem, Barree," Carlos said, his English heavily accented. "I show him rope."

He slapped me on the back and pointed at a huge pile of filthy aluminium pots and pans stacked up by the sink.

"First jobs. Wash up!" Carlos slapped me again and laughed.

Lunch was over by about three. I had done sink loads of washing up, scraped burnt rice from paella pans, cooked some chips and waited a few tables. Well, taken out bowls of olives and bread. It appeared you had to be multi-skilled to work at Bodega Jubarry: demanding work. Suited me.

Barry drove me back into town after lunch. The shocks on his dusty beige Mercedes rattled as we crossed the main road and hit the potholed roads on the outskirts. The ashtray was overflowing with butts. We drew up outside an orange stone apartment block.

"Not bad," Barry said, surveying the building. "Nice and quiet, anyway."

I looked back across the dusty street to the unfinished

development opposite, its pre-formed concrete slabs piled up, windowless, like the ghost of a building. Two industrial-sized wheely bins spilt their contents onto the road. Several skinny cats with Egyptian heads sniffed at the scraps.

"See you back around seven?" Barry asked.

"Sure," I said. "Thanks, boss."

He gave a throaty chuckle and winked at me, then placed the cocktail stick he used in place of a cigarette between his teeth and drove off.

I let myself in with the keys Tony had given me. The apartment was warm and stuffy: thermal, aluminium-lined curtains had been drawn across the window to keep out the heat of the day. I drew them back and slid open the picture window, which led to a sliver of a balcony with a plastic patio chair. The apartment was positioned at the back of the building, over the air-conditioning duct, looking out onto a narrow backstreet full of parked cars and cats. At least I wasn't overlooked. Maybe that was why I'd been given it. Basically, I was tucked away in the shady arse-end of a semi-occupied apartment block in a town that was down on its luck.

Whatever it was, it was going to be home for a bit.

There was one main room with tiled floors and white-washed walls. A round table with two high-backed chairs at one end; a small TV and a heavy wooden Spanish coffee table at the other. Off the main room was a bathroom, a tiny galley kitchen and a bedroom.

Instinct and training combined, so my first move was to sweep the place for bugs. I checked the curtains, behind the doors, inside the kitchen cupboards and even in the ceiling lights. There were plenty of the insect variety – dead flies, spiders and mozzies – but no surveillance equipment as far as I could see.

I went into the bathroom and felt the panel on the side of the bath. It took a couple of tries, but once I had the knack, the side came away easily. As promised, there was a stash of stuff behind it: a fake driving licence and all sorts of other cards; a few bits of surveillance kit; a transmitter that looked like a plug adapter; some standard magnetic bugs; listening devices; a button camera. A Spanish mobile phone with various SIM cards. A new laptop with a dozen memory sticks, an iPad – which I immediately booted up – and then the Baikal, boxes of ammo and several knives and nasty-looking knuckledusters.

For the moment I just out took the iPad, the cards and some money. There was at least three grand in euros, so I wouldn't have to worry too much about the €200-odd Barry had promised me a week. I was about to put the panel back but then picked out one of the knives.

It was a short, wide-bladed, vicious-looking thing, no more than ten centimetres long. It had a knuckleduster grip, which the blade folded into, and felt good in the hand. I closed the blade and pocketed the knife.

Just in case.

TWENTY-FIVE

I arrived back in town early. It only took me five minutes on the moped and I enjoyed the ride, cutting through the familiar backstreets and down to the harbour, still wondering why I was back in the same town. I stopped by the pontoons and strolled down to look at the yachts where I'd been working only a short time before with Gav Taylor. Some of them had gone, but one or two were still there, hatches locked and no sign of Adie. I was confident that if he had been there, he wouldn't have recognized Pedro Garcia.

When I got to Jubarry's, Carlos was bringing out small trays of tapas from the kitchen and putting them in the display cabinet at one end of the bar. I helped him line up Spanish omelette, meatballs, fried baby green peppers, potato croquettes, chorizo and grilled prawns. Jubarry's wasn't the best place in town to eat tapas, but there was always something to nibble with a drink.

A couple of Spanish workers drifted in for a beer and I served them while Barry was still upstairs. They smoked as they chewed bread and sucked the brains from a plate of prawns.

"The boss sleeping," Carlos told me, making a drinking gesture followed by a loud snore and a hands-together sleeping mime.

I polished tables and laid out cutlery in the restaurant. A few tables began to fill on the terrace as the sun lowered, and at around eight the Spanish families began their evening stroll around the cafés and bars of the harbour area. They looked glamorous, healthy and happy in the golden, early-evening light.

My eyes followed an absolutely stunning girl as she crossed the plaza. She was tall, like a dancer, and moved with a cat's ease. She caught me staring as she came closer and I broke my gaze. She walked right up to the restaurant and I thought she was going to say something about me gawping at her. I felt like a plum. She was so cool and beautiful and there I was, staring at her with my mouth open.

"*Hola*," she said. Her voice was deep and husky. She walked straight past me and into Jubarry's. I caught her scent as she brushed by: floral but musky, almost hippyish. She was wearing a tie-died wrap-around skirt and I could see the shape of her legs and bum through the thin fabric. Nice ankles, bare, brown feet in Brazilian flip-flops. A tight, yellow T-shirt that revealed that her top half was every bit as good as the bottom. Big, black, ringletted hair.

She made me feel hungry.

If she wanted a drink, I was going to make sure I served her. I rushed inside and dipped behind the bar, popping up as she arrived at the counter top.

"*Beber*?" I asked.

She almost laughed, showing even, white teeth. I must have looked comical in my eagerness to serve her.

"*No, gracias*," she said. "You speak English?"

"*Si.*" I nodded, and she smiled again. Without saying another word, she stepped behind the bar and opened the door that led upstairs to Barry's apartment.

"You can't go ... *no pasar*," I said feebly, but really I would have let her do anything she wanted. I would have robbed an old lady if she'd asked me to.

"Yes, I can," she said, taking an apron from the back of the door and tying it over her skirt. "I work here." She held out her hand. It felt long-fingered and warm. "Juana."

I spent the rest of the evening like a puppy. Running around after Juana, making sure she had everything she needed while she waited tables. Some gallant part of me felt that she was too good to be doing this work, that somehow I should rescue her.

Actually, who was I kidding? I didn't feel gallant. I didn't want to rescue her at all. She seemed perfectly capable of looking after herself. She was confident and assured and looked above it all, the small smile that played at the corners of her mouth suggesting that she treated it all as a game. What I really wanted was to kiss her from head to foot and lie naked in a rumpled bed with her, drinking her in, while the sun shone outside.

Barry and Julie finally came down around ten-thirty. Barry had spruced up in a clean striped shirt and did the rounds of the tables, dispensing his sickly smile, while Julie sat at the bar and drank gin. I refilled her glass regularly and she winked at me each time until her wink became a blurred, two-eyed blink and a grimace.

Barry gave us a break at eleven and I stood out the back of the restaurant, drinking Coke with Juana while she smoked. The only other girl – woman – I knew who smoked was Anna. I didn't mind it; Anna made it look sexy. The way Juana put a Fortuna to her full lips didn't look unattractive either. A lot of the Spanish girls still smoked. I'm not a health and safety officer.

"Your English is good," I told her.

"You have to speak English here or you don't get work," she replied. I nodded. Every bone in my body wanted to chat her up, impress her, but I had to keep reminding myself that my cover persona was a little bit slower.

"Why's your Spanish not so good?" Juana asked.

"I've lived in England for most of my life," I explained. "My dad is Spanish, but I never see him." I found myself putting a Spanish-accented lilt on my English. I felt easier talking to her from behind an accent.

"Me neither." Juana took a puff of her cigarette. Seeing her inhale deeply, I realized that I equated smoking with people under pressure. Either stressed, like Anna, insecure, like Cath, or, perhaps like Juana, a bit more emotionally volatile.

"What happened to yours?" I asked. "Your dad?"

"We don't talk about him," Juana said. She put her cigarette out. "*Vámanos*, Pedro," she said. "Work." And we went back inside.

Around eleven-thirty, a white Porsche Cayenne drew

up outside and parked slap bang in the middle of the cobbled pedestrian area. No one made a peep of complaint, but the crackle of electricity as the men and women who got out, slammed doors and sat at the best table out the front could be felt right through to the kitchen.

I watched from the bar as Barry hopped around nervously and Juana went across to the table, smiling broadly and handing out menus. On her way back to the bar the smile left her face just as quickly as it had arrived and she rolled her eyes at me. She obviously knew these customers.

All four of them spoke English in loud voices. The loudest of the men at the table wore a bright Hawaiian shirt and had wavy blond hair styled in a mullet that must have gone out of fashion thirty years ago. In a rasping voice he ordered champagne for the group: two perma-tanned beauties and a stocky bloke who chewed gum ferociously and wore a lot of gold jewellery.

Barry clicked his fingers at me, eager to please the new arrivals. I found an ice bucket behind the bar and filled it. On his instructions, I got a bottle of the proper French stuff, Bollinger, from the fridge and took it out with four glasses. No cava for this lot. Barry was still fawning over the table when I got there, his banter jumpy and punctuated with nervous laughter. He looked pleased to see me so he could change the subject.

"Here we go," he cheered. "Vintage Bollinger, first one's on me."

I placed the four glasses on the table and popped the cork as I'd been shown by Tommy Kelly back in the day. The trick was not letting it fly, but twisting it and easing it out with a quiet pop. Discreet and not showy. I poured three glasses carefully, tilting the glass at an angle as I'd been taught. The fourth glass I had to lean over to fill. The woman righted the glass while I was pouring and the froth shot to the top, spilling over and splashing on to her dress. She squealed dramatically, and the temperature around the table plummeted.

Barry's face dropped.

The bloke with the wavy mullet grabbed a napkin and pawed at the woman's lap and then her knockers, mopping up overenthusiastically, and the woman started laughing.

"Any excuse, Terry," she howled, tugging at the neck of her dress, exposing more cleavage, and the bloke laughed too.

Then Barry laughed. "Sorry about that," he gushed. "Pedro's our new boy."

"Not for much longer if he sprays the good gear over Sylvia," the one called Terry said. He mimed a pistol shot at me.

Barry looked from one to another, decided that they were all finding it funny, and laughed louder.

"Not the worst thing she's had sprayed over her tonight!" Terry wheezed.

His date slapped him playfully and they roared louder. It was clearly not their first drink of the night.

"Anyway," Terry laughed, "Sylv don't drink much..."

The others waited in anticipation of the well-worn pub joke.

"...she spills most of it!"

Their mouths flew open in abandoned laughter, none wider than Barry's. He shook his head and slapped his knee, mopping imaginary tears from his eyes, as if in disbelief that anything so funny could have been said, here, tonight, in his very own bar.

"Tell us one of yours, Tucker." Terry nudged the other man at the table, who was more muted in his laughter.

"You know I ain't good at jokes, Tel," he protested. The girls egged him on, but he sat deeper in his chair. Terry seemed disproportionately disappointed that Tucker wasn't joining in. The smile creases disappeared from the corners of his eyes and mouth. The women stopped laughing too.

"Tell us a fucking joke, Tucker," Terry barked. "Tell us a joke. Now."

Tucker squirmed uncomfortably for a moment, then pulled himself to his feet. "I'll show you the one-eared elephant." He looked eagerly from face to face for approval. The girls smiled, urging him on, but Terry's expression was stony.

Tucker pulled the pocket of his trousers inside out and went to undo his flies. The girls laughed ... the joke seemed to be that merely the suggestion of what he was about to do made it funny. Terry looked on, unsmiling.

"Go on then," he said. "What you scared about, you knob? The cat got your dong?" He stared hard at Tucker.

"That's the joke, Tel," Tucker pleaded. "You don't actually get the old chap out."

"Do it," Terry commanded.

Tucker swallowed hard and proceeded to unzip his

flies, then limply exposed himself to the table – and anyone else who was brave enough to be watching.

Suddenly Terry burst out laughing, slapping Tucker on the back and shaking his hand. "You fell for that, Tuck!" he roared. "I was having a laugh!"

Tucker looked somewhere between tears and laughter, but managed to get a grip.

The party, and Barry, collapsed again into helpless laughter.

"*Número dos!*" Terry shouted, waving the empty Bollinger bottle at Barry. Barry flicked his fingers at me and I went to find another. Juana had it ready behind the bar.

"Who are *they*?" I asked. I already knew the type. I had hung around with plenty of them while working for Tommy Kelly.

"He's called Terry Gadd," she said, waving her fingers at her neck to indicate the mullet. "The one with the hair. He's not a nice man."

"I guessed that," I said. I took the next bottle to the table. Barry patted me on the back and urged me to pour.

"Careful this time, Pedro," he said. "Then get some food for this table. Tapas, olives, anchovies and that." He followed me as I left the table. The Spanish couples who were eating inside were beginning to leave, annoyed by the raucous behaviour out front. Juana, everyone's favourite waitress, cleared their tables with apologies and liqueurs on the house.

"Be very nice, kid – anything they want," Barry confided. "No questions. Mr Gadd's offered us a sweet catering job this weekend. Top dollar, champagne all night."

I nodded, impressed.

"All leave is cancelled," Barry slurred. "We're going to pull out the stops and show them the kind of spread Jubarry's can put on."

"Sure," I said. It was what I was here for, after all.

"It's a birthday party." Barry leant in close and I could smell sour, anxious shit-breath. "Someone special."

"Who?" I asked, chancing it. I was right to try. Barry was pissed and full of it. He tapped his nose and held his finger to his lips in the way only drunks do.

"Mr Kelly." He winked.

I felt myself go cold.

"Patsy Kelly."

TWENTY-SIX

Donnie sat on his new information for a few days. Chewed it over in his mind, and then over and over again, until it was like a spent piece of gum in his mouth, lacking flavour, surprise or satisfaction. It had hardened into a chewy lump of fact, bound to be spat out at some point.

As the information became used and familiar, Donnie began to dissect Dave's parting shot.

Be careful who you tell.

Dave must have known that there were very few people Donnie could share the news with. Who was he going to tell? A couple of nightclub bouncers? His ex-girlfriend? Cogs began to clunk into place and Donnie wondered if by feeding him the gen, Dave had meant Donnie to share it with the one big contact he still had. Maybe Tommy wanted Patsy to know that he was being moved to a less secure environment, and that from there he would be able to exert his influence more powerfully.

The thought firmed up in Donnie's mind.

Get back in, Dave had said. That could only mean getting back in with Patsy. Eyes and ears. Reporting back to Dave. In with Tommy as well. All bases covered. Donnie felt the surge of a new mission begin to take hold.

He was sitting outside a backstreet café in the port. He'd finished his coffee and first brandy of the day and sat back, enjoying the sun on his face. He began to think that a line of marching powder might be just the thing to liven up another dull day in Paradise. Something to kick-start his mind and give him the confidence to think bigger. He shuffled in his seat as the waiter brought him another café solo and a brandy, crossed his legs and studied his shoes. He'd bought this one good pair since he'd been here. Light Spanish moccasins. They were expensive and the leather was soft enough to deal with his swollen feet – and the occasional crippling attack of gout in his big toe. He looked at the shoes, stretched at the toe joint, scuffed and beginning to go through at the soles. In a rare flash of insight, Donnie likened the shoes to himself. Quality – well made from good materials but beginning to get scuffed and battered through hard usage. Ready to be binned or repaired. Donnie was of the opinion that quality gear should be maintained and repaired. He always took his suits to the dry cleaners, ironed his own shirts and sewed on buttons where necessary, if clumsily. He was like that, he thought. Repairable. Just needed brushing off and dusting down to be as good as new. Back in the game.

That brandy was good stuff.

Encouraged by his train of thought, Donnie heaved himself out of the café chair and through to the lavabos at the back of the bar, where he unfolded a paper wrap and treated himself to a large line of the granulated white powder. He snorted it through a rolled ten note on top of the toilet cistern and wiped up the

164

remainder with his finger, rubbing it across his gums. Hygiene wasn't at the forefront of his mind.

Donnie unrolled the ten and slapped it on the bar on his way out. Seizing the moment, he took out his mobile and speed-dialled the number for Casa Pampas. Terry Gadd answered.

"Yes, Don?" he snapped. "What do you want? If it's money, don't ask. If you've had enough of the job, fuck off and your cheque will be in the post. Everything's going jolly well and I don't need you kicking off. Keep it tidy down there, mopping up the wallahs, and your position in the firm is safe. OK, Don? Nice to talk to you, you old c..."

Donnie was silent, his hatred for Terry Gadd hardening in his bowels. He let the silence continue.

"Well?" Gadd asked. Donnie's silence had momentarily put him off his stride.

Donnie coughed. Put on his nearly-posh voice. "I would like to see Patsy," he said deliberately. "On his own."

Gadd was silent for a few seconds too. "It's his birthday," he rasped. "He ain't seeing no one. There's a photographer here. Celebrity photographer, from Lundun."

It was as if the presence of a photographer superseded all other business. Donnie knew the syndrome. Tommy, if he had a weakness, was a bit infected himself. If anything showbizzy came his way — meeting a celebrity or someone who had once been on telly or in the pages of Hello! — he went all soppy. A few years before, Tommy had had his photo taken at a do with his arm around the Scottish TV presenter Lorraine Kelly.

Crime had become the same as all other industries, Donnie thought. Celebrity endorsement would cure all ills.

"I think he'll want to talk to me," Donnie said, undeterred.

"Fuck off, Don," Terry Gadd said.

The line went dead.

Deflated, Donnie, went back into the bar and knocked back the last of his brandy and coffee. Then his phone went off.

"What is it, Don?" Patsy's voice.

"I got something I think you should know. Can't talk on the blower."

"Get a cab up here," Patsy told him. "You've got five minutes with me. If it's shit, you're brown bread."

Casa Pampas was full of noise and excitement. It was Patsy's fiftieth, and there was going to be a bash the next day, Saturday. Donnie felt about half his normal size, diminished as he always was here, tiptoeing across the slippery tiled floor of the hall. Felt he should have taken his shoes off, like you did in posh houses back home.

There were kids in the pool this time, chaperoned by Patsy's ex-wife Jacqui and her Botoxed mates. They were all blonde highlights, tits, legs and Liz Hurley bikinis, drinking around the pool. Either Jacqui hadn't wanted to be in the photos or she hadn't been asked. Donnie stepped into the vast living room that led to the poolside, where the shoot had been set up. A spiky woman with tortoiseshell glasses and a linen trouser suit shot Donnie a look that could have frozen molten lead at a hundred metres. She was running the set-up; clipboards, studio lights and bottled water. She looked completely out of place, but what she was being paid at London fashion rates, Donnie guessed, she wasn't grumbling. She put a finger to her lips and Donnie stood silently in the background, as welcome as a fart in a space-suit. The photographer, a complete, dyed-in-the-wool woofter to

Donnie's eyes, danced around behind the tripod with tousled hair and a white shirt open to the waist.

"Lovely, that's great. Fantastic. Look to me…"

The lights popped and Donnie looked at Patsy, sitting on a designer throne-like affair with his three kids, Chantelle, Storm and Victoria, at his feet. Chantelle and little Victoria were dressed as fairies and Storm Kelly sported a tiny black pin-striped suit and a trilby.

Patsy was something else. Donnie could have sworn he was wearing orange make-up, and his suspicions were confirmed by the slight stain on the collar of his frilly white shirt. He wore a purple velvet suit and crocodile loafers with the distinctive gold Gucci snaffle glinting in the lights. Patsy shook his wrist to make sure that the Rolex with the diamond numerals got in the shot. His hair had been brushed into a smooth red meringue and he smiled, giving the full effect of white, American-style dentistry.

"Lovely, great," the photographer said. "Got that. If the kiddies could change into the Bo Peep stuff, we'll move on."

Donnie thought it looked like a gyppo's wedding.

The lights went dead and Patsy stepped off the set and came over to Donnie, looking like a cross between some poncey French king and Liberace.

"Birkin," Patsy said. "Best photographer in the world, bar none. He only goes by the one name. All the best smudgers do that. He'll get this in Vogue, Tatler, Vanity Fair, whatever. He's done Naomi Campbell and the Queen. All legit, Don. Show the Russians we've still got it. Class."

Donnie nodded. Tommy would never have allowed his celebrity photos to be published. They were for his study and for silver frames on top of the grand piano.

"Kids look lovely," Donnie said. "And you look ... special."

Patsy gave him a glance, making sure he wasn't taking the piss. Donnie gave nothing away.

"You got five minutes," Patsy said. "While I get changed."

Donnie followed Patsy to a bedroom, where another set of clothes were laid out. There was a tailcoat, silk waistcoat, buttoned breeches and buckled shoes. Donnie watched while Patsy stripped to his pants, looking almost vulnerable in frilly shirt and bare legs with socks.

"Well?" Patsy asked, struggling with his breeches.

"I got some information, Pats."

"Where from?"

Donnie coughed, shuffled his feet. "You'll understand, I have to keep my sources secret at this point, et cetera. But straight from the horse's mouth—"

"Stop fannying about," Patsy barked. "What?"

"I have conditions," Donny chanced. Patsy Kelly stopped still and hoicked the breeches up to his waist.

"You're priceless, Don, you know that? Conditions? You waste of space. Fuck off."

Donnie stood his ground. "Nothing big, Pats. I just want to be back up here, in the firm. Not doing street-cleaning duties."

"What have you got?" Patsy asked.

"I've got word from Tommy," Donnie said.

Patsy paused for a moment while he considered. Donnie had his attention.

"OK, here's the deal," he said. "If what you've got is of the slightest interest to me, you can come back up here and lick my bath out every day. Clean the whole gaff up with your tongue. Deal?"

"Whatever you say, Patsy."

"Give."

"They're moving Tommy from Belmarsh."

Donnie could see from Patsy's expression that this was news.

"When?" Patsy asked.

"Dunno yet. I can find out." Donnie attempted not to sound eager.

Patsy Kelly thought for a moment. Put on the waistcoat. "OK, Donnie boy, I want a full report of whatever your 'sources' tell you. And I can find out who they are, so don't muck me about, understood?"

"You got it," Donnie said, swelling.

Patsy pulled the tailcoat over his shoulders, looking like something out of a Hollywood Dickens film. If they'd ever done the porn version. He went to a drawer in his bedroom and pulled out a roll of fifty euro notes, then handed them to Donnie.

"If you're useful, I might reassign you some duties, OK?" he said. "Not a word to Terry or anyone. Don't let me down, Don."

Donnie nodded. Trousered the money. New shoes, he thought.

"Welcome back," Patsy said. "Now piss off, I'm making movies."

III

Tercio de Banderillas

Tercio de banderillas *("third of flags"). In this stage the three banderilleros each attempt to plant two sharp barbed sticks into the bull's shoulders. These weaken the bull but also anger it, resulting in even more ferocious charges.*

TWENTY-SEVEN

We were all at Jubarry's by six in the morning on the Saturday, yawning and bleary-eyed. I don't think Barry had been to bed.

Juana had been off the night before, but even she looked tired. There was a puffiness under her eyes and her hair was wet, straight from the shower, but she still looked lovely. Although I'd only known her a few days, she kissed me on both cheeks when I arrived, like an old friend. She made me feel safe and warm, in touch with another real human being. I realized I'd hardly thought about Sophie since I'd clapped eyes on Juana.

Barry jumped around the kitchen, twitching and coughing instructions, less than useless. He drank strong small coffees by the bucket load, which made him jumpier than ever.

Carlos seemed to run on different fuel from everyone else. Years of producing breakfast, lunch and dinner for hotels full of package tourists meant that a party for a hundred or so was a walk in the park for him. He'd

173

been in the kitchen for forty-eight hours non-stop, making bread rolls, cold soup, vegetable stews and salsas that would form the basis of the buffet. The tourist slump had meant that Carlos could recruit a cheap army of freelance seasoned caterers for the day, making it look like Jubarry's had a staff of thousands.

They grilled prawns, stuffed mussels, steamed clams, split lobsters and battered squid until there was an ocean of cold seafood on platters, ready to go. The hake in green sauce and paella would be produced on-site.

Carlos ran around like a conductor on whizz, layering platters into the back of a couple of Transit vans hired for the occasion. Serious-looking Spanish women in black clothes clucked among themselves and tended the loading.

Barry, on his fifteenth fag of the morning, took me and Juana aside. "I want you two front of house. Meet and greet, make sure everyone's got a drink, *comprendez*?" He took a deep pull. "Ninety per cent speak English, so you can do the how d'you dos and Carlos's lot can do the service. Make me proud."

Barry took a double vodka from the optic behind the bar, and seeing his hand shake I would have been surprised if he made it through the day.

Of course, I knew who Patsy Kelly was. And over the past few days I had found myself wondering whether I'd been planted here. Was it just a coincidence or had I been drawn, by my own stupid instinct, into the nest? No one had told me to come to Spain to begin with. I thought I'd come with Gav Taylor out of choice, but my paranoia made me wonder if there had been a bigger plan.

Fate? Surely not.

Coming across another member of Tommy Kelly's family in my first week was more than coincidence. I had a growing feeling in my gut that I'd been stitched up again, so before I left that morning I'd armed myself with a handful of bugs, my mobile and the knife that I liked – well if not *liked*, the knife that made me feel safe.

With the food all loaded, we piled into the vans and several cars and drove across the motorway and up into the hills above Benalmádena, where Patsy Kelly lived, hidden away behind acres of olive trees and winding, rocky roads.

Casa Pampas wasn't visible at first. All that grew out of the cactuses and prickly pears was a white wall, and all that could be seen at the entrance was a steel gate surrounded by cameras and barbed wire. The house was set back somewhere behind this barricade.

My heart started thumping as we waited for the gate to be opened. I was trying not to be overdramatic about it, but there was something almost symbolic in the gate: my portal back into the world of the Kelly family.

However, this house couldn't have been less like Tommy Kelly's period property back in London. It looked like everyone's idea of a villain's house. White walls, palm trees, glass and chrome everywhere. I tried to look straight ahead as I carried in trays of food, not wanting to appear inquisitive, yet incapable of stopping my eyes from darting left and right, wondering if I would catch sight of the man himself.

It was still only nine in the morning, so I guessed the family was still in bed. Besides, we weren't in the main part of the house. We were setting up outside, on the vast patio area and in the pool house. We put up circular gas burners for the paella pans and to cook the fish, which for the moment was kept in cold boxes that I stacked inside the pool house.

It was impressive inside, in a flashy kind of way. The floor was made up of dark grey flagstones, cool under-foot, and the walls were lined with smooth wooden planks. A jukebox stood at one end, and near it a pool table. There was a big black-and-white photo of the Kray Twins on the wall and, hanging next to it, a pair of giant-sized red boxing gloves. At the other end of the room there was a steel-topped bar with a shelf above it, groan-ing with every known colourful cocktail ingredient, and there were optics filled with the usual stuff – gin, vodka, whisky and rum. There was beer on tap and fridges were stocked with bottles of different brands.

The whole place felt like a cool American bar.

I remembered where I was and why I was here, and slipped a small magnetic mic from my pocket and attached it to the underside of the bar. It may not have been the ideal position, but I knew from experience that you had to seize the moment. I didn't know if I was ever coming back. I heard someone come in and quickly popped up from beneath the counter.

Fortunately it was only Juana.

"What are you doing?" she asked.

"Trying to keep all this stuff cool," I said.

"As long as you're not stealing drinks," she retorted, and smiled.

"I'm not a thief," I protested.

"Don't even think about it," she said. "These are pretty dangerous people."

"I know," I said. Juana narrowed her eyes at me. "I mean ... I've heard.

TWENTY-EIGHT

When he finally came out of the house, there was no doubt about which one was Patsy Kelly.

Guests had started arriving at 12.30 p.m. and the lane outside Casa Pampas suddenly became clogged with Porsches, Ferraris and four-by-fours representing every luxury brand. The crowd was exactly what you'd imagine at a villain's birthday party in the sun. There was an explosion of shirts that looked like splashes of coloured vomit. There were lightweight suits in pale and pastel shades. Feather-cut hair and highlights. Plenty of jewellery.

And, as the joke goes, that was just the blokes.

There were some local dignitaries, too: Spanish men with moustaches, slicked-back hair and shiny suits. Juana recognized one as the local mayor and another as a minor politician from Mijas.

Of course there were a few heavies as well, bullet-bonced in white shirts and reeking of aftershave. The women were just as fragrant but their outfits more varied, jockeying for position as the lowest cut top, the highest split thigh, the most exposed back.

In my experience, villains' wives tend to fall into two categories: the faithful girls who have been with them and stayed loyal since way back when; and the second wives and girlfriends who tend to be twenty years younger than the gnarly old arms they're hanging off. What both types have in common is that they make the effort. This lot were buffed, shined, manicured, pedicured and waxed to within an inch of their lives. Whatever they had was on show, whether backs, fronts, legs or teeth. They were like prize ponies, there to reinforce the status of their owners.

Patsy Kelly's girlfriend was at the top of the pile. She wore a dress split to the waist, showing brown, oiled, gym-toned legs that rippled like those of a thoroughbred. The back of the dress was scooped down to the cleft of her buttocks and the front looked as if two small bald blokes were trying to escape from it.

My breath came in short bursts as I caught my first sight of Patsy Kelly. The family resemblance was clear: Patsy was a redder-headed, coarser-looking version of his elder brother. His skin was more tanned, the teeth bigger, whiter. His eyes were harder; not cold, but hooded and angry, darting around, checking on everyone and everything.

When it came to clothing, Patsy Kelly parted company with his brother completely. Tommy was all understated Savile Row suits and suede shoes. Patsy looked as if he might be doing a Las Vegas show: linen frock coat, frilly shirt and crocodile loafers. He had rings on at least four fingers; gold, with one flashing a large stone. Heavy gold chain dangled from his wrist and around his neck.

There were murmurs of "Pats" and "Patsy" as he stepped out onto the patio. Handshakes and back slaps were exchanged and more champagne was poured.

The thing about serving drinks is that no one is even looking at you. You might be invisible for all the thanks you get, and this crowd's manners weren't all that. Not that I minded; invisible was fine by me.

The lunch was served from giant paella pans and people sat eating under umbrellas at café tables set around the pool. I poured more champagne, sangria and Rioja and the pitch of the conversation became louder and rowdier with each drink, almost drowning out the flamenco guitarists who were playing on the far side of the pool.

I helped clear up and took the opportunity to slip inside the house, where the kitchen was open for washing up. I dumped a pile of plates in the dishwasher and considered. There was no one around except for one of our guys, washing up at the sink. I felt under the worktops and found an overhanging lip. I dug in my pocket and brought out a small bug, sticking it underneath, out of the way.

Encouraged by my success and the quiet in the house, I ventured through into the open-plan lounge, which was furnished with leather furniture, thick rugs and big, tacky lights. I planted another behind the steel uprights of a bookshelf, then slipped through to the hallway.

There were several doors off the hall and stairs up to the next level. I had half a mind to nip up the stairs, but I heard a toilet flush and one of the doors near me opened, leaving me frozen to the spot. Terry Gadd, the man with the blond mullet who I had seen at Jubarry's, came out. He sniffed and pinched his nostrils, looking straight at me. He was followed by a woman; not the one I had seen him with before, but a brunette of even more generous proportions, also wiping her nose.

"What you looking at, tinkle?" he asked. I was caught out.

"*Lo siento*," I said. "Lost."

"Kitchen's that way." He pointed at the door at the side of the hall and, feeling simultaneously stupid, guilty and terrified, I thanked him and went back outside.

The dancing started at around six and I continued to pour drinks. Terry Gadd caught my eye once or twice and I looked away. I had been stupid drawing attention to myself like that.

The band played "La Bamba" and people did that drunken jive thing, spinning around and laughing. The mayor and the politician sat together with their wives. They drank moderately, covering their glasses with a hand when offered, looking a little out of place. Others sat around, quietly sloshed, chatting and smoking.

I think I was the only person to see the sniper.

I was standing near Patsy Kelly, and being one of the few sober people left in the place I still had my wits about me. I don't know why I was looking up, but something drew my eye to the roof. It was only as if a shadow had passed, but I kept my eye on the tiles and saw the movement again. As my eyes adjusted to the lowering sun coming from behind the roof, I saw it was the top of a head, and, and, pressed to it, the telescopic sights of a gun.

And I could see where it was aimed.

I would probably have saved myself and plenty of other people a lot of bother, had I just watched and let the planned course of events unfold.

However, instinctively I shouted to Patsy to look out. He'd had plenty to drink and was slow turning round, but I leapt over and pushed him as the gun went off – and a woman sitting at a table near the pool took the bullet destined for Patsy Kelly. The woman next to her shrieked as blood spouted from her friend and another shot ricocheted off the tiles around the pool. Suddenly screams went up from everywhere, the music stopped and men drew pistols and looked for the source of the gunfire.

A second gunman appeared on the roof and, along with the first, sprayed bullets across the patio of Casa Pampas. People ran for cover inside the house and the pool-house bar while Terry Gadd and a couple of others shot randomly up at the roof. Patsy Kelly was well inside by the time the would-be assassins had skidded down the slates and away into the scrubland behind the house. When Terry Gadd scaled the back wall, they were long gone.

One of Patsy's heavies had taken a shot to the head and was lying in a pool of blood. I looked across the patio to where the first woman was lying, bleeding, across a table. She looked dead, her dress soaked black with the blood. There were two more bodies on the poolside: another woman, motionless, and a man, clutching his thigh and groaning. I looked around for Juana but could see her nowhere. I suddenly had a horrible premonition and crept out from under the roof to look in the pool.

There was a body there and, to my instant relief, I realized that it wasn't Juana, but a small boy in a black suit, his fedora hat floating beside him in the bloody water that curdled around his body.

I dived in.

TWENTY-NINE

Donnie's new shoes were pinching.

He was seriously pissed off. The day before, he'd driven up to El Corte Inglés, the department store just outside Málaga, and bought himself a nice new pair of daisy roots. They were soft leather, like before – Spanish, but in the low light of a dark club they could be mistaken for Gucci. In the shop he'd thought they fitted like a glove, but today, after walking around in the heat, they were nipping his toes on one foot and rubbing the heel of the other into a blister.

He'd really bought them so he'd have something new and smart to wear to the birthday party, but it wasn't until he had phoned Terry Gadd the night before that he realized he wasn't invited.

"You may be back in," Gadd had said, "but you're staff, Don. Not family."

The rejection had hurt. The bottle of single malt he'd bought for Patsy was unwrapped and consumed. In England he had definitely been part of the family: a long-serving driver, hit man and minder, trusted enough to ferry Tommy Kelly's wife and kids around. Trusted enough to murder anyone who got in the way.

To be rejected by the younger brother was a big, dry slap in the face.

By Saturday lunchtime, Donnie consoled himself by driving down to the beach and paddling his hot, sore feet in the surf. A couple of beers later, he was feeling marginally better and after a few more he began to feel human. Or as close as he ever got.

By six in the evening he was rolling drunk, walking from bar to bar, propping up various counters and smoking, talking to anyone who dared communicate with a drunk who looked as if he could walk through brick walls. Donnie barely noticed the sirens that raced up into the hills as the sun began to set, stuck as he was in a drunken conversation with an English bloke in a bar.

His tongue loosened by beer, vodka, wine, brandy and cocaine, Donnie found himself overcoming his dented pride by bragging.

A lot of them did it down here, Donnie knew, bigging themselves up to make it sound like they were connected; blokes who boasted that they had worked with the Krays years back, as if that still gave them protection. If everyone who reckoned they'd played a part in the Brink's-Mat gold bullion robbery had actually been there, there would have been about a thousand villains on the job. The Brink's-Mat robbery of twenty-five million pounds' worth of gold bars from Heathrow Airport, back in the 1980s, had certainly set a few up in business – but not even a tenth of those who claimed to be connected.

Donnie had never mouthed off like that. He had never needed

to, as he'd always been confident about his protected place in the Kelly firm. And the ruthlessness of the Kellys had never been in question, nor its bankrolling of jobs. The Kelly firm had been pivotal in making the Brink's-Mat job come off but had never felt the need to boast. Now Donnie felt like a large turtle without its protective shell: needy, vulnerable and drunk.

Bragging.

He talked about keeping the Eastern Europeans at bay and whacking small-time Spanish dealers. He talked about protecting nightclubs back in the UK and running cocaine up the Channel.

By the time the English bloke had bought him two more large vodkas, he was talking about the big Romanian and Russian names who had moved in, about how he was trusted by Patsy Kelly and how he even knew about an important prison move that was taking place in England.

Donnie clumsily tapped his nose to emphasize the secrecy of the move. A secret now shared with the stranger and anyone else who was listening at the bar.

The bloke hadn't appeared particularly interested. In fact, Donnie barely remembered anything about him by the end of the evening, save for his nasal voice, unremarkable, unlined face and crinkly hair, and could hardly recall anything he'd told him. Couldn't remember when and on what terms they'd parted.

It was only when he was fumbling in the pocket of his jacket for his apartment key later that night that Donnie pulled out the creased photo the man had given him, asking if Donnie knew the bloke in the picture. Donnie couldn't see straight and put the photo back in his pocket, where he forgot about it for some time to come.

*　　*　　*

I woke up looking straight at her beautiful face. A mass of dark curls spread across the covers and long, black lashes stayed firmly shut. Where her face was pressed against the pillow, her lips were pushed out into a pout and I leant over and kissed them. Her eyes flickered and I kissed her again. Her eyes opened.

She looked surprised to see me for an instant, then appeared to remember and her face relaxed into a smile.

The day before had turned into a bit of a bun fight, to say the least. I had finally found Juana at the end of the day, trembling and traumatized after the bloodbath she had witnessed at Patsy Kelly's poolside.

I had hauled the kid out of the pool and pumped the water out of his chest, not even realizing, as I saved him, that he was Patsy Kelly's son. Helping Kelly dodge the bullet *and* rescuing his son and heir, I felt I was becoming a bit of an unwitting patron saint to this family who had dogged my life for the past year and more.

The kid had honked up some pool water and jerked back to life, breathing in rasping spasms. I'd taken his little suit jacket off and found that his arm had been merely nicked by a bullet. There was a lot of blood, but the wound was superficial. In fact, once he was out of danger, I was sure that in time both he and his father would be proud of his first wound.

There had been a lot of screaming, shouting and confusion, and after half an hour a couple of ambulances had snaked their way up from the town. At the final count there were several walking wounded, a few more serious casualties and two bodies: the English woman who had caught Patsy's bullet in the throat, and Ricky Barker, one of Patsy's minders. Both dead as doornails. One of the more seriously injured was Barry, who had taken two or three bullets in his lower abdomen and bellowed and roared with pain. They were pouring brandy down his neck as his light grey slacks darkened with blood and his wrinkled face paled with the loss of it. He eventually passed out and was stretchered away, closely followed by a wailing Julie. No one else seemed too bothered about him. Patsy and son were safe.

The Spanish police put in an appearance and made some perfunctory notes, looking vacantly at the roof where the assailants had escaped. Really, they must have known that this sort of crime was out of their league. It was the kind of incident that would be settled by the involved parties, not by a couple of Spanish plods.

We started to clear up the catering stuff and filled the vans while Patsy Kelly and his family licked their wounds indoors. Terry Gadd saw us off the premises, assuring Carlos, who was shaking like a leaf, that we'd still get paid. Juana and I dumped the empty platters and crates back at Jubarry's and locked up, with no appetite to keep it open any later.

We walked into town, away from the port and into the backstreets, where we both felt a little more secure. We held hands on the way, needing each other's company. We stopped in a quiet tapas bar down an alley, shared a carafe of red wine and picked at some olives. The place smelt of wood smoke, and a guy picked out quiet flamenco on his guitar, drowned out by the football that the patron was watching at the bar.

We went back to the flat, clung to each other for a feeling of security. We held each other tight, then tighter still, then we kissed and pulled each other's clothes off. Eventually we slept a bit and woke up late morning.

"This town is getting worse," Juana said. I got out of bed and drew back the curtains, letting in midday light. "It has always been bad, but now it is becoming a battlefield."

She told me about her wayward father and his drug problem, and how her mother had struggled to support her. I was certainly able to relate to that. I told her as much as I could about my situation. I felt I knew her already; we felt familiar and easy talking together. We just clicked. We got on to the subject of mothers and how protective they can be. Juana seemed to be as protective of her mother as her mother was of her. She said her mother always seemed to go for the wrong men.

"And you?"

"I choose carefully," she said. She rolled back and stretched, pushing the sheet away unselfconsciously, displaying her long brown body.

"So why me?" I asked, part probing, part looking for flattery.

"I feel comfortable with you," she said. "And I don't think you're as dumb as you act."

I laughed. I put my hand on the flat of her stomach and felt the rise and fall of her breath. She rolled towards me and put her hand on my waist, then let it trail down to the scar on my stomach.

"How did this happen?" she asked.

"Boring," I said. "An operation. Or maybe I should have told you I was gored by a bull, or got into a sword fight over a girl..."

"Would you fight a duel for my honour?" She leant over me and her long, dark curls formed a curtain around my face as she planted small kisses on my lips. I could smell the faint muskiness of her hair and the sweetness of her breath.

"To the death," I said, wanting to keep hold of the moment. I returned her kisses and stroked her back, feeling her smooth bottom under my hand.

"Promise?" She shifted and climbed on top of me. The feeling of her body brushing the length of mine made me tingle. My breath came in short bursts.

"Promise," I said.

At that moment, I would have promised the world. And then some.

THIRTY

"Do you know what the hell's going on here, Tony?"

I used my hotline to Tony Morris as little as possible. It had been made clear to me that my deep cover meant I was to communicate with London only in emergencies, but I was angry and scared.

I had waited until Juana left to see her mother to make the call. I needed to talk to someone else, to play out and share the horror of the past twenty-four hours. After all, I wasn't long out of post-traumatic stress rehab.

"You OK, kid?" Tony enquired. He might have been asking if I'd caught a cold.

"Yeah, just fine," I said, sarky. "Yeah, you've only put me in a restaurant that just happens to service another branch of the Kelly family and their lovely friends. So I work my nuts off all hours of the day and night to cater for a party where the birthday surprise is that half the guests get mown down by machine-gun bullets. Ta-dah!"

"You're not hurt, are you?" Tony asked, concern nearly perceptible down the line. I considered a moment.

I wasn't hurt. But how many milliseconds, how many centimetres stood between me and one of those random bullets?

"No," I said finally.

"So there you go," Tony answered. Safe and sound, his tone implied.

It was like my mum telling me not to be so silly when, as a kid, I *almost* fell off my bike. *Almost* came off the swings.

Almost took a bullet to the head.

"Listen," Tony continued. "We know it's kicking off over there, but we also know you can handle it."

"Why me?" I asked. "You chucked me in right at the deep end. You never mentioned anything about Patsy Kelly, and you've delivered me right to his doorstep. Cheers."

"And would you have gone if we'd told you that you'd be dealing with Patsy?"

"No," I said.

"There you go," Tony answered. Point proved.

"I thought I was free of the Kelly business."

"You're our *expert* in the Kelly business," he said. Despite myself, I felt a quick rush of pride. "No one has been closer to that family, no one knows it from the inside like you do. There's no one else we could have sent in, Eddie. They'd have sussed me, or Anna, or *anyone* else in five minutes."

Eddie.

Tony had slipped up, used my classified name rather than my code name. I realized he wasn't quite as cool as he was pretending to be. He was on edge.

"Pedro," he corrected himself quickly.

"You called me Eddie."

"It's OK," he backtracked. This is our one-to-one. It isn't recorded. This is your helpline, remember?"

"Good evening, Samaritans," I joked. "I've been stitched up by people I thought were looking after me, and find myself in a basket full of bullet-spitting cobras. I was thinking about jumping out of the window to my death. Can you help?"

"You're not, are you?" Tony asked, concern suddenly clearer in his voice.

"Leave it, Tony." I said. "Do you take me for a sap?"

Silence.

"Don't forget, this is part of a deal, mate," he reminded me. "A deal that keeps you out of the nick."

I half-suspected them of setting me up with the drugs bust in the first place. If I had never worked for them, I would never have found myself in Stoke or in rehab with Mr Stitch Up, aka Gav Taylor.

But then again, I didn't know who I would be now, or what I'd be doing if Tony hadn't recruited me.

That's life.

Tony continued. "If it makes you feel better – and I shouldn't be telling you this – Baylis has been over there a couple of times, gathering intel." My heart sank.

"I thought he was after Serbian war criminals or something," I said. "He told me he'd moved on to bigger things."

"Mate, if there's one thing you should have learnt by now, it's that it's all linked. I've told you before. Any warlord worth his spots is at some point going to be involved in all the other illegal trades: drugs, guns, money laundering. They need to raise funds either to fuel a revolution or to feather their own nest when it's all gone tits up. They can't exactly try and overthrow a small Eastern European state, then, when it doesn't work out, go and get a proper job, can they?"

I supposed not.

"So they go to places where there's fast bucks to be made, where they can hook up with other people like them. Bigger picture, kid, bigger picture."

"Yep."

"Baylis is on it. He's on the trail of some Serbian warlord who's supposed to be holed up down there. Keep your ear to the ground."

"Working for Baylis again?" I said. "Great."

"He's good at his job," Tony reminded me.

Tony had a knack of making me feel like hanging out with the villains – whether it was in South London or southern Spain – was a breeze compared with what was going on in the big, wide, dirty world.

"Let me tell you," he continued, "we're keeping a close eye on what's going on down there and if, for one moment, I think it's going to blow up and that you are in personal danger…"

I waited to see where this was going.

"…we'll be on it like a sack of newts."

"Nice one, boss," I said, smiling at his phrase. "Thanks for the heads-up," I added, batting back the kind of corporate jargon I knew he liked to hear. "I'm on message."

Even though I had little faith in Tony's pep talks, I always felt an almost paternal warmth come from him down the phone. I knew he wasn't perfect, but I liked the man. After all, I'd known him all my life. Like it or not, he was part of my background, part of who I was, part of the person I had become.

"Reassured?" he asked.

"Yeah, thanks," I said, knowing what he wanted to hear.

"Keep calm and carry on." He hung up.

I wasn't calm and I didn't want to carry on at all.

THIRTY-ONE

We tried to keep business as usual at Jubarry's.

Barry was still in hospital up in Málaga hooked up to a drip. They had operated on him to remove the bullets, but they had trouble repairing his torn gut. No doubt years of poor diet and a daily bottle of spirits had done little for his internal health. He never looked that great on the outside.

Julie went to see him most days. When she wasn't at the hospital, she was upstairs, hitting the bottle and feeling sorry for herself.

Carlos ran the kitchen, but without Barry fidgeting and fussing around him, he seemed a bit aimless and distracted. I would often find him missing or out the back on his mobile when we had orders to complete. Instinctively, or following my training at the Iberico, I found myself stepping up to the plate, driving orders along, carving ham, serving tapas, uncorking wine, waiting tables with Juana. We weren't rushed off our feet, but there was a steady stream of custom and we began to find our own rhythm.

A week to the day after the Kelly party, Juana came into the kitchen looking worried.

"Pedro," she said. "He's here." She did the thing with her fingers to describe Terry Gadd's mullet. "He wants to see you."

My stomach lurched. A lunchtime visit from Terry Gadd couldn't be a good thing. I wiped my hands and took off my apron, unconsciously smartening myself up to go front of house, or maybe to face a man as dangerous as he was unpredictable.

"All right?" he said when I appeared. He wore his customary twisted smirk, as if he was keeping something to himself. He threw some keys on the bar – Playboy Bunny key ring, black car key – and gestured for me to pick them up. I did. "Come outside," he instructed.

My heart was thumping as I followed Gadd into the street. Paranoia chewed my gut as I tried to remember what he may or may not have seen me do at the house the week before. Maybe he'd found a bug. I half-expected a hail of bullets or at least a blow to the back of the head I squinted as my eyes adjusted to the bright sunlight.

Gadd was standing next to a shiny red car, its convertible roof folded back. It had tan leather seats and a matching steering wheel. Nice touch.

"Alfa Romeo Spider," Gadd croaked.

I made admiring noises.

"Drive," he said. He pointed at the driver's door. I hesitated; in all the movies I'd seen, an invitation to drive was usually a one-way ticket to your own shooting.

"Where am I going?" I asked shakily. I glanced back at

Juana, who stood in the doorway of the restaurant, chewing her lip.

"Anywhere you like," Gadd said. His face split into a hoarse laugh, showing flattened, piggy teeth. "It's yours."

I looked at him blankly.

"The kipper's yours, a present from Mr Kelly."

I finally found my voice. "What?"

"Mr Kelly is giving you this car," Gadd spelt out. "As a thank you for saving the kid."

"I didn't really…" I began.

"And he reckons you pushed *him* out the way of a shell."

"I just did what anyone would have done," I said, regaining my composure. I really didn't want to be credited with saving Patsy Kelly from a well-deserved bullet. "I can't take the car." Now it was Gadd's turn to look as if he couldn't believe what he was hearing.

"You what?" he said. His face became more serious.

"It just doesn't feel right," I said. "I can't take it."

Gadd shook his head and scratched at the back of the blond mullet. "No, no, no, *no*," he said. "You don't understand. If Mr Kelly says he wants you to have the car, then you have the car, *comprendez*?" He spat white phlegm into the gutter. "Patsy'll be very offended if he hears that you even tried to refuse it."

I stood, looking at the Alfa Romeo. It was a nice car, but it came loaded with a boot full of heavy baggage.

"I don't want it," I said.

"You ain't got a choice." Gadd laughed. His usual white Porsche Cayenne roared into the square and the driver swung the door open for Gadd to get in. He jumped in and opened the window. "Just take it, you dry lunch," he called out cheerfully. "And say thank you very much next time you see him."

I watched the Cayenne disappear out of the plaza and up the side street that led away from the port area. I turned to Juana, who shrugged, confused.

"Looks like we have a car," I said.

"I hate that man, Pedro," she said. "He is like a devil. That car is bad luck."

"I know what you mean, babe," I said. "But you can't be superstitious over a car. It looks like I haven't got any choice."

We closed after lunch and I persuaded Juana to come and try the car out. She reluctantly agreed.

It felt good.

I had grabbed a CD that we'd been listening to a lot late in the restaurant – a Ministry of Sound Ibiza mix – and by the time we were doing 90 km/h along the dual carriageway with the volume up full, we were laughing and singing along with the wind in our hair.

We had quickly forgotten about Terry Gadd, Patsy Kelly and bad luck.

I pulled down off the coast road and tried the car out on the bends, testing its road holding, flooring it on the straights. Juana shouted at me to slow down, but when I looked across at her, nothing could disguise the suppressed smile at the corners of her mouth and her exultation as the wind whipped her hair across her face.

I felt alive; my nerve endings singing with the thrill of it all.

We parked up in a small cove with a thin stretch of sand and a few rocks that opened into a deep pool of clear green Med. No bar, no restaurant. No one.

I kicked off my Havaianas and hopped across the hot sand, pulling off my T-shirt and dropping my shorts at the water's edge. I jumped a few steps through the surf, then dived in. I surfaced and looked back to Juana on the shore. She was daintily untying her tie-dyed sarong and taking off her vest, laying them out in a neat patch on the beach with her bag.

"Come on!" I shouted. "It's lovely."

Juana got in slowly, and I watched as the ocean rose up her shins, then over her knees and her brown thighs until she took a lady-like dive and did a lazy, natural crawl out to where I was, chest-deep in the warm sea.

I pulled her close and kissed her, then a solitary cloud appeared above, changing the bright orange light to warm grey and pouring rain on us. The heavy raindrops burst on the surface of the water like bullet traces, and in the temporary coolness the sea felt extra warm.

I held her tight; my toes gripped the smooth sand and Juana wrapped her legs around my waist. We stayed like that for a while, holding, kissing, until the cloud emptied and blew further along the coast.

Once we had dried off on the sand, we drove back towards Benalmádena along the coast road, stopped off at a beach bar and ate sardines grilled on sticks over the embers of an open fire.

We sipped Coke, watched the sun lower and ate until it was time to go. The memories of that afternoon were etched into my memory by the sun.

A rare, perfect afternoon.

The mood had changed as the light turned golden and we headed back, so I tuned the radio to a local rock station. Between the interference, the Rolling Stones crackled out "Gimme Shelter". It was one of my brother Steve's all-time favourites. A Desert Island Disc. I didn't want to bring Steve back to mind right now.

Didn't want to go there.

I was over his murder, and I suddenly realized I was over a lot of things. Since I'd been here I'd hardly spared a thought for Anna Moore, Cath, therapists or anyone else who had been the focus of my emotions for the best part of a year. Barely even spared a thought for Sophie Kelly. I'd moved on.

I was living in the sun, with a job I enjoyed and a beautiful, grounded Spanish girlfriend. We were getting on fine, working and playing together, far away from the scabby nightclubs that I'd frequented with Gav Taylor. Juana made me feel like I belonged; one of the natives.

I was really beginning to fall for her.

I looked across at her and smiled. She smiled back at me; wide, white grin and brown eyes. Full, dark pink lips. She reached over and stroked my cheek with her palm, as if she had been reading my thoughts. It felt like our relationship had deepened to a new level that afternoon.

She felt in her bag and pulled out a pack of Fortuna. She dipped her head into the footwell to light a cigarette, escaping the wind that funnelled across the open top. Lit it on the third attempt.

"You wanna give those up," I shouted over the wind and the music. "They'll kill you."

Juana exhaled, flicked the first ash into the slipstream and laughed. "If your driving doesn't kill me first," she shouted.

"Death by driving is quick," I joked. "Smoking, slow." I took the turning into Benalmádena.

"You make it sound like immortality is an option, amigo," she said.

I took the thought on board as I drove through the shabby backstreets into town.

THIRTY-TWO

Barry died that Wednesday.

There was no weeping and wailing as such. Julie came down early that morning, looking marginally worse for wear than usual. She'd been at the hospital till 3 a.m. when poor old Barry had given up the ghost.

"He's gone," she told us flatly. From the resignation in her voice you'd think she had been expecting it not just for the last two days, but for as long as they had been here on the Costa.

Juana, Carlos and I managed to hug her thin shoulders, but there was no give in her.

"Pneumonia got him," she said. "Complications." As if three bullets in the intestines hadn't made the difference.

The funeral was late one afternoon the following week, in a small cemetery above the town. There were few mourners: one or two broken-nosed faces from the criminal fraternity; some of the silver-surfer expats who used Jubarry's; us – the staff; and Terry Gadd, loitering on the edges, representing the Kelly family.

Patsy wasn't appearing in public at the moment, it seemed. He'd sent his wife and kids back to England after the shooting and rumour had it that he barely left his room.

While Barry was being interred in dry, red Spanish soil, my eyes wandered to a figure who had joined the circle of twenty or so mourners, shuffling uncomfortably as if his shoes didn't fit. He was standard-issue bouncer but bigger than most, with a wide, muscled back that strained against his thin summer jacket. He was dark-tanned and shaven-headed with two gold earrings and a Zapata moustache. He looked familiar. I began to feel a queasiness in my stomach.

I lost sight of him as the party turned away from the grave and back to their cars for the real business of the funeral. The wake.

Jubarry's was closed for other business that evening, but once we had started serving drinks and tapas, the numbers swelled, tripling from the few that had been at the graveside.

With Julie playing the merry widow, sitting on a banquette in the corner surrounded by a gaggle of wrinkled, tanned witches, I found myself playing host.

I managed to grit my teeth and smile while resenting every drink I poured. I played up my "Spanishness", making Pedro Garcia a bit like Manuel off "Fawlty Towers", nodding politely and agreeing every time some Thames Estuary voice whined "Barry would have loved this". Or "It's how he would have wanted it."

I seriously doubted that Barry Ambrose, having sold

up in Orpington twenty years before, would have wanted to die in the arse end of Spain due to a hail of bullets to the gut.

I ducked across the restaurant to make sure the widow's needs were being attended to. Ready with the bottle.

"He always wanted to be buried in the cemetery in Penge," Julie whined. "Next to Mum and Dad, and his nan."

"Aah," the witches chorused sympathetically, while still managing to hold out their glasses for more.

"But, you know," Julie explained, "with the flights being what they are now ... a coffin and all that."

"Yeah..." the witches sympathized.

"Cost us two hundred quid to send Darcy's wedding presents via Ryanair," she said.

"They reckon they're going to start charging a quid for a piss next," one of the witches piped. There was a moment's pause while they checked the widow's reaction.

"And fifty to join the Mile High Club," Julie retorted to a mass of throaty giggles

"Not exactly British Airways Club class, is it?" Another joined in. "That's where I joined the Mile High, when I was modelling. Free ... with a complimentary glass of champagne."

The lady mourners around the widow collapsed into titters as I refilled their glasses. I guessed that Julie was dealing with her grief in her own way.

I felt a tap on my shoulder. I turned and Terry Gadd was in my face. He grinned at me.

"How's the motor?" he asked.

"It's great," I said. "But I can't—"

He drew me away from the ladies by taking my bicep between thumb and forefinger and turning me around. It didn't hurt, but he was clearly in charge.

"I'm offski," he said. "And I don't want to hear any more about the poxy wheels. OK?"

"OK."

"You've done a good one here tonight," he said. "I've been watching you. You've made everyone feel … comfortable. You're good at it. It's appreciated."

"Thank you," I said. "I just—"

"Stow it." He put his tobacco-smelling finger not to his own lips but to mine.

Juana must have been watching and passed by, bottle in hand, her eyes defensive, nervous.

"You guys OK?" she asked. "Can I get you another drink?"

Terry Gadd smiled and shook his head to dismiss her. I gave her a look that told her I could handle it. I wasn't sure that I could. As she passed, Gadd followed her with his eyes and turned to me.

"You getting some of that, Spunky?"

I shrugged, giving nothing away. He gave my bicep a squeeze, his thumb almost inflicting pain this time.

"Lucky boy," he wheezed. "Prime, Class A crumpet. Nice one."

He laughed. Loosened his grip. "*Nice* one," he said again. He stroked my cheek, not quite a slap but almost friendly, then turned to leave. "I'll be in touch."

*   *   *

The evening started to wind down about 2 a.m. It was still busy but with most people just sitting at tables, mumbling quietly, pouring themselves what was left of the hundreds of bottles that had been opened in Barry's memory. On Barry's tab.

Juana and I were behind the bar, taking a breather. I had put on a bit of chilled Brazilian music and now picked at a plate of fried anchovies and drank the first cold beer of the night.

Then the big bloke came in.

He'd obviously had a few, but he'd not been at the wake. He lurched over to the bar and scraped up one of the bulky wooden barstools and positioned it under his heavy arse.

"Hello, *guapa*," he said to Juana. She rolled her eyes at me and went to serve him.

"What would you like, Vic?"

"Large brandy, beautiful," he slurred. His voice came rumbling from deep in his chest, marinated in years of booze and cured by a million cigarettes.

But familiar.

Juana placed a tulip-shaped brandy glass in front of the man, grabbed a bottle from behind the bar and filled it. "On the house," she said. He picked up the dainty glass between fat thumb and forefinger and drank half of it.

"'Ow's your mum?" he asked. Juana pursed her lips in a dismissive, non-committal way.

"She's fine."

"Will she see me?" the big man asked. He drained the other half. I watched, sipped beer, analysed. There was almost a pleading whine behind the gravel that lined his throat. He held his glass out for more, as if he needed the sauce to be able to talk.

"I don't think so, Vic." She pronounced it *Bic*.

I saw the shadow of rejection flicker across his face. His body deflated half a stone.

He couldn't see me, I was just another waiter. His blurred eyes were on the pretty girl. I looked at him; stripped away the tan, the earrings, the moustache. Put a little more stubbly hair on his head. Put him in an ill-fitting, tight, English winter-grey suit. And then I knew who he was.

I think I had half-known from the moment he turned up at the cemetery that afternoon.

But now I knew *exactly* who he was.

THIRTY-THREE

Donnie staggered out of the Bodega Jubarry.

The night air was still warm, but the additional oxygen to his brain made him feel very pissed. A day on the lash was no novelty to Donnie, but he'd been on a beano for over two weeks now.

Caning it.

He'd worked out why; it was because he felt rejected. Clearly Valerie was having nothing more to do with him since he'd got shot. And working for Patsy Kelly – an honour he'd sacrificed his love life for – had also gone tits up. Word had got back to Patsy that Donnie was a loose cannon around the bars, and the firm had brought the shutters down once again, extra paranoid after the shooting.

Donnie had called Dave Slaughter in England a few days after the assassination attempt on Patsy Kelly, pleased to have information to pass on. Hot information.

"I know, Don," Dave had said. He'd known within an hour of the shooting, it turned out. "Word is, some Serbian bunch was behind it."

He asked Donnie for a witness's view of what had happened,

and Donnie had to admit, shamefaced, that he hadn't actually been invited to the party.

Dave was the closest Donnie got to having a mate. He'd known Dave for twenty years, but now he could hear the disappointment in his voice.

"I thought you was my eyes and ears over there, Don?" he growled down the phone. "I can get news quicker by bleedin' carrier pigeon or going on Google Earth."

Donnie didn't know what Google Earth was.

"Any more news about moving the guv'nor?" Donnie asked, hoping for a grain of information coming the other way.

The silence that followed was clearer than words. Donnie was getting the message: he was washed-up, completely useless and not to be trusted.

Donnie swayed in the street for a moment as he recalled the conversation, then tried to focus. He felt an alien sensation in his chest, like indigestion. It crawled up his throat, restricting it. The feeling continued to his nostrils and behind his eyes. He couldn't remember the last time he felt like this, if ever. Donnie's huge chest rose as if taking in a deep breath, then let it out with a shudder and a loud moan.

A sob. For the first time since he was a baby, Donnie realized that he was crying.

He took out a packet of fags, and as he did so his phone dropped out of his pocket onto the street. The screen cracked across, and finding an outlet for his feelings, Donnie stamped on it until it was a small pile of smashed plastic and circuit board.

Feeling better, he placed a cigarette between his trembling lips and lit it.

He heard a noise and saw two young Spanish men coming across the square towards him, not aggressive but swaggering and cocky. They were talking loudly and laughing, like they'd had a good night. Donnie felt jealous. He wiped his sleeve across his wet face and pulled himself together. He took a few faltering steps across the square. The men crossed his path, unlit cigarettes dangling from their lips.

"Tiene una luz?" one asked Donnie, making the sign for a lighter with fist and thumb.

"You taking the piss?" Donnie slurred, misreading the gesture through blurred eyes. He swung a fist, so slow that the Spanish guy was able to dodge it, causing Donnie to lurch forwards.

Seeing Donnie's aggression, the men's expressions had changed. They were no longer friendly, nor frightened of a lumbering drunk, however big he might be. The second man took advantage and, clearly with some martial arts training under his belt, let off a kick to Donnie's chest that sent him flying. Donnie toppled back onto the street, his head hitting cobbles. The second man came back with a kick in the face and, through his drunken fog, Donnie felt his cheekbone crack and his nose break. He could taste blood in the back of his throat and saw pinpricks of light flashing in his skull. He felt his stomach and ribs cave in under punches, kicks and knee drops. Felt the terrible ache as his testicles were stamped on.

Donnie wanted it to be over. He wished they would just shoot him to put him out of his misery.

Headlights swept the square and the Spanish boys delivered a final kick to Donnie's nuts before running off.

* * *

It was about half three by the time we finally locked up. The square was quiet and we hardly noticed the dormant shape in the gutter some metres away, partially illuminated by a street light.

A low moan drew our attention to it.

"Drunk," I said. I took Juana's arm, drawing her away, not wanting a scene.

"It sounds like pain," she said. She looked back. "It's Vic."

She broke away from me and rushed over to the kerb. "*Bic?*" she asked.

Reluctantly I followed. In my opinion, the man in the gutter was better off dead. After all, he had shot me twice and left *me* for dead.

"Leave him," I said. "He's pissed." But she was already crouching by his head.

"Oh my God," she said. "Look."

I joined her and tried to see his face in the street light. It was a complete mess, with split, swollen lips and puffy black eyes. Blood poured from his nose, which had been bent across his face, and his shaved head was scored with scratches and cuts. Juana rolled him over and he groaned in pain.

"Vic?" she asked. He groaned. "We need to get him to hospital."

I sighed like a spoilt kid. "It's half three in the morning…"

She fixed me with stubborn brown eyes. I couldn't explain to her that I wanted no part in helping Donovan Mulvaney, the Kelly thug who had tried to murder me.

The man I was pretty sure had also killed my brother.

"Get the car," she said.

"Why don't we call an ambulance?"

"It will take hours. What is your problem? This man is dying. Get the car."

I sulkily kicked a fag butt on the ground as if it was a football. I saw the remains of a smashed mobile phone near Donnie's feet. Knelt down and found the SIM card behind the battery – you never know... Then I got up and went to find my keys.

We squeezed Donnie into the front seat, after levering his huge bulk out of the gutter. Juana sat wedged in the little seat behind me and I took the road out of town towards Málaga. No one spoke and the atmosphere weighed heavy in the car, punctuated by the hulk's groans every time I hit a pothole or took a bend too fast.

"Why are you being like this, Pedro?" Juana whispered in my ear.

"It's four in the morning and, believe it or not, I've had quite a busy day."

"I thought you had a good spirit."

"I do have a good spirit," I said. "But this guy's one of them. He's a thug and I don't like it. It won't end well, believe me."

"He's a human being," Juana said.

I looked across at the battered lump. Almost, I thought.

THIRTY-FOUR

We drove back as the sun was coming up across the sea, and even Benalmádena looked pretty in the cool of early morning.

"Let's go to bed," Juana said.

I gave her a cheeky glance, but with my body aching from fatigue and my eyes blinking and gritty, I wasn't really serious. I was almost hallucinating with tiredness. Jubarry's had to be open in a few hours and it felt like our responsibility.

I woke up next to Juana feeling marginally rested after three hours' kip. I showered, as hot as I could stand, and let the needles of water massage some of the stiffness out of the back of my neck. I made us *café con leche* and fried-egg sandwiches while I listened to Juana singing in the shower.

She had a good spirit, I thought. She took life's knocks and still got up singing the next day. I could learn from her. I felt contented as she sat down opposite me at the small table, wet and loosely wrapped in my towel, and wolfed down an egg sandwich. Juana had really started to relax around me, opening up more. A few nights before, she'd told me about her hopes and dreams; how she wanted a nice flat, like mine, a secure job, a man she could trust. Even though she had a couple of years on me, she suddenly looked younger and more innocent as she outlined her simple plans for the future.

I felt heavy-hearted that Juana would never be able to fully trust me.

We drove into town in the Alfa, around eleven. Quite the husband-and-wife team on the way to work, me still only eighteen and her twenty. It felt like we'd been doing it for years.

Carlos had opened up early, so the few punters around before lunchtime would had been served coffee, pastries and whatever without much ceremony.

I drank more coffee once we got in and started to feel a bit buzzy, ready to cover lunches and light duties, looking forward to a kip in the sun after.

Never make plans for an easy ride. Life always gets in the way.

Lunch was quiet, as expected. One or two regulars came in for a beer and some tapas or sat outside with grilled lamb cutlets and chips.

At 1 p.m. Terry Gadd walked in. Always guaranteed to put me on edge.

"Hello, stranger," he said. He seemed cheered by the fact we'd seen each other just twelve hours before. He grinned. "No peace for the wicked, eh?"

He was wearing a hideous shirt: turquoise with pink

flamingos. It nearly made my hallucinations return. His eyes darted around.

"Anyone about?"

I gestured at the empty bar and the table on the terrace, where two Spanish widows in black sipped hot chocolate.

"Juana and the chef are out back," I told him.

"Good," he said. Then, pointing to the kitchen, added, "You wanna watch him with her though, john." He made a gesture with his fist and locked it into his elbow. I got the gist. "Wait there."

He went and stood in the sunlight in the doorway and made a call on his phone, like a bouncer outside a club.

Seconds later, Patsy Kelly walked in, followed by a shaven-headed monkey who acted as if he was about to throw some kung fu moves. He cased the joint then went back outside, minding the door.

Patsy Kelly was dressed to be inconspicuous: black shades, black shirt, tight black trousers and purple suede Tod's. Gold chain. He probably thought he was slipping in like a shadow, but he couldn't have made himself look more like a villain if he'd tried. It was dark inside and he took off his shades at the bar. Now I was able to see his eyes, he looked tired and worried. He'd lost weight.

He held out a big hand, which I took. Felt the rasp of ostentatious rings. Smelt the cologne transferred to my own hand.

"*Buenos días, amigo*," he said. "Pedro, isn't it?"

Gadd affirmed with a nod. So did I.

Juana poked her head out of the kitchen and, seeing who it was, darted back inside.

216

"Listen," Patsy said. "Terry tells me you like the car."

"I, er…" Behind Patsy, Gadd put a finger to his lips. "It's great. Thank you."

"It's just a small token of my esteem," Patsy said. The phrase sounded clumsy coming from his mouth, as if he'd picked it up from a TV show or something.

"You don't know me," he said. "But I come from a big family. It's important to us, family."

His words reminded me of the patter from a hundred gangster movies.

"Aren't you going to offer Mr Kelly a drink?" Gadd asked.

"Sorry," I said. The mention of the surname always pulled me up short. "What would you like, Mr Kelly?"

"Thank you," Patsy said with forced politeness. "I'll have a large vodka and … no, tell you what, can you mix a Bloody Mary?"

I nodded.

"Give me a large Bloody Mary, all the bits." He lit a cigar.

"And I'll have a beer," Gadd joined in. "I'm as dry as a camel's ring in a dust storm."

I poured Gadd his beer to shut him up, then, my hand trembling a little, set about making Patsy his Bloody Mary.

"You see, we're like aristocracy down here," Patsy continued.

I took a chilled stainless steel cocktail shaker and poured two measures of vodka from the optic … and one more.

"Or a bunch of gyppos," he said, with a self-deprecating

laugh. The rich cigar smoke drifted across the bar, bringing back a vivid memory of Tommy Kelly in his study.

I squeezed half a lime on top of the vodka, added a splash of fino sherry and three shakes of Worcester sauce.

"Whichever way you look at it, we take care of our own," Patsy said. Terry Gadd agreed.

Three drips of Tabasco. Celery salt. Knife-end blob of horseradish. Mix it with a swizzle stick. I'd been well taught.

"And you, Pedro, have looked after me." Patsy sounded almost sentimental.

I wiped lime peel around the rim of a frozen highball glass and rolled it in cracked black pepper. I filled it with ice and poured the mixture from the shaker over it.

"So I want to look after you," he said.

I tried to keep eye contact with Patsy as he spoke, to show I was listening, but I didn't like his drift and my preparations kept me busy. I cut a small slice of lemon and put it in the glass, then sliced a baton of celery off a stick in the chiller. I didn't think he'd appreciate a paper umbrella. I pushed the celery into the drink and placed it on a mat in front of him. He looked at it, held it up to the light and took a sip. Smacked his lips and picked a grain of pepper from his lower one.

"Not sure about the gravel round the rim," he said, wiping the rest of the pepper from the glass with his finger. "But that's the best bloody drink I've had this year. Get his recipe, Tel." I thanked him. He took a large gulp and the Tabasco connected with his taste buds. He drew his lips back across his teeth like a dog. "Terry says you're good. He's been watching you. Seen how you handle yourself. So here's the deal."

He took a large bunch of keys from his pocket.

"Bodega Jubarry," he said. He waved the keys in front of me. "This place. Yours."

"But I thought Julie…" I started. Widow Julie wasn't around. She was probably still nursing her grief with a bottle of cava by one of her mate's swimming pools.

"Julie-shmoolie," he cut in. "She can't wait to get out of here. We've arranged a flight and removals for her so she can go back to live with her old mum in a bungalow in Orpington.

"Spend more time with her family." Gadd grinned, holding his glass out for another beer.

"Anyway, I've been paying the effing rent here for years," Patsy Kelly said. "And I'll pay yours. You take opening stock, food and all that. Make a nice tidy living and I'll make sure all the accounts are sorted, bish, bash, bosh. You look after me and I'll look after you. Deal?"

He held out his hand again. I knew there were only two options with a Kelly handshake: either take it and agree terms, or face whatever shit they chose to heap on you.

I shook Patsy Kelly's hand.

Done deal.

THIRTY-FIVE

I spent most of the afternoon walking up and down the beach, trying to explain to Juana what had gone on. All thoughts of an afternoon snooze in the sun evaporated, along with a lot of other ideas for a quiet life.

She'd been listening through a crack in the kitchen door as much as possible, but when I filled in the gaps she held her head in her hands in despair, telling me that it was a very bad idea.

I already knew that, thank you.

She told me I didn't know what I was getting myself into, like she was the expert on crime down here. Of course, she'd had her brushes with it through her mum and her old man, but I couldn't let her know that I probably knew a hell of a lot more about it than she did – as the scars on my stomach testified.

Thinking about my scars, and perhaps cruelly, I reminded her that it was she who had insisted we took some old lag up to hospital in the early hours. Leaving me sleep-deprived, so that when something like this happened I could barely see straight, let alone make good decisions.

She took note.

After I'd had a swim, and Juana had looked out at the sea and smoked a few Fortuna, she calmed down a little. Although she was usually calm, when things didn't go right, Juana showed some Hispanic genes and went off like a bottle of pop. Shouting and ranting and stamping.

I quite liked her passionate side. She made me feel like I had ice in my veins.

Maybe I do.

"Things needn't change," I insisted, sitting down next to her on the sand.

"No?" She looked straight ahead at the sea.

"We'll have the same responsibilities as before, but we'll be in charge and the money we make will be ours."

"You think so?" she said. "We won't own this place, it will always be owned by those *criminales*."

"Listen," I said. "Maybe this way, we can put some money aside, then move on. Open up something of our own somewhere else. We could rent somewhere together."

She looked at me, weighing up the idea. "Can we do that?" she asked.

"'Course," I said. "If we work hard at the business, we'll be out of there in months. We can set up together once the summer season's over. In the meantime I have a flat, we have a car..."

She put her head on my shoulder and her arm round my waist. I think I was winning her over. "You promise, Pedro?"

221

"Promise. I'll take you away from here."

All Juana wanted was some security and a better life. Take away the criminal connections and I guess I looked like a dynamic young bloke who was making his way. A sense of security and a better life was what I was searching for too.

I knew, in my heart, that *I* had also been seduced by a similar deal. And now I was trying to keep her on the same terms, a better life perhaps, but on the wrong side of the tracks.

What choice did I have?

By the time we walked back towards the bar for the evening, I think I had convinced her that our life here could be good.

The evening crowd was just beginning to gather for drinks before dinner; the time of day when the Spanish come out and stroll around the harbour area to see and be seen. This tradition was one of the things I liked best about Spain. For them, the working day was over, but they didn't go indoors to eat dinner on a tray and watch crap TV till they crawled to their beds. Whole families came out, drifting from bar to bar – a drink here, a snack there, never getting drunk – before settling down to a family dinner that went on until after midnight. I never knew how the kids got through school with this lifestyle. Everyone seemed to exist on three hours' kip a night.

I looked around the bar with a new sense of ownership, feeling I'd stepped up a level.

Juana was serving a family inside, so I took a moment

to nip into the kitchen and grab myself a snack. I sliced off some Serrano ham and wedged it into a roll with a tomato. I was about to take a mouthful when my phone buzzed against my leg. My phone hardly ever rang – certainly not the little one I kept tucked deep in my pocket at all times.

My lifeline.

I fished it out and checked caller ID. It was one of the London numbers. Not Tony's.

"*Hola?*" I said, just in case.

"*Hola*, handsome," a woman's voice said coolly. Anna.

"Ysobel?" I asked, using her code name.

"*Si, Pedro.*" She sounded as if she was messing with me.

"*Qué tal?*"

"*Bien*. Listen, cut the Español for a minute. I've got a bone to pick with you."

"Yes?"

"Why aren't you talking to me?"

"I thought I was meant to keep shtum until something big happened," I said, back pedalling.

"So when there's an attempt to assassinate one of our major targets, and you're there to save his life, I don't get to know about it?"

I was silent for a minute. "I didn't…" I began.

"You called Tony," she said. "He's not your case officer."

She was right. When the birthday shooting put the wind up me, my instant reaction had been to turn to Tony. Anna was terrific; efficient and strong. But maybe I'd got a bit too close to her. In London, it had sometimes felt like I was the one protecting her.

"We need to talk," she said. "And if I don't get a drink soon, I might die of thirst. I want something dry, white and cold with some olives."

"Where are you?" I asked. I was beginning to twig.

"Sitting out the front of your bar. Now get a move on."

THIRTY-SIX

I took a bottle of white Torres Rioja from the chiller and pulled the cork out fast. I put it on a tray with a glass and plates of olives, anchovies, bread and garlic mayonnaise.

I wasn't counting on kissing her.

I rushed towards the terrace, passing Juana on her way back to the kitchen.

"You OK?" she asked.

"*Si*, fine, *guapa*," I said in Spanglais.

"You look funny."

"I am funny." I kissed her fleetingly on the cheek and went out into the evening light.

It was typical Anna: sitting alone at a table, looking fresh and immaculate, like she'd just stepped straight out of a shower via a hair salon. Smoking a cigarette. She was dressed in her regulation crisp white shirt, three buttons undone to show the low-cut vest underneath. Just low enough to make any bloke act the fool in front of her.

I put the tray down on her table and noticed a middle-aged man with his family, a regular, casting glances in her direction and smoothing his hair.

"Señorita," I said.

"*Gracias.*"

"Why are you here?" I kept my voice low and hoped my body language looked as if I was just being smarmy to a good-looking customer as I put plates on the table. I poured her some wine.

"Day trip," she said. "Well, two-day trip, if we're being pedantic. I arrived this morning, go back tomorrow."

I looked around. Juana was coming back outside. "I can't talk here," I said.

"No, of course." Anna crossed her legs, showing a pale knee from under her wrap-around skirt. Strappy sandals, pretty feet. I couldn't help but look. "Meet me at the marina in half an hour. I'll have a quiet drink, ignore you, then wander down there."

"Looks like we're going to be quite busy here," I said.

I saw Anna clock Juana as she served the next table but one. The look couldn't exactly be described as sisterly. Anna took out her iPhone and began to appear interested in it.

"Well, take a break," she said, pretending to read something on the phone. "You're the boss, aren't you?"

I was, I thought. But putty in Anna's hands.

I made feeble excuses to Juana. I was popping out to buy cigarettes for behind the bar … and a bottle of Sambuca. We were nearly out, someone might order one. She looked at me and cocked her head.

"Don't be long, we're getting busy."

"Sure," I said. A couple of Carlos's waiters were still knocking around, so she wouldn't be alone. But I already felt I was somehow cheating on her.

I nipped out the back way through the kitchen, bought a carton of Marlboro Lights and a bottle of Sambuca from the supermarket down the road to get my story straight, then jogged the few hundred metres to the marina.

Anna was sitting on a bench looking out at the boats, halyards and cables clanking in the light sea breeze. As I approached, she pretended to check her phone.

"What kept you?" she asked.

"Came as quick as I could," I said. "Why are you over here? You could have phoned."

"So could you," she said.

I had no answer.

"Baylis comes over now and again," she said. "He thinks he's got a lead on the Serb, up in Mijas."

I knew the town she meant. Pretty, well-heeled, up in the hills.

"Nice place," I said. "Has he got a finca in Mijas?" I trotted out the old joke from these parts.

"Very funny," she said.

"Sorry."

"So I thought I'd hop over with Ian for a day or two, just to see how the land lies."

"Did you know about Patsy Kelly being here?" I asked. She shot me a sideways glance.

"We know all sorts of half-information," she said. "It's not until we get a man on the spot –" she squeezed my leg – "that we can really get the inside track."

"So you and Tony knew what you were setting me up for?" I persisted.

"Of course we knew Patsy Kelly was down here," she admitted, coming clean. "He was peripheral to our enquiries; he was pretty much an exile. Trust you to become big showbiz buddies with him so quickly."

"It was a complete accident," I said. "We were catering for his party. Before that we only ever saw his sidekick, a bloke called Terry Gadd."

Anna took a deep breath and I thought she was going to tell me about Gadd's track record. If she was, she thought better of it.

"You're being naive," she said. "We know that plenty of bars down here have criminal connections. All our investigations, whether it's about the Irish, Russians or Eastern Europeans, they all bring us down to the Costa on a regular basis. And to Corfu, Split, Brindisi, wherever. EasyJet's made our work easier. There's a hub of activity here. We watch as many clubs, bars and boats as we can, but we're only human. Although we have the technology, we don't always have the manpower. Government cuts hit *our* work as well, you know."

I had never considered that perhaps they – *we* – had to work to an ever decreasing budget, like all public service industries. Including getting the cheapest airfares.

I suddenly saw Anna as a manager for an international company rather than as an intelligence agent. Given her abilities, she could have probably switched jobs overnight for a better salary and less aggro. But she clearly loved her job, for all the grief it entailed.

"Having said that," she continued, "we had a bit of intel about the bar where *you* work, slap bang next to the harbour, where the rent was paid by one of the Kelly family businesses. So it was interesting. I hear you're in charge now?"

"Yeah, kind of," I said.

"So who's the girl?" she asked.

I looked at her and maybe imagined a hint of jealousy. I was mentally preparing what I might tell Anna about my new, wonderful girl when I saw a yacht manoeuvring into a berth. *Sea Dog of Ramsgate.*

"Don't look now," I said in a low voice, "but that's the boat I was living on."

Anna was good. She took an imaginary call on her phone, scanning the harbour as she did so.

I saw Adie, Gav Taylor's mate, in waterproofs and salopettes, gear you didn't need unless you'd been out into the Atlantic and down the North African coast. The sails had been furled out on the water, but he was fussing on deck, stowing stuff in lockers.

I stood up to get a better view. There was another bloke in waterproofs on deck, tying buffers to the taffrail, baseball cap pulled firmly down. Couldn't swear, but from his limp I was pretty sure it was Gav Taylor.

"Go," Anna said.

Neither of them would have known me from a bar of soap, I realized. I would have looked totally different from the dirty blond bloke who had hung around with them months before. But I needed to go anyway. I had a restaurant to run.

"Leave this to me," Anna said. She was already filming on her phone's camera. "I'm here till after lunch tomorrow. Come and find me as early as you can. I'll text you where I'm staying."

I went to kiss her but thought better of it, turned and headed out of the marina.

"Who was that woman?" Juana asked.

"Which woman?"

"The woman at the table outside," she said. "She seemed to know you."

Anna had been pretty subtle, and I, as far as I knew, had just behaved like a waiter with a pretty customer. Maybe it was a bit careless of Anna to turn up on the doorstep; it was as if she enjoyed the risk. In any case, Juana clearly had a sixth sense for this kind of stuff.

I shrugged, acting dumb. Juana seemed to want to keep digging.

"When she went, you were off pretty quick..." She made a whooshing gesture with her hand and whistled to illustrate the speed of my exit. I looked at her and we made eye contact. I wished we hadn't: Juana had a coal-eyed look that could burn through your soul.

"I don't know what you're talking about," I insisted. I put the fags behind the bar and plonked down the bottle of Sambuca. She shrugged, but she clearly didn't believe me.

Despite trying to look nonchalant, I felt so guilty that my head throbbed as I wrestled with my conscience. Sweat poured between my shoulder blades. I hadn't actually *done* anything, I thought. And when I had gone out, I justified to myself, all I was doing was my job.

My real job.

I reached for Juana's wrist, but she twisted her arm away from me and stormed into the kitchen, swinging the door closed behind her.

THIRTY-SEVEN

I woke up alone.

Juana had told me she was seeing her mum the night before. I didn't argue. I guessed it would be better for her to have a bit of a sulk and then calm down at her mum's rather than give me the third degree all night.

I was kind of flattered that her passion was matched by a feeling of jealousy. Then again, from my standpoint, I wasn't sure if that kind of possessiveness was a good thing. Juana wasn't needy exactly, but I guess she was prickly when it came to being messed about by men, like her old girl had been.

But whatever I thought about it, the one thing I couldn't do was actually tell her the truth.

Anna had texted me her hotel address and demanded that I be there to meet her at 8 a.m. It was uncharacteristically early for me and I felt pretty bleary. Even early nights didn't get me in bed much before three. I took the old moped out of the underground car park, and I was pleased to see that Anna's hotel was in the opposite

232

direction to the port and Juana's mum's place on the outskirts. I was unlikely to bump into anyone, but I still parked in a backstreet and cased the front of the hotel before I went in. Basic fieldcraft.

It was a bright, sunny morning and not yet hot. This was a smarter part of town. The street had been hosed down and I could smell flowers, hanging fresh in baskets in front of the hotel. I'd come straight from the shower and wore a navy blue Lacoste shirt and beige chinos. Ray-Ban Aviators. Espadrilles. Smartened up, sharp enough to look like a young European tourist at home in a four-star hotel. I took the lift up to the third floor and found Anna's room.

I knocked on the door and it swung open as Anna concealed herself behind it. The room was humid with the aftermath of a bath, and light, citrus perfume hung in the air. She closed the door behind me.

She was wearing a hotel dressing gown. It was open, revealing some pretty classy underwear in peach-coloured silk.

"I was just getting dressed," she said, looking at me and smiling. She didn't seem to be in much of a hurry. She pulled me towards her, put her arm round my waist and put her face to mine, lips parted. I was glad I had brushed my teeth before I left.

Her breath was minty and fresh, and as her tongue found its way between my teeth I felt my hand rest on her bare hip, stroking the curve of her waist. I felt hot, and guilty and confused.

She pulled my shirt up over my ribs and I had to raise

my hands, as if in surrender, for her to lift it over my head. Then she spun me round and pushed me towards the bed. I toppled backwards as my knees hit the edge. Anna laughed and pushed me onto my back, climbing on top of me. She tugged at the waist of my chinos as she pinned me down.

"Now, let me remind you what you've been missing," she said, kissing me, and I kissed her back then pulled away.

As I lay on the soft hotel bed looking up at the ceiling fan, feelings of guilt churned in my stomach. I was cheating on Juana, no two ways about it, and it didn't feel right.

"What's the matter?" Anna asked.

"Nothing," I said.

My tiff with Juana the night before had given me pause for thought. I thought about her before I went to sleep; dreamt about her. She was the first thing on my mind when I woke up. She was everything that Anna wasn't: passionate, loyal, warm. In Juana I had a real human being with blood in her veins, and I had found an emotional connection with her that had been missing in my life. I would have been mad to mess with that.

Anna sensed my reservation. She shrugged and pulled on her dressing gown as I got up off the bed.

"OK, that's that out of the way,' she said, businesslike, as if the sexual heat was something she could turn on and off at will. "Now, work."

She poured coffee from a thermal jug and we sat together at the small table in the hotel room as if the previous few minutes hadn't happened at all.

Anna took a cardboard folio from her bag. It was marked GARCIA and had a government stamp on it, declaring it Top Secret and Confidential. There were papers on Patsy Kelly, and one she singled out on Terry Gadd.

"So. You know this one, right?" she asked.

"Know him? We're practically best mates."

"Nice friends you have."

"I'm joking. He does all Patsy Kelly's running around. He comes down to the restaurant when Kelly wants to get a message to someone."

"Well, don't get too pally with him. He's a nasty piece of work."

"I think I know that," I said dryly.

"He got off a murder charge five years ago in the UK," Anna said. "Stabbed an undercover copper in his own back garden. Gadd was under surveillance and he caught the copper hiding in the bushes. No questions asked, he stabbed him there and then, straight through the heart with a sharpened bayonet."

"Nice," I said. "How did he shake that one off?"

"He said that the bayonet was part of a collection of antiques. Claimed self-defence, that he was attacked on his own premises. Self-defence so savage that the knife went all the way through and stuck out of the bloke's back. But the jury bought it."

"Or maybe the jury had been bought?" I ventured.

"It looks highly likely," Anna said. "A lot of juries that have anything to do with the Kelly family seem to vote in favour of the defendant. They literally get away with murder. I'd love to make something stick on Terry Gadd," she added, "but he's pretty clever. We think he's been here on and off for nearly ten years now, but he's also been spotted in Jamaica and South America. He's very well connected. I know plenty of people who would like to see him collared and sent home. Dead or alive."

"And Patsy Kelly?"

"He's the focus for all the other activities in this area. When Tommy was in command, he was the one we needed to keep an eye on. Patsy was just the kid brother, his every move sanctioned by Tommy. But now Tommy's inside, Patsy seems to think it's his birthright to take control of the business."

"Can he?"

"Patsy's more likely to slip up than Tommy; he's nothing like as smart. He thinks he's got the nuts to dominate the whole drugs trade down here. Our bet is that he hasn't, but he's having a good try at monopolizing the cocaine trade by bringing in massive quantities from South America. We suspect Terry Gadd is the brains behind it."

"Why don't the Spanish get on Patsy's case?" I asked.

"Of course, we work with the Spanish police, but from their point of view at least they know who they're dealing with. Patsy's had the business tied up for a long time, so he's like a guard dog against all the other, smaller traders that might have a go at setting up here. Plus he's probably – no, certainly – paying a few of them to keep it sweet."

"And now I'm on the same payroll," I said a little bitterly. "Again." Anna looked at me and raised her eyebrows.

"Who better?" she asked. "You know more about that family than anyone else. And God knows why but they seem to like you."

"Great," I said.

"Maybe they get the sniff that you're as dodgy as they are. Takes one to know one?" She raised her eyebrows again, this time questioningly.

"Do I take that as a compliment?"

"Take it how you want," Anna said. "But there's clearly something about you that Tony, and I, spotted a while back. You have a certain charm, you make things happen, and you seem to have an ability to assimilate yourself into your surroundings wherever you are. People, and villains in particular, warm to you."

My ego began to swell a little.

"Plus you have an ability to land yourself in the middle of a load of shit."

Ego deflated again. For all my usefulness, I was obviously also troublesome to them. Like a difficult teenager who occasionally pulled a good result out of the bag.

"So," I said, "let me get this straight. I have to run a bar, work my butt off for the Kelly family and deal with psychopaths like they're my mates – at great personal risk. Then lie to people I genuinely like, all for some faint praise from you lot?"

"You've just given the textbook definition of working undercover, Eddie. Deep cover. You have to be like them, talk like them, do the deals. To all intents and purposes, you *are* one of them."

"So what's in it for *me*?" I asked.

Anna laughed. She pulled the bathrobe and tugged it tight around herself for comfort. Shrugged. "What's in it for me?" she countered. "Sometimes you just have to do things for the greater good."

I felt trapped, and she could see it from the look on my face.

"Listen," she said. "You know, if things got really sticky, we could pull you out. But for the moment it's not that bad, is it?"

I thought back to Jubarry's, to Juana, the flat, the afternoons by the sea. Remembered living in rainy Stoke-on-Trent with the old girl.

"Guess not," I said.

"So give me a kiss and let's go to work, eh?"

She leant over and kissed me on the mouth, then gathered the papers up.

"One more thing." She opened another folio and took out an A4 sheet. There was a passport-type photo printed on the page. A dark man with big, swept-back hair and a moustache. Underneath was a candid shot, grainy, taken on a phone camera, of the same man sitting at a table in a restaurant.

"Something rings a bell," I said. "But there are a hundred Spanish blokes knocking around the square every evening who look like that. It's a pretty standard look in these parts."

"This one's not Spanish," Anna said. "He's Serbian. His name is Dragomir Radic, although he won't be using that name, he'll be passing himself off as Spanish or South American or something. He's a smart bloke. Trained as a doctor and then a lawyer, so he could reappear in any guise. Baylis thinks he's down here."

"So what's he done?"

"Well, apart from escaping the UN forces in Serbia nearly twenty years ago with a bank's worth of euros, he personally orchestrated and oversaw the slaughter of two hundred Muslims from his own village."

I remembered Baylis telling me about men like him and saw what Anna meant about doing things for "the greater good". Reminded myself that I was a small cog in the bigger set of wheels.

"He organized the trucks to take them out into the fields – grandfathers, fathers, boys and male babies – and then watched while they were gunned down. Watched while the local militia clubbed any remaining signs of life out of them."

I shuddered. Violent British drug runners suddenly appeared small beer compared with this kind of whole-sale murder. Anna had taken the wind out of my sails. The trump card I'd felt I was holding for this meeting had been out-trumped. So I changed tack.

"It's probably not important," I said. I fished in my wallet and found the SIM card I had found near Donnie's beaten body. "But I think this might be the SIM card from Donnie Mulvaney's phone."

Anna looked at me, open-mouthed. "Donnie?"

"He's here as well," I said. "If it's what I think it is, it might be useful. Could be some contacts, recent phone calls, you know." She took the SIM between finger and thumb.

"Of course it will be useful," she said.

I turned to leave. I needed to get to work. Anna stood up.

"I'll see you soon. Talk to me, Eddie."

I nodded.

"You're good," she said.

THIRTY-EIGHT

Juana looked daggers at me.

It may have been a guilty look on my face that betrayed me, but I couldn't be sure. It was only 10.30 a.m., so I wasn't even late, but when I arrived she was waiting on the terrace in front of Jubarry's, smoking.

"Where have you been?" she asked.

"Nowhere," I said. Stupid answer.

"I've been trying to call you."

"My battery's dead. I couldn't find the charger. Why? What's up?"

She jerked her head back towards the restaurant and followed me in through the door. She guided me through to the kitchen.

There were two Spanish blokes stacking up polystyrene crates and another taking them down to the cellar. The back door out to the goods entrance in the alley was open. Juana looked at me questioningly, like this was something I'd organized.

"They were here when I arrived," she said. "Carlos is

off. They had a key to the back and let themselves in.

"*Cuál es este?*" I asked one of the guys loading the boxes.

"*Gambas,*" he replied. He gave me a consignment note that said there were twenty crates of frozen prawns. We already had prawns. And this delivery was enough to last until the middle of the next decade – if we were planning to cater for several weddings ... and funerals. I studied the consignment note and wondered if it was some kind of deal Barry had done before he popped his clogs. But there was no mention of the late Mr B Ambrose on the form.

Besides, delivery men didn't tend to let themselves in.

I started to get shirty. "*No mas,*" I said to the guy. But the crates just kept coming. He gave me one of those Spanish shrugs and pointed out the back. I went out into the alley, where the refrigerated truck had reversed.

There he was. Gav Taylor. Acting like the overseer, smoking a fag.

My mouth went dry as I forgot for a moment that I looked completely different. Even so, my heart was in my mouth at the thought of approaching him, but when he looked at me I had little choice.

"*Hablas Español?*" I asked, knowing very well that he didn't.

"No, pal. What's your problem?" I felt a little relieved – he didn't have a clue who I was. I switched to English. I put a little more *Spaneesh* in my accent just to make sure.

"I didn't order this stuff. I run the place," I said.

"No problemo, pal," he said. "It's taken care of."

"Not by me it isn't."

Now my initial fear had subsided, anger surged up inside me. I'd had quite a morning already. I was angry with Anna for manipulating me, making it difficult for me to be straight with the new girl in my life. A girl I really liked. I'd had this bar thrust on me, with all its responsibilities, under the jurisdiction of a psychopath, just to be able to feed intelligence back to London. And now I was being mucked about by the flaky ex-squaddie who'd stung me with a kilo of coke so he could slip through with a bigger haul. I felt blood rush to my face and my fists tighten by my sides. I was absolutely ready to lay him out. I looked at his cocky face, still slick with the sweat of last night's toxins, and as he took another drag from his Benson and Hedges I could see exactly where I would hit him. I took a step forward to smack him, and would have done … if Terry Gadd hadn't appeared from behind the truck.

"All right, lads?" he asked. Chipper. "Wassup, Pedro? You look like you've got the blouse on ".

Gav Taylor chuckled dryly. "Nearly done," he said. Looked at his watch.

"What *is* all this stuff?" I asked Gadd. "I never ordered it."

"'Course you didn't, treacle," he said. "I did."

I was so fired up, I might have had a pop at Terry Gadd at that moment. But he was used to this kind of thing.

"Pedro, Pedro … me old mate," he said. He put a strong hand on my shoulder. "Get used to it, son." He steered me back into the kitchen, his strangler's hands kneading the corded muscle across my shoulders. "You're in the import and export business now. Goods in, goods out. You don't even need to know about it."

"It's on my watch," I said. My mouth was still fuelled by adrenalin, ready for a scrap.

"No it's not, you shit bag," he said. "All you need to do is mind the bar, serve the food, keep the opening hours and be nice to all our friends, and life will be sweet."

"Yeah, but I'm sitting on top of this." I'd begun to get the idea. Seen something like it before. "Whatever it is, it's my name above the door." Gadd looked like he was considering this idea.

"Oh, yeah. It is, isn't it?" The expression on his face changed and he guided me down the cellar stairs. "Since you seem to be a member of the awkward squad, and you're not going to cock a deaf'un to all this, then maybe I have to explain it to you clearly."

He shoved me down the remaining steps into the cellar and opened a box. There was a layer of what appeared to be frozen prawns – maybe they were plastic, I don't know.

"I don't like your attitude, Pedro. You've always had a funny look on your face as far as I'm concerned." He grabbed me hard by the neck and forced my head down into one of the poly crates. "All you need to know is that they're fuckin' prawns, all right?"

Gadd swept away the first layer of shellfish, and beneath them were white blocks of what could have been ice. "And underneath, there's the stuff which you didn't need to know about. But now you do. Because you

244

pushed me. And if you breathe a word, you're as dead as them prawns, and you will leave this place, like them, in little pink bits, frozen in a box. Do you understand?"

He rammed my face into the crate, bringing my nose into sharp contact with the hard plastic lumps in the box. I saw stars and felt the metallic taste of blood as my lip split. I nodded. It wasn't good enough for him.

"Do you understand?"

Terry Gadd punched me, as hard as I'd ever been hit, in the stomach. The wind left me and I doubled up on the concrete floor, gasping for breath.

"Do you understand?" he hissed.

"Yes," I wheezed.

"Good." He kicked me in the stomach again for good measure and I thought I was going to die fighting for breath. Then he lifted his leg up and stamped his heel down hard into my groin. I curled into a ball, my mind a white world of pain.

Gav Taylor came limping down the cellar stairs. "That's the lot," he said.

Terry Gadd straightened his shirt and went back up the stairs, job done. He'd got his message across; got the terms of the deal straight.

Gav Taylor looked at me writhing on the ground.

"You fookin' tosser," he said. "You could have avoided that."

THIRTY-NINE

Juana found me sobbing on the beach.

All traces anger or jealousy or whatever it was had gone. She sat stroking my back while I continued to hold my sore gut and aching nuts, rocking back and forth on the sand, crying out my anger, pain and frustration.

I had kidded myself that I was in a safe place under the protection of Patsy Kelly. I couldn't have been more wrong.

"Shh, shh..." she whispered. I dried my eyes with the back of my arm.

"I can't go on like this," I said. My first thought had been to contact Tony or Anna, but I knew I couldn't go bleating to them so soon. Tony had already baled me out big style.

"What's happened, Pedro?" Juana asked softly.

"I've been totally stitched up," I said. "They've filled the cellar with cocaine, and if the place gets busted it'll be me who takes the rap. We're sitting on a time bomb."

"OK. This time maybe we go to the police. Explain

exactly what has happened…" She had the good grace not to say that she'd told me so, but I laughed at her naivety.

"Baby, the first *guardia* we talk to would be on the phone to Kelly. He pays them all, surely you know that? They have the whole town tied up. If I say a word, I'll be dead meat."

Juana stroked my hair, running her fingers over the back of my head. She kissed me lightly on the ear and cheek and I began to feel a little better. I turned to kiss her back but she held my face between her hands, stopping me, fixing me again with black eyes. I knew now that I had begun to rely on Juana for her strength and her loyalty. Her clear judgement between right and wrong.

"So, who was that woman?" She certainly didn't give up easily.

I considered for a moment. "No one" was not going to wash. "I love you," I said. "And I hope you feel the same about me. But if I tell you who that woman was, you will think very differently about me. You may not want to be with me any more."

She kissed me on the lips, then pulled away. "I love you, too, amigo. But if you don't tell me, I won't be staying around anyway."

I knew I couldn't tell her. But then if I wanted her to trust me… Breaking every rule in the book, I decided I would give her the economical version of the truth.

That I'd been caught in a drug sting, but I was innocent. That I'd been arrested and had done a deal with the authorities that had brought me back here, gathering any information I could about the drugs coming into the country. That "the woman", Anna, was an officer who came to check up on me from time to time.

"She must be pretty pleased with your progress," Juana said.

I thought for a minute. They never seemed particularly pleased with me. "I dunno," I said. "They don't know about this recent development."

"You will tell her?"

"I guess so." My brain was whirring with possibilities. What Anna had said they could do if things got really sticky. The beating from Terry Gadd had really knocked me for six. I decided I would call her after all. "I think I'll tell her that it's getting too hot for me here, and that I want out."

A look of pain flashed across Juana's face.

"And I'll take you with me."

It was quiet back at Jubarry's: only a few covers in and the regular barflies. I stayed in the kitchen most of the afternoon, or upstairs in Barry and Julie's flat during the quiet period. I was in no mood to talk to anyone or be sociable, so at nine Juana suggested we leave the running of the place to Carlos and the duty waitress. I couldn't wait to leave, claiming a stomach bug, and Juana led me out by the hand.

I felt a shift in our relationship. She seemed stronger and more capable than me, as if she was taking charge, protective and maternal. I liked the feeling and I squeezed her hand as we walked across the square. She squeezed mine back.

"It'll work out OK, amigo," she said. She smiled and

kissed me. Not passionate but soft, her lips warm and comforting on my lips, her fingers combing through my hair.

"Where are we going?" I asked.

"To my mother's," she said. "You need some home cooking and a glass of wine."

The apartment block was in a dusty suburb. It had green window shutters and whitewashed walls with peeling plaster. We walked up to the second floor. Tomato plants bearing fruit sprouted from olive oil cans outside the front door.

Juana's mother, Valerie, wasn't quite what I was expecting. She was bigger than her daughter, not fat exactly but sturdy.

"*Encantado*," I said.

She looked at me warily through dark eyes, sizing me up, and shook my hand. The flat was small but spotlessly clean and a small table was laid with a bright red spotted cloth by the open windows. Juana poured me some wine from a jug and sat me at the table. She and her mother spoke rapid-fire Spanish in the kitchen at such a speed, I could only understand bits of it. I heard Juana explain how I'd been hit by a villain. Her mother rolled her eyes, having heard it all before. I hoped Juana wasn't giving away too much.

Her mother put a plate of tapas in front of me: serrano ham, chorizo, cheese. "You have come to a bad town, kid," she said. Her English was good. She touched my cheek, checking for bruising. "Eat," she said.

I had little appetite but I picked at slices of ham until Valerie brought a *cazuela* to the table full of *arròs al forn*

– baked rice with smoked sausages and pork. The two of them sat down with me and watched as I spooned some onto my plate. It smelt great and I found my appetite, the food warming the empty void I felt in my stomach, the wine slowly returning my confidence.

By the time I had finished the home-made flan, we were chatting easily and laughing. It felt good to be in a proper home again. Valerie clearly protected Juana like a tigress, and Juana loved her right back. At the end of the evening Valerie enveloped me in strong arms and pulled me to her in a hug. Over her shoulder I could see Juana smile and knew I had made the grade.

I slept on the lumpy sofa bed in the living room. Valerie wasn't the kind of mother who would put up with any monkey business under her roof.

I woke up to sun streaking through the window, not having a clue where I was. My instant reaction was panic, and then the events of the previous evening came back to me, reinforced by the sound of Juana making coffee in the kitchen. I got up and pulled some trousers on, then drank milky coffee with Juana, sitting on the narrow balcony looking across the suburbs while she smoked a cigarette. I wanted to stay here, away from the action. I didn't want to go back to work at Jubarry's and to everything it represented. I made up my mind that I would call Anna and try to bale out. But first we had to go and open up.

Valerie saw us off at the door, wrapped in a dressing gown. She hugged me and kissed me on the cheek. It was like being hugged by a marshmallow. She kissed her daughter all over the face, holding her beautiful features between the palms of her hands, then looked at me.

"Look after her," she said. "She is very precious."

"I know," I said, and vowed to do exactly that.

"That was quick," Anna said at the other end of the phone. "I've only been back a day and you're calling me already."

"Things have changed," I told her. "A basinful of stuff has just come in, a shipment from somewhere. Gav Taylor's involved in it, but Terry Gadd's the man looking after it."

"Stuff?"

"Charlie, I think."

"How much?"

"It's major. About thirty crates, each holding eight or ten parcels the size of a bag of sugar underneath a layer of prawns."

"Smelly," she said.

"They're fake," I told her.

There was a pause as she mentally calculated. "Let's say, conservatively, that's eight kilos per box, total 240 kilos. With a street value of around fifty quid a gram, we're talking nearly twelve million quid's worth."

"Shit." I panicked. "If I get caught with that on the premises…"

"Don't," she said. "But I'll do what I can to protect you. I'll inform the top brass here that you're bringing in high-level intel and they can square your immunity with the Spanish police and customs."

"No, don't, Ysobel. Someone will leak something. The Guardia are so tied in with the villains – you said

251

so yourself. It would only take one loose tongue and I'm dead in the water. I'm more spooked by Terry Gadd than all the Spanish lot put together."

"We need to move on this," she said. "If that kind of quantity gets onto the market, Patsy Kelly will pretty much have the complete monopoly. Is the stuff secure?"

"Yes. It's in the cellar and the place is locked up every night with alarms and everything."

"OK, but for our information and your protection, I would like you to try and log it in some way. Get some evidence of it. Mobile phone photos texted straight to me and then deleted would do. A pic of all the crates and one of the contents. You can do it after hours, can't you?"

My stomach sank. There was no way I wanted to go back down in that cellar.

"Ysobel," I said. "I want you to pull me out. You said if things got really sticky … well, now they are."

"From what you've just told me, the last thing I can do right now is pull you out. I needn't remind you, this is a big deal. As big as it gets."

"What if I get your evidence for you? Will you pull me out then?"

She paused. "I'll see what I can do."

"And Juana will have to come too," I added. I knew I was pushing it. "She'll be in too much danger here."

Longer pause. Even over the phone, I sensed Anna's female hackles rise.

"Just do the job you've been asked to do, Pedro Garcia, and we'll take it from there."

I'd been told.

252

"When do you want the photos?"

"Soon as. You never know when they might be moving it again. If it looks like they are on the move, let me know straight away. We'll need to step in."

"Sure."

"You can do it," Anna said. "You're doing great, but you're going to have to man up."

I was about to protest, but she had gone. The phrase rung in my ears.

Man up.

FORTY

I waited a couple of nights, but, I decided, if gathering evidence of the massive cocaine haul tucked away in the cellar of Jubarry's was my ticket to freedom, it needed doing sooner rather than later. Carlos had knocked off and it was Juana's night to see her mum.

I locked up the front around 2 a.m. then went back into the kitchen. I took out my iPhone and fired up the camera, which had a pretty good lens for low light. The outer cellar door was unlocked, which was not unusual as Carlos would have been up and down during the evening. I pushed the door back and crept down the stone stairs, my heart thudding against my ribs. The bulkhead cellar light shone yellow overhead, and in the corner where the boxes were stacked I could see that the poly lid had been taken off one of them.

I froze for a moment as I saw the shadowy figure of Gav Taylor hunched over the box, slicing a chunk off one of the lumps inside. The prat had a pair of earphones in and hadn't heard me coming.

I tucked myself tight against the wall, half concealed by a brick pillar, then pressed the shutter on the phone. I'd forgotten to switch the flash off and Gav looked up, a rabbit in the headlights. He yanked the buds from his ears.

"What the fook're you doing?" he asked.

"I could ask you the same," I said. Gav Taylor didn't scare me.

"I thought you'd been warned."

"Not by you I haven't," I said. "And part of the warning was to keep a safe eye on the stuff in my cellar."

"It's got nowt to do with you, mate," Gav said. "You're just the fookin' barman. So sling your hook. I've got work to do."

I took another picture. "So you won't mind me sending this photo to Terry Gadd, then, just to make sure it's all OK, you being down here taking chunks out of his cocaine?" I glanced up the stairs. I was pretty certain that he was here alone, that he wasn't doing this on anyone else's behalf. "I'll send it now if you like?"

"Give me that phone." He took a step towards me. "Delete the picture."

"Not until you apologize."

"What for?"

"You stitched up a very good friend of mine. He got caught at Manchester Airport with a key. You planted it."

Taylor shrugged.

"And I reckon you dobbed him in so you could slip through ahead of him."

"Yeah, what a mug," Taylor said. A look of suspicion

255

passed over his face. "How the fook do you know? What's your game?"

I ignored the question. "So now he's facing a seven-year stretch. And he thought you were his mate."

"There aren't any mates in this business, pal," he said. "Just acquaintances. Now, give me that phone."

I withdrew the phone as he took another step forwards, but, with a practised flourish, he spun on his good foot, crashing his steel shin across my leg. It felt as if my own shin was splintering with pain. I dropped the phone and Taylor launched himself to try and pick it up, but I managed to smack a hard right hand into his face as he leant down. He dropped onto the floor, scrabbling for the phone, and I jumped on top of him, my knee on his back, pulling him by the hair. He grunted and swore at me as I reached round and grabbed my phone. I shoved it in my pocket, then knee-dropped on his back, attempting to wind him. The cellar was a bit tight for a ruck and I didn't want to get cornered down there, so I let go of him and headed for the stairs. But with both of us limping, he was soon up and behind me, dragging me back by the waist of my trousers as I tried to climb the steps.

"Come here, you fooker."

I struggled my way to the top, my shin screaming in protest, but the adrenalin kept me going. I tried to turn and kick him back down into the cellar, but he was clinging tightly to me now, shoving me towards the bar.

Whatever he had or hadn't learned in the army, he was a pretty tenacious fighter: hard, wiry and vicious. I'd only ever seen him brawling drunk, but this time he had his wits about him. He threw me backwards and I felt myself lose balance and fall against the end of the bar, sliding to the floor. His fist flew into my face and I defended myself as best I could. I didn't want him busting my veneers or anything else that might reveal me as the bloke he'd stitched up. His wiry hands grabbed my hair and banged my head against the tiles. He punched me in the mouth and I felt my fake teeth crack. I found a bit of leverage and rolled him off me, landed a blow in his eye and another on his nose. That set him back a little and I was able to pull him up by his collar and smack him again in the mouth.

My blows had connected and he was bleeding from the nose and lip. I staggered to my feet, spitting out the loose teeth, and he pulled himself upright against the bar. He launched himself at me again, tearing at my face and pushing me through the swing door into the kitchen. We were locked together now, his fingers clawing for my eye sockets and my right hand desperately thudding into his ribs while my left hand tried to prise his fingers off my face.

I roared and spat as I felt his fingernails at my eyelids, losing my contacts, and I bent his little finger back so far it felt about to snap. He yelled and loosed his grip and I managed to pull away, but only as his hand found a thirty-centimetre cook's knife lying on the work surface.

He looked at me suspiciously but the kitchen was dimly lit and I guessed I was too dark-haired, battered and bruised for him to recognize me clearly.

"Who *are* you?" he asked, gasping for air.

I looked around desperately, but there were nothing I could use to defend myself. He swung the knife at me, but his efforts were easy to avoid. I clearly knew more about this kind of fighting than he did and was able to back away around the worktops. I reached out and grabbed a steel omelette pan. I now had a small, gladiatorial shield against his sword. As Gav Taylor lunged forwards again, I parried the knife. It clanged as it deflected off the steel and I was able to get a glancing blow to his shoulder with the pan. He swung the knife back and I stepped away.

He was using his weight all wrong. Even with a long knife, I had been taught, you needed your attacker to come into you so your weight was firmly on both feet, then their forwards momentum would do the work for you.

I deflected a few more slashes and stabs, reversing, holding up my pan, using it like a steel bat, but I needed something else to even up my chances. I swiped a bowl of olives onto the floor between us and the mushy fruit and oil turned the kitchen floor into a skating rink. I felt behind me, where I knew there was a pot of utensils. I tipped it out and grabbed the short, blunt oyster-shucking knife from the pile. Gav was slithering towards me and if I stepped back much further, I would be cornered.

I drew him into me again, and he slashed the knife across, missing my throat by millimetres. He brought the knife back, slicing down, and I got inside the blow, twisting his arm away, dropping the pan and grabbing his wrist. I brought my knee up into his Jacob's and pulled him towards me. We fell into a contorted embrace, me trying to twist the knife free while he tried to get the fingers of the other hand into my eyes.

The pain in my eyes was excruciating and he had the better of me now. With my free right hand I clenched the oyster knife and swung my arm up, as hard as I could, in a final bid to throw him off. Blinded by his fingers, I felt the knife hit something hard, then give a little.

It was a strange sensation as Gav Taylor's body jerked and spasmed against mine, as I tasted hot blood seeping between the fingers that still covered my face. As his body ceased shaking and went limp against my own. An anticlimax as he slid down to the floor, the handle of the oyster knife sticking out from blood-matted hair just above his temple.

Now I was finally able to open my eyes, I looked down at him, stunned, as the enormity of what had happened crept over me. My scalp tingled and throbbed and my face ran with cold sweat and warm blood. I had managed to do what a roadside bomb in Afghanistan hadn't.

I had killed Gav Taylor.

FORTY-ONE

"Calm down, calm down." Anna's voice sounded tired but steady on the end of the phone. "We won't get anywhere if you panic."

It was easy for her to say.

My heart was pounding so hard I thought it would burst, I was choking on snotty tears and my brain hurt trying to come to terms with what had happened. My hand shook as I held the phone to my ear. Before making the call I had stood looking at the body for, I guess, minutes, frozen to the spot, not knowing what to do.

"Deep breaths," she said. "It was self-defence."

"I killed him," I said. "I took his life."

For all the hatred I had built up against Gav Taylor and the anger at being stitched up by him, it was still a life. The life of someone I knew.

"You can't think like that at the moment," Anna said. "We can go through the rights and wrongs later. For now, it's damage limitation. One option is to leave it as is and let the chef discover the body in the morning."

"That's never going to work," I said, panicky. "Everyone knows I was the last one there. If the police get involved, they'll be all over me. They'll be down in the cellar. And I won't get any protection from Gadd."

Anna thought for a moment. "Here's what you're going to do. It's, what, nearly three in the morning over there?"

"Yes."

"So you've got a good few hours to clean up. Is it messy?"

"There's quite a bit of blood, and the kitchen's a tip."

"Listen," she instructed. "Take a scene-of-crime photo and text it to me straight away. Then move the body out to the back while you clear up. Do this one step at a time. If you panic, you're stuffed."

"OK," I said.

"Clean up all the kitchen surfaces, wash any knives or anything that might have been touched, then once all that's tidy – and this is the critical bit – clean the floor. Swab it down first, then bleach it and dry it. Check for footprints to and from the kitchen. Fingerprints on doors. We want the place as clean as a whistle."

"OK," I said again.

"When you've done that, deal with the body," she said calmly. "Think of it as just another drug-related death on the Costa del Sol. Probably one of several tonight."

Her words didn't make me feel any better.

An hour and a half later I dragged Gav Taylor's corpse out by the heels, cling film wrapped around his bloody wounds. There was plenty of cover and shadow in the back alley to hide him away. I had scrubbed and swabbed and tidied until the kitchen shone like new. Anna had suggested the possibility of dumping the body in the harbour, using one of the barrows the sailors use along the pontoons. I rejected the idea: the harbour was busy all through the night. Suddenly I had found myself becoming as practical as Anna.

I took two black bin bags outside and rolled the body over. I couldn't bear to look at the face and averted my eyes as I pulled the first bag over the head and down over the shoulders. I stuffed a key of cocaine inside his jacket to keep the story straight if he was ever discovered, then I put the second bag over his feet. I felt the artificial limb as I pulled the bin bag over his legs and, along with it, a renewed surge of guilt. But, like Anna said, I had plenty of time later to consider the rights and wrongs.

She had promised that as long as the body was tucked away out of sight, she would get someone to deal with it. Like she disposed of bodies on a weekly basis. Hidden down a dark alley, there was nothing to link Gav Taylor to Jubarry's or to me. If the police took any interest at all, Taylor would be written off as yet another statistic in the Costa's dismal roll-call of drug casualties.

Panting with the effort, I hauled the wrapped body down the alleyway and tucked it tight into a corner where it couldn't even be seen in daylight. An area of crushed cans, needles, plastic bottles, rats and feral cats. Somehow fitting for a louse like Gav. I covered the body with flattened-out cardboard boxes; I couldn't wait to make him disappear and get myself away from there as quickly as possible.

With Gav finally hidden under several layers of stinking card, I walked back, took my filthy, bloody clothes off in the kitchen and put them into another bag. I checked my watch: just past 5 a.m. I padded, naked, up to the flat vacated by Barry and Julie and had a shower. I found an old grey suit in a cupboard and a white vest. Complete with flip-flops and my face a mass of swellings and cuts, I looked quite a picture. I had to get back to the apartment before Carlos or anyone got in. After locking the back door from the inside, I checked the kitchen again and let myself out by the front.

I zigzagged through all the tiny side streets on the moped. I didn't want to be stopped by a stray police car: my strange appearance and bag full of blood-stained clothes might just have raised suspicion. As soon as I could, I ditched the bag in a row of bins behind some shops, then wound my way back to the apartment just as the sun was coming up.

I paced the room, swigging from a bottle of sticky Spanish brandy, but it didn't seem to settle my nerves. It looks so easy when someone gets hit in the movies. Bang! Dead. Move on.

I could still smell Gav's breath, his body odour, his blood under my fingernails. And now, by my doing, he no longer existed.

I had knocked back too much brandy and I suddenly felt the acidity rise in my throat and a wave of nausea creep up from my chest over my face. Dropping to my knees in front of the toilet bowl, I retched and heaved. Not much came up; I'd eaten nothing for hours.

Finally I lay on my bed, waiting for the morning to come, looking at the water stains on the ceiling and only seeing Gav Taylor's face in them, staring accusingly back at me.

I must have eventually drifted off, because when I opened my eyes again it was nearly ten. The memories of the night before came rushing back, hitting me like a body blow. I sat bolt upright and looked at my phone. No messages. Nothing unusual there; I didn't communicate with Juana much by phone. It pissed her off at first, but I think she understood my reluctance to use it. Now I needed to talk. I pressed her number.

"*Hola, guapa!*" I said, trying to sound normal.

"Where are you? You sound strange."

"I got into a bit of trouble last night," I said. "I got mugged, but I'm OK, I think."

She gasped. "Are you sure? You aren't hurt?"

"I'll live. Are you there already? I'm late."

"Don't worry, it's quiet in the restaurant. Carlos is here."

"Good," I said. My leg was shaking. "Fine. I'll be in soon."

"No hurry," she said. "But there's something going on in the alley behind. The police were there earlier. It makes me nervous."

The blood drained from my face again as I cut the call. I ran into the bathroom and retched dryly into the sink.

FORTY-TWO

Donnie sat in the car facing out over the harbour. He looked at the domed apartments that surrounded the marina and watched as a Chinese junk ferried tourists from one side to the other.

His life had improved, marginally.

In the days since he'd recovered from the beating he'd taken, he'd been on the wagon and cut down on the fags. The painkillers required to dampen the agony of a broken nose and collarbone, three fractured ribs and a ruptured spleen did not work well with a diet of forty fags and twenty-plus units of alcohol. The drinking wasn't helping him, he'd concluded, and he needed to straighten out. Needed to get his life back on track if he was to have any future at all.

He'd made a decision.

He'd called Dave Slaughter and explained his predicament. Pledged his undying loyalty once again to the Tommy Kelly branch of the family and told Dave that as long as he was sober, he could be really useful to them. He'd got some new information from a British doorman he'd met at the hospital. A doorman with a couple of Albanian bullets rattling around his gut.

Dave had wired him some money, sorted out a phone and a car and put him in touch with a couple of bods who could give him the odd driving job or security work. Donnie knew he was in the last-chance saloon and had vowed to Dave that he would do anything for him, no task too big or small.

His job today was to collect a package from a bloke off one of the boats. A sample. He'd been told to look out for an ex-service-man with a limp answering to the name of Gav. It was getting hot in the car and the guy was already twenty minutes late.

Donnie got out and smoked a fag, flicking his ash down into the greenish harbour water. Tiny fish flocked to the surface as the ash hit, in the hope that it might be nutritious. He waited another ten minutes, then locked the car and walked down to the pontoons. Sweat patches were beginning to show under the armpits of his light jacket, which he was only wearing to conceal the Baikal tucked into a shoulder holster. There was little activity on the yachts, just the odd middle-aged man tinkering about, repairing a hatch or retying a rope. Keeping out of the way of the missus, Donnie imagined, envying them a little.

After an hour, he became impatient. He hated ringing Dave with anything but positive news, but this clearly wasn't shaping up.

"Dave? Don."

"Yes, Don."

"It's a no-show, Dave."

"What do you mean, a no-show, Don?" Dave sounded angry. Donnie felt guilty, like it was his fault.

"The geezer ain't turned up, Dave. I been here an hour."

Dave swore on the other end of the phone. "What's going on down there, Don?"

"Nothing, far as I can see, Dave. All quiet on the western front."

"I don't like it, Don. Last night this wanker promised he'd get a sample of the blow and get it to our contact."

"Tell me about it, Dave," Donnie said. "The tip-off was good. Maybe I can help."

"It's a big effing deal is what it is. That's all you need to know." Dave sighed. "It's the second thing that's gone Pete Tong today and I don't like the smell of it."

"What, Dave?"

"They're not moving Tommy after all. Just found out, the guv'nor's staying in Belmarsh for the foreseeable."

"What?" Donnie felt a hot flush of shame. He had not been exactly discreet with the information.

"Tommy thinks they never intended to move him," Dave said. "Thinks they wanted to see how quickly information would leak out and get back to them. Thinks the prison authorities or whoever just put it out as a red herring to see who got excited about it. You didn't hear anyone discussing it down there, did you Don?"

"No, Dave. Like I said, I'm a bit out of the loop." Donnie wiped guilty sweat from his brow. Not only had he told Patsy about the move, but he had an idea he'd not exactly kept it under his hat while he was in his cups.

"It's not the end of the world. Tommy's still well in control where he is, but a move might have made him a bit more comfortable."

"Right," Donnie said. "Well, let me know what I can do, Dave."

"There's a lot of gear on its way in and it looks like Patsy's trying to corner the supply. It's one thing keeping the small-timers out, but we've got deals to fulfil ourselves. Long-standing arrangements. We can't have Patsy monopolizing it. Tommy's not very pleased with him. Not at all. He's upset some of our best customers, so we need to sweeten them up, get them back onside.

"So what can I do?" Donnie asked.

"For a start, find this limping gimp," Dave said. "He's our contact. Find out where they're keeping the gear. Then we need to get a half-kilo sample to this Serbian, whoever he is. Then I'll give you further instructions. And mind yourself, Don.

"Sure."

"Bad things happen in threes."

IV

Tercio de Muerte

Tercio de muerte (*"third of death"*). In this stage the matador re-enters the ring carrying a red cape stretched over a wooden dowel, and a sword. From the point at which the first pass is performed, the matador has no more than fifteen minutes to kill the bull.

FORTY-THREE

I got myself into Jubarry's as quick as I could, although every bone in my body resisted returning to the scene.

"You look terrible," Juana said when she saw my face.

"I feel worse."

"Go back home," she said sympathetically.

It was weird, but now I was in the restaurant with Juana I didn't want to go back to the apartment. I felt all over the place; maybe it would be better to be here if anyone started asking any questions, rather than hide away.

I didn't have long to wait.

I couldn't keep myself away from the kitchen. I needed to have a look, to make sure everything was as it should be. Carlos was tidying out there. He said hello, and sympathized with my bruised face, but otherwise everything was normal. Knives in their places, floor clean, cellar door locked. Despite myself, I was drawn to the rear door of the restaurant. It was still locked, so I guessed no one had been out back since the night before. I opened it up and walked out into the sunshine. It was really beginning to stink out there from several days' uncollected rubbish beginning to rot.

I broke into a sweat as the image of Gav Taylor's dead body returned to me again. Then my heart beat harder as I watched our neighbour, a hairdresser, turn into the alleyway followed by an inspector. I placed myself across the back alley as if to block it from their view.

The hairdresser was a stocky, loud man with chestnut-dyed hair who made big gestures with his arms when he spoke. I waved nervously to him, but he ignored me, too busy gesticulating at the row of wheelie bins. I guessed he was complaining about how they weren't emptied frequently enough and that the stinking refuse was affecting his business. Our food waste was probably making most of the smell. But with a dead body in my back alley and a cellar full of cocaine, a health and safety inspection was not what I needed.

The neighbour pointed at all the rubbish on the ground, then began to flip the lids of the bins open, one by one, to show how full they were.

Clouds of flies rose up from each bin, and as my neighbour got halfway down the row, the inspector had clearly seen enough and slammed the bin lid down again before more flies could escape. The alley was now swarming with flies and I felt them hit my head, crawl into my ears and across my eyes.

An image of Gav Taylor's face, crawling with maggots, flashed through my mind. I almost wanted to shout out, tell the men that there was a body in the alley. Confessing would have been almost preferable to the terrible tension and stomach-churning fear of being found out.

The hairdresser gave a resigned shrug as the officer made notes, then spoke into his mobile, increasing my paranoia. Who was he calling? Someone who would inspect the area more closely? Maybe he wasn't complaining about the rubbish, but telling the officer that he had seen something suspicious the previous night. All sorts of possibilities, both far-fetched and realistic, bombed around my brain. The two men finally turned and left, and my eyes were magnetically drawn to the alley behind me.

Gav Taylor's bin-liner-wrapped body had gone.

An hour later, Donnie Mulvaney came into the bar. He looked hot and short-tempered, overheated in a summer jacket. There was a new scar across his nose, pink and fresh against the leathery brown skin of his face.

Juana went to pour him a beer, but he waved his hand, asking for orange juice and soda instead

"You can tell your mum I'm on the wagon."

Juana raised her eyebrows.

"I want to thank you for what you done the other day." He sounded almost shy. "There's not many who'd have done that."

"*Da nada*," Juana said. It's nothing.

"Let me buy you both a drink."

We refused, but Donnie wasn't having it. He ordered a bottle of cava and Juana and I reluctantly poured ourselves a glass. Donnie looked uncomfortable sitting across the bar from us, watching us drink. He didn't really have any small talk, so it was an awkward moment while we all looked at one another. Donnie pretty quickly seemed to forget that he was on the wagon, or perhaps he didn't consider fizzy wine a drink, and he poured himself a glass, then rapidly drained most of the rest of the bottle. He ordered another. Juana and I sipped another glass each while Donnie did the same to the next bottle. There were no other customers in, so we became a captive audience for Donnie, who was difficult to refuse. By the third bottle he was acting like we were all old friends.

I was anxious; worried about what had happened to Gav's corpse. I reminded myself that the bruiser quaffing cava in front of me had murdered my own brother and had tried to kill me, too. Now, like him, I could add a killing to my CV.

He appeared to be in the money, judging by the roll of euros in his pocket. When he left, he pressed some crumpled notes on the counter. I began to sort them out, but among the crumpled notes there was a picture of a man. I recognized it immediately: a black-and-white photo of a man with a moustache and swept-back hair. It was the photo that Anna had shown me. I pushed it across to Donnie.

"Who's that?" I asked. He picked it up and attempted to focus.

"Dunno," he said. "Some foreign bloke." He put the picture back in his pocket. "Listen," he said. "This is between us." He leant in conspiratorially, placing a heavy paw on my neck and breathing alcohol fumes into my face. "I'm looking for a bloke with a limp. Can't miss

him. Northerner, Kev … no, Gav, he's called. Very important. If you see him, let me know…"

Donnie winked and crushed up at least another fifty
in notes, stuffing them into my hand. I watched, shaking,
as he tapped his nose and weaved out of Jubarry's.

Wherever his body was, Gav Taylor was already
haunting me.

FORTY-FOUR

"No way," I said. I meant it.

"That's the deal," Anna said. "I've spoken to Baylis. We bust a gut to get that body out of the way by daybreak, but you'll have to use the opportunity to step into Taylor's shoes and get another step closer to Patsy's business."

"But Terry Gadd can't stand the sight of me," I pointed out. I remembered the pain he could inflict, and I had only had a small sample.

"Use your charm, Pedro Garcia," Anna said. "The boss likes you. He may be using you but he'll remember that you saved his boy. The Kellys are sentimental about all that family stuff. You should know that better than most."

She was right. Saving Patsy Kelly's kid from drowning did cast me in a good light, but I sometimes wondered about Anna's judgements.

Also, the fact that Donnie Mulvaney was looking for Gav had really rattled me.

"You know what to do. Take them the evidence, tell

them what you know," Anna said. "And while you're there, make sure you wire the place a little better. We're getting very little intel from the bugs you planted."

"A few days ago you told me just to gather evidence of the cocaine and then I'd be out of it," I moaned.

"A few days ago I hadn't banked on you killing someone, had I?"

I finished the call and went back into the bar. "I have to go out this afternoon," I told Juana.

"Where are you going? I'll come with you."

"I don't want you to know," I said. "I can't take you with me."

Juana grabbed my wrist. "Is it that woman again?"

"No. She's in England."

"When is this going to end, Pedro?"

"I dunno. Soon, I hope." I really had no idea, but instinctively I felt that with all the bad vibes and toxins hanging around in the air, mixing and mingling together like a boil, before long something was going to burst.

"What do you want, ball-bag?" Terry Gadd asked.

"I'm here to see Mr Kelly."

I had been back to the apartment to pick up a few bits and pieces: magnetic bugs, surveillance devices and suchlike. Then I'd got in the Alfa and driven out of town. The afternoon was hot and I had the roof down. I was still shaky with nerves, but I put my foot down on the bends and opened up the throttle along the motorway to give myself a jolt of adrenalin. I put a CD on, a mix of old-school rap and hip hop. Public Enemy, "Harder Than You

Think". The sinister beats of Dr Dre's "Next Episode" followed, so packed full of "mofos" and "my niggas" that by the time I got out of the car at Casa Pampas I was almost walking with a pimp roll.

My pumped-up courage soon deflated when Gadd answered the door.

"Why do you want to see him?" he asked.

"I've got some information I think he'll be interested in."

"You talk to *me*, winkle. *I* talk to Patsy."

"What if I said it was about Gav Taylor?" I asked. "I expect you're wondering where he is."

Gadd looked at me for a moment and narrowed his eyes, then stepped back and let me in.

A couple of Patsy's heavies were hanging around reading English red tops and smoking while Patsy sat through in the big white lounge with the view over the Costa. There were lines of cocaine chopped out on the glass-topped table, which surprised me. I thought rule number one was never to touch the gear.

"To what do I owe the pleasure?" Patsy asked. His eyes had lost some of their aggression and he looked at me flatly, gesturing for me to sit down. I sat on the armchair to his right, and as soon as I could I slipped the small transmitter I'd palmed between the cushion and the arm as if it was a lost coin.

"Er, you—" I nodded to Terry Gadd— "asked me to keep an eye on the stuff in my cellar. So I have."

"And?" Patsy said.

"Well, I heard something the other night, so I went

down there and found that guy with the limp ... Gav Taylor, is it?"

"What about him?"

"Well, he was helping himself to the, er, merchandise you have down there."

"How do you know he wasn't just keeping an eye on it, like you?" Gadd asked.

"If carving chunks out of it counts as keeping an eye, then he was keeping an eye," I said. I took my iPhone out of my pocket and Patsy Kelly flinched slightly. It was beginning to feel like he was as jumpy as I was. I called up the camera roll on the phone and scrolled through. I had already downloaded the scene-of-crime pictures of Gav's dead body onto a portable hard drive back at the apartment. I didn't want them to see those.

I found the picture of Gav up to his elbows in cocaine and gave it to Patsy Kelly. He looked at it, studied it carefully and handed it to Terry Gadd. Gadd spat out the C-word.

"Where is he now? The effing..." Gadd spat a few more choice anatomical terms.

"He took a big chunk and did a runner," I said. "I tried to stop him, but he cut up rough." I pointed at the yellowing bruise beneath my eye.

"Do you know where he's gone?" Patsy asked.

"No." I shrugged, played dumb. "England?"

"Doubt it," Gadd said.

"But he said something about a Serbian ... I don't know if that means anything to you?" Anna had primed me to spin them a line, tell them something that would unsettle them. Patsy and Terry Gadd exchanged glances. I had clearly hit the right spot.

"Can you leave us alone for a minute?" Patsy said.

I got up and left the room. I walked outside and sat on a recliner by the pool, out of sight of the main house. Checking around me, I plugged a small earpiece into my ear. One that connected to the transmitter I'd put in the armchair minutes before.

"I told you!" I heard Patsy shout. "He was your bitch."

Gadd mumbled some excuses about Gav Taylor. How he'd come recommended. Patsy raised his voice. He sounded emotional.

"I've never seen you like this. This is no time to lose your bottle, Patsy," I heard Gadd say. "We've almost got it tied up. You can't roll over now."

"This Serbian fucker's running rings around us, who-ever he is. It's getting to me, Terry. If he's everything I've heard about him, we need to cut a deal."

Terry Gadd grumbled some more, his hoarse voice mostly too low for the transmitter to pick up, then I heard him tell Patsy he thought he was frightened.

A few minutes later Gadd called me back inside.

"Why did you come up here?" Patsy asked.

"I thought you'd want to know," I said. "You asked me to keep an eye out. If I hadn't come and told you, you'd have blamed me if gear went missing."

"Are you bent, Pedro?" Patsy asked.

I paused. "I've been done for attempting to smuggle charlie, if that's what you mean."

"Yes, that's the kind of form I was thinking about..."

"More to you than meets the eye," Gadd said.

"We've got another shipment arriving shortly," Patsy told me. "Then we need to start moving the stuff around sharpish. We need someone on the spot. Will you help?"

I felt uneasy, but I knew that I had convinced them – that I had just crossed the line into their territory.

"Do I have a choice?" I asked.

"No," Patsy said.

FORTY-FIVE

The next consignment was due to arrive sometime later that week.

I realized that now, whether I liked it or not, I was guilty by association. I knew too much. I had become Gav Taylor's replacement as runner or overseer or whatever, and Patsy Kelly knew I wouldn't put a foot wrong for fear of my life.

He was right.

I began to regret my bold step. Terry Gadd would as soon kill me as look at me if there was even a whiff of my being up to something. And of course I *was* up to something. I'd have to be very careful about feeding back intel to Anna.

I also wanted to protect Juana from the knowledge that I was working closer to the villains, and I couldn't tell her about Gav Taylor. I'd been honest with her up to a point, but even so I was adding on so many layers of lies that I could hardly remember what the truth was myself.

I became edgy all the time we were at Jubarry's, then

when we went back to the apartment I couldn't sleep. I'd have a few beers and Juana would watch TV, looking at me disapprovingly.

"You drink too much."

"I'm sorry, babe, I'm just jumpy."

I really appreciated her caring about me and couldn't imagine my life without her. She had become my emotional bedrock. She was the most beautiful girl, and when we were together I would be totally distracted: absorbed by her face, her hair and her body, but then my mind would drift back to the bad stuff. When I did get to sleep, images of Gav Taylor would appear, spewing garbage from his dead mouth, surrounded by a cloud of black blowflies. I could hear the buzzing in my sleep, smell the filth and the rot and the blood.

The smells of death.

I would wake up pouring with sweat and cling to Juana, burying my face in her hair. In my waking mind I thought I was protecting her, but at night it was she who made me feel safe. I wanted to disappear into her curls, to pull the duvet over us and stay there for ever.

She burst into tears one morning before we headed off for Jubarry's. It had been a restless night. I'd been shouting out in my sleep.

"I don't know how much more of this I can stand," she told me.

"I'm sorry," I said guiltily. "I didn't mean to get us in this mess."

"I feel sick all the time, like something bad is always about to happen."

I felt it too, but didn't say. Juana didn't know quite how bad things already were. I tried to smile and convince her, and myself, of Anna's half promise.

"I'll get you away from here soon," I said. I tried to believe my *own* promise. I had a vague notion of us back in England, somewhere green and leafy: secure, away from the heat and the red earth of the Costa.

As soon as we got in to work that morning, I had a call from Terry Gadd, summoning me to Casa Pampas after the lunchtime shift.

He was really getting his two pennyworth out of me, getting me to fetch this and fetch that, check out certain boats in the harbour. Keeping me on the run, keeping me on edge, so that I felt he was watching me all the time and that I was at his beck and call 24/7.

Gadd would even send me out for packets of cigarettes if Patsy ran out. They had me by the short and curlies, and of course the London office wanted me dug in there as deep as possible. I had no room for manoeuvre, but despite the pressure I began to take it in my stride. Soon, working with them felt completely normal, as if it had never been any other way.

"D'you get seasick?" Gadd asked me when I arrived. He snorted a line of cocaine from a mirror.

"No," I said. I had sailed with Tommy Kelly, although nothing too rough.

"Good," Gadd said. "Because the shipment's due in at the weekend. And you're going to get it."

"Where from?" I asked. "I can't really sail."

"Don't panic," Patsy Kelly said. He thumbed his nose

and sniffed, his eyes darting around edgily. "You won't have to control the boat yourself. You'll just have the navigation coordinates for the pickup. I need someone I can trust."

I must have looked very blank, scared or both.

"I *can* trust you, can't I?" Patsy asked.

"Sure." I nodded. "Of course you can."

"If I can't trust you, you're dead in the water anyway. So, let me tell you how it all works," Terry Gadd said. The charlie was making them both far more talkative than usual. "In the old days, when we was working more out of London, we'd have to deal with a load of middle men and the gear would take about five stops on its way over. Trouble with middle men is they put their mark-up on it, and price goes sky-high. So what we've done down here is create a direct relationship with one or two Colombian growers who airdrop it somewhere in the Moroccan desert just over the water."

"Then we got plenty cheap labour over there who drive it to the coast in bashed-up vegetable trucks," Patsy continued. "Out to Casablanca or a bit further up, where there are no coastguards, then onto a fishing boat – which we meet on a nice, anonymous charter boat just outside Spanish waters."

"Cut out the middle men," Gadd said. "And now we're into such big quantities, we can bring the price down further, widen the user base, do wholesale deals, monopolize the trade. Bish, bash, bosh."

"Very tidy," I said.

"But it makes people jealous," Gadd said.

"The Spanish?" I asked, innocent.

"Albanians, Romanians, the young Spanish kids who think they can have a go…"

"Serbians?" I chanced. Patsy Kelly banged the glass table with his fist.

"I don't want to hear another fucking word about the Serbians!" he shouted.

Then, right on cue, Terry Gadd's phone rang.

"What?" he yelled. "When?" He looked at Patsy. He looked worried. Threw me some car keys. "Drive," he said.

FORTY-SIX

The bar was a couple of kilometres further up into the hills. You could hardly tell it was a bar from the outside. The windows were barred and the building itself wasn't much more than a concrete bunker. It had a small sign on the front that read FLANAGAN'S. There were a couple of anxious-looking blokes and a woman hanging around outside. Expats.

It was hot, and when I braked into the small car park, a cloud of reddish dust hung in the air

Patsy and Terry Gadd got out. They hadn't spoken on the way other than to give me the merest grunt of an instruction.

One of the men gestured to a black Range Rover parked over in the corner. Gadd walked across to it and looked in through the window. I watched his expression change, saw the expletives form on his lips.

Patsy followed him, and out of curiosity, so did I.

The side window was open, and inside, a man lay back in his seat, looking like he was having a rest. At least you could tell it was a man by his unshaved lower jaw and the stray teeth that hung from it. Most of the rest of his head was missing: there was a huge hole where the ear should have been and a great spray of blood and bits across the windscreen. Laying across him, as if cosying up, was another man. I could only just see him through the window, but his face was twisted and contorted, as if he was pressing his face against glass. Black hair glued with blood stood in spikes around a hole in his head, and a milky eye, almost hanging out, stared blankly at me. Dead bodies don't look at peace, with their eyes shut like they're having sweet dreams, they look twisted and tortured as if they're still in pain. A big green fly landed in the gore.

I felt nauseous and turned away.

Patsy was holding his head in his hands, like he was going mad; two more of his men down. Gadd walked back to the group.

"We didn't hear nothing, Terry," one of the men said.

"Curtis and Tony often came up here at dinner time," the other said. "Someone must have been waiting for them."

"We didn't see no one," the woman said.

"Some people are saying the Serbians—" the first man started.

"Shut the fuck up," Patsy snapped. "Just get it sorted."

We drove back in silence.

When we arrived at Casa Pampas, another car was waiting. An official-looking blue Mercedes. A short Spanish man with a moustache and a comb-over got out, followed by his driver. I recognized him from Patsy's birthday party. I heard Patsy let out a deep sigh, as if his troubles would never end.

"*Buenas dias*, Señor Kelly," the man said.

"Señor Dominguez," Kelly said. "Please…"

He ushered the man in through the gate, and offered him a seat in the shade around the pool.

"Señor Dominguez is the mayor," Patsy told me. I nodded and we shook hands. "Get him a drink, will you."

The mayor and his driver refused anything other than water, which I brought as quickly as I could, not to miss anything.

"My nephew's life support was switched off yesterday," I heard the mayor say. "It appears that it was one of your men who put him in hospital in the first place."

"I'll find out who and deal with it," Patsy assured him. "If it *was* one of ours, you have my sincere apologies and you must let me know how much—" The mayor waved Patsy's offer away.

"It's not quite so simple, Señor Kelly. It means that I am finding it hard to protect you. My brother-in-law, Jesus Ybarra – his father – is district commissioner in Mijas, very important. You and I have always had a good understanding, but you must realize that the English are not quite the force they once were here."

"That's about to change," Patsy said, wrong-footed.

"We are building relationships with some of the new arrivals. We can do deals. They are keen," the mayor added.

"'Course they're keen," Patsy said, beginning to sound rattled, "because they want a piece of my action."

"I'm not talking about the small-timers, Mr Kelly. There are some very big businessmen already investing in the area. They are helping to build the town's economy back up."

"Like we've done," Patsy said.

"With respect, although you have contributed in the past, very little has gone back into the local economy recently."

Patsy Kelly was fuming. He clearly wasn't used to being talked to like this. Terry Gadd kept it shut.

"Who are these people?" Patsy asked.

"There is a Russian company building the new marina just along the coast," the mayor said.

"We know about them. All financed by a load of arms sales and Es."

Señor Dominguez shrugged. "As you know to your advantage, I don't look too closely at the source of the money. My brother-in-law has just been approached by a Serbian organization keen to do business here."

Patsy looked mad. If the mayor had been anyone else, I was sure he'd have killed him. "I've heard enough about these Serbians to last me a lifetime," he spat.

"All I'm saying, Mr Kelly, is that there's been a lot of bloodshed these past few months and now I think it is time to make a truce and share some of the business. Work together, no?"

"Let them come and talk to me if they want to know what's what," Patsy said sharply.

"I think it may be more a case of you talking to them, Mr Kelly."

Patsy didn't say anything.

"You will come to the *corrida* at the weekend, as my guest?"

The mayor's driver produced a stiff envelope and handed it to Patsy, who opened it and took out an invitation to the bullfight. It was part of Benalmádena's fiesta of the Virgen del Carmen, one of several festivals that went on during the summer months.

"You will meet the Serbians then," Señor Dominguez said. "I will introduce you and we can talk business." He stood up.

I escorted the mayor and his driver back to the gate and closed it behind them. When I arrived back at the poolside Terry Gadd was on the phone.

"Stav, you testicle!" he shouted. "Did you put that Spanish kid in a coma?" He listened. "Why am I not surprised?" He finished the call. "It was that slab of shit Mulvaney."

Gadd looked at me as if he'd just realized I was still there. "What are you doing here?" he asked. "Piss off! I'll tell you when we need you."

I did as I was told, and as I shut the gate I heard Patsy Kelly put his boot through a glass-topped table, sending shattered glass all across the poolside.

He wasn't having a good day.

FORTY-SEVEN

"Looks like the next shipment's coming in over the weekend," I said. "I'm totally bricking it."

"Isn't there some kind of festival going on?" Anna asked. It was late in the evening and I'd nipped out to make the call.

Garlands of white paper fluttered above the square. Several doughnut stalls and stands selling deep-fried churros and caramelized peanuts had begun to line the pavement.

"Yeah, it's this weekend," I said. "It's called the Virgen del Carmen. They take the statue from one of the churches down to the port. It's supposed to protect people at sea."

"Hope it works for you," Anna commented. "Funny time to pick for a drop."

"Makes sense to me," I said. "The whole procession goes down to the port then out towards Malapasquera beach, then there's fireworks. Everyone will be focused on that."

"Who are you going with?"

"Dunno yet. But I don't think PK will be anywhere near. He's going nuts. He's doing plenty of blow and it's making him edgy."

I told her about the hit by Flanagan's bar, and about the mayor's visit and how ruffled Patsy Kelly was getting about the Serbians.

"Does Baylis actually know where this Serb is?" I asked.

"If he does, he's not letting on. But between you and me, I don't think he does. We're just getting intel that he's in the area, building up contacts. If it's rattling them, that's good enough for the moment. I don't need to tell you, but let me know as soon as you get details of the drop."

"Sure," I said. "But if I'm going to do this, you will pull me out of here straight away, won't you?"

"I said we would as soon as possible," Anna said.

"And Juana," I pressed. "I've promised her. It will be too dangerous for her to be even in the same country if you bust twelve million quid's worth of cocaine out of Juharry's."

"I'll do what I can," she said.

Juana was back at the restaurant.

I'd been leaving most of the work to her while I'd been seconded to Patsy Kelly and Terry Gadd. It was getting busy towards the festival weekend, so we'd taken on extra staff, including Juana's mum, who was helping behind the bar. Valerie was an experienced pair of hands.

I felt guilty for having plans that would take her daughter away from here as soon as I could.

293

My phone rang around 10.30 p.m. Gadd.

"All right, bollock chops? We're on. Tomorrow night. I'm gonna text you the details. Basically you'll meet a geezer called Adie down on the pontoons. *Sea Dog of Ramsgate* the boat's called. 8 p.m. Don't cock up," he said, "or I'll cut your girlfriend's throat."

My knees went weak.

He texted the details five minutes later, plus the coordinates for where we were to meet the incoming boat, *Selim*.

An hour later Ian Baylis was on the phone. It was the first time in months that I'd spoken to him. Never my favourite thing to do: I always felt he was trying to catch me out.

"Anything to report?" he asked.

"Are we safe on this line, Nimrod?" I said, using his code name, toeing the line. I walked across to the shadows on the other side of the square, where no one could see me.

"As houses."

"OK, the pickup is tomorrow night. I've only just got the coordinates but it looks like it's some way out at sea, Strait of Gibraltar maybe."

"Perfect timing," Baylis said. "Text me the details, we'll be there."

"What?" I said. "You'll be where?"

"We'll intercept the drop. I can get the Guardia and the British Coastguard from Gib' across there in a joint operation."

"Whoa, I agreed to do the pickup," I said. "Not be

right at the centre of a heist! Two things: first, the Guardia are as bent as a bottle of chips; as soon as they get a whiff of this, someone at Patsy's end will be tipped off. Second, it would be better to land the stuff at Jubarry's; that way you get both hauls in one place. I'm sure Gadd at least will be there. None of them are coming out on the boat. That's why they've got muggins here doing the pickup. They've threatened to kill Juana if I mess up."

"You're thinking above your pay grade," Baylis said drily. He paused. "But what you say makes some sense. We'll hold off until the consignment is safely landed, then our chaps on the ground can take care of it."

"Thanks, Nimrod," I said. "I think it makes sense." Stupidly grateful, even though it was still me doing the dirty work.

"OK?" Baylis said.

"Sure," I said. He rang off.

It wasn't OK. I knew the score down here better than Baylis. I'd been the man on the spot, but he always acted like he had superior intelligence. Maybe he was picking up intel that I knew nothing about, from surveillance … or from other agents I didn't know. I was sure I couldn't be the only person working undercover out here. You could just never spot them. I walked back across to Jubarry's.

Juana looked tired. Donnie Mulvaney had wandered in and was talking to her mother across the bar, sipping Coke and laughing politely at her, like butter wouldn't melt in his mouth. It struck me how I'd got used to hanging around people like Donnie, Terry Gadd and Patsy Kelly. I realized how small my pool of friends was. In short, I didn't have any here. The work prevented it. I was lucky to have Juana. Without her I would have been completely lost.

I suddenly felt very tired. I needed out. I went out back and checked that everything was securely locked and bolted. Carlos was still in the kitchen.

"You OK, boss?" he asked. I shrugged. "You look *fatigado* … ti-red." It was nearly time to close. "You go home," Carlos said. "I lock up here." I didn't like to leave the locking up in anyone else's hands, but I needed to get away.

"Make sure you do the double bolts and the dead-locks," I said.

"Sure, sure, sure," Carlos said, shooing me away. "Go get some rest."

Good old Carlos. I thanked him, said goodbye to Juana and walked out of Jubarry's.

Just one more day, I thought.

FORTY-EIGHT

Saturday dragged.

We got in early and it was busy right off the bat. Even the roughest towns in Spain have an air of excitement when there's a fiesta on.

We were serving coffees and pastries. There were some tourists in town, but for the most part holidaymakers stuck close to their resorts and the beaches, and to the bars and 24-Hour Square at night. Any local culture pretty much passed them by.

I could see why it was a good day to try and slip vast quantities of cocaine into town. In the winter, any activity down by the harbour was scrutinized. On a day like this there was so much else going on: outdoor discos in the plazas; fairground stalls on every street; balloon sellers walking up and down. By lunchtime the Spanish were pouring themselves bottles of wine and drinking beer like the English expats.

I did my best to keep across the customers, but Juana could see I was jumpy. I'd told her I had to go off in the evening and she knew not to ask me where.

Late afternoon, brass bands started assembling in the town, brought in from surrounding towns and villages. From the restaurant we could hear the distant rap of snare drums and blare of bugles and trumpets warming up. Outside the church across the plaza, men dressed in white were gathering, ready to shoulder the effigy of the Virgin for a procession around the town before heading down to the harbour. The air of ritual increased my tension, and I was glad I would be away before the festival got going.

By evening I was on pins. I kept checking my phone, hoping that there might be change of plan or that I might be called off.

Nothing.

When it was time, I went down to the harbour and found the familiar pontoon. I knew *Sea Dog of Ramsgate* of course, and Adie who was waiting on deck for me, but pretended I didn't.

"Pedro?" he asked. I nodded. He threw me some salopettes and a waterproof jacket. "Put these on, it might get a bit wet out there."

"We sailing?" I asked.

"Nope," he said and laughed like I'd asked a stupid question.

Ten minutes later we waddled down another pontoon, then across to a more industrial, concrete mooring where there was a medium-sized diesel boat chugging at rest. It had a cabin, with a couple of cushioned seats and a bench around the inside of the hull.

A Spanish guy stood at the wheel, smoking a

strong-smelling cigarette. Combined with the stink of diesel, fish and sweat, I hoped it wouldn't prove too much for my nervous gut.

We shook hands. No names. Another Spaniard was taking care of the ropes at the stern of the boat. He nodded to me and Adie, and we nodded back. I wrote down the coordinates for the skipper, and within a few minutes we were motoring out of the harbour.

I stayed on top in the fresh air as we chugged past the pontoons towards the open sea. I watched the town recede into the distance as the drumming became fainter. Festival lights were beginning to come on around the harbour, lighting up the domed apartments on the quayside, making the place look almost magical.

An hour later we were out at sea, heading down past Marbella, the coastline just visible as a streak of lights in the distance. No one spoke much. Adie fussed around on deck, clearing crates and making space. I went into the cabin and checked the chart. The skipper pointed to our location with a diesel-stained finger. We were well out into the Strait of Gibraltar, a couple of centimetres away from our rendezvous point on the map. It was dark out at sea now and I scanned the horizon for other vessels or lights.

Nothing.

A few kilometres further on, the skipper cut the engine and dropped anchor, the chain rattling loudly as it plunged into the calm sea. The four of us sat in near silence, just the faint sound of the waves lapping against the hull of the boat, drifting on the anchor.

Adie checked his watch and brought a torch out from the cabin. He took a bearing on the compass, then flashed several times across our starboard side. There was no response. He flashed again, then seconds later a faint light flashed back in the distance.

"That's our man," he said.

My heart started pumping hard. I was desperate for this to be over, desperate just to land the stuff, then hopefully get quietly arrested and spirited away as promised.

Life is never that simple in a business like this.

The lights of the boat drew closer. It was bigger than us, wide-bodied and low in the water, coming from the south. As it came closer still I could see orange floats and nets draped over the back, an old-fashioned Moroccan fishing boat.

My hand tightened on the gun I had tucked into my waistband, more for a sense of security than any thought of using it.

The boat chugged alongside us and I could see a couple of dark figures on its deck and the name *Selim* painted on the side. The figures and our guys exchanged ropes and pulled the two vessels side by side. Once the boats were hitched together, the men on the other boat shifted some pallets across the deck to a position underneath their winch.

The chains on the pallets tightened as the winch arm lifted them one by one into the air, and one by one deposited them onto the deck of our boat. There were twelve cartons altogether, plastic-wrapped against the damp. We stacked them centrally and covered them with a tarpaulin.

No money changed hands. That was clearly taken care of at a different level. The job was done and we began to unhitch the ropes and bring the anchor back up.

That was when the alarm sounded.

Two rapidly approaching spotlight beams flashed across the sea, fixing us in their glare. They were joined by another, larger beam powerfully sweeping the surface of the water, its klaxon roaring out a throaty warning that fixed us to the spot. I swore, and the crew of our boat looked around like cornered rats, searching for an escape that didn't exist.

The Moroccans on the other boat ran around in a frenzy, starting up the engine and trying to chug away. But the approaching boats were coming far too fast, quickly gaining on us. Cutting across the beams I could see a RIB speeding towards us with several men on board.

A flare from the largest boat shot into the darkness. Its white light revealed not only the attempted escape of the Moroccan fishing boat, but also the heavy-duty vessels approaching us. One looked like a British Revenue and Customs cutter, grey and armed. The other had the distinctive green and white hull of a Guardia Civil patrol boat.

Baylis had clearly suckered me. He'd completely ignored my warnings and had gone his own sweet way, with his usual disregard for me or my opinions.

The British cutter fired a couple of shots at the Moroccan boat to slow it down.

Our boat was going nowhere. I froze to the spot and watched as the official boats came closer and closer, circling us like sheepdogs.

The first to reach us was the RIB, and while two men kept the engine running, four more, armed to the teeth, climbed aboard and waved automatic weapons at us.

"Down!" one shouted. I had the pistol in my waistband but didn't for a second consider using it. I hit the deck, as did Adie and the two Spanish men. I felt a heavy foot on my back, while another set of hands frisked me, finding the gun and removing it.

Then I felt another hand, this time on my head. It lifted me up by the hair until my face was looking up. A man in black was standing over me, looking down via the end of his automatic weapon. Next to him, kneeling beside me, holding onto my hair and looking pleased with himself, was Ian Baylis.

FORTY-NINE

The Guardia Civil vessel hitched up the Moroccan fishing boat and began towing it towards the coast.

I was handcuffed and separated from Adie and the other guys. I knew it was standard procedure to keep defendants apart, so it didn't look suspicious. I felt relieved. Soon I would be out of the game and on a flight home.

The customs cutter escorted our boat back along the coast, armed SBS men lining each side of their boats in case of attack. This was a major haul for customs, potentially preventing a few million quid's worth of cocaine flooding southern Spain and beyond.

Baylis stood with me on deck. He was keeping up the official tone, but nothing could disguise how chuffed he was with this result.

"Pretty smooth operation, I think you'd have to agree, Elgar?" Elgar had been my code name while operating as Eddie Savage.

"From your point of view maybe," I said. "But I'm the

one standing here in handcuffs. If they get a scent of this ashore, then Juana is at serious risk. I told you not to intercept it out here."

I was feeling seriously paranoid about Juana. I knew Gadd would have no hesitation in carrying out his threats.

"Send two texts," Baylis instructed. "One to Gadd to say that the pickup was successful, the second to your girlfriend…"

"Saying what?"

"Suggesting that she makes herself scarce. While the fiesta's on, it will be easy for her to disappear into the crowds."

"I thought you were protecting her," I said, my heart sinking.

"I have a couple of people on the ground, but as you know, our resources are stretched, particularly when such a big deal is going on. Everything else, including people's personal safety, is secondary."

I began shaking with barely contained rage; once again, my trust had been abused and I had been made false promises. I had been played, without any regard for my safety or Juana's.

The difference between the organization I worked for and the crims, I thought bitterly, was that the villains were true to their word; did exactly what they said they were going to do. When they delivered on their threats, they were brutal, but at least you knew where you stood.

Baylis had my cuffs unlocked and I took out my phone and texted Gadd:

Pickup successful. PG.

Keep it simple, I thought. Then, to Juana:

*On way back. Leave Jubarry asap. Go somewhere
safe. Txt me later. P. XX*

"It's a good night to disappear. She can go to friends or somewhere," Baylis said.

I wasn't reassured. "She only really has me to rely on."

Baylis nodded. The lights ashore began to come into focus and the occasional rocket burst into the sky off the coast.

"Quite the ladies' man, aren't you?"

I shrugged. I knew I had only her to rely on. I wouldn't have survived out here without her.

Baylis got on his phone. He was liaising with someone ashore, speaking in a clipped, coded way. Then he came back over to me, rubbing his hands together.

"Everything in place ashore," he said. "As soon as we land, I'll authorize confiscation of the Jubarry haul. I have several armed plain-clothes SAS and Spanish specials lined up. They'll all be around the square and the back alleys when we go in. Should be more than a match for Terry Gadd and his thugs. If we can bring him in as well, it will be a bonus."

I looked at my phone. "He's not acknowledged my message yet," I said.

"Would he normally?"

"I don't get many messages from him," I said. "But

you'd have thought that with this amount of gear, he'd be on the case."

Baylis nodded. He was thinking. "Try him again." I texted Gadd again.

"Perhaps he's sensed something. Doesn't want his phone tracked," I suggested. "They're totally paranoid about the Serbians getting wind of this deal."

"The Serbs have put the wind up Patsy Kelly, have they?" Baylis smiled in his usual self-satisfied way.

"Patsy's been on tenterhooks since they attempted to shoot him. At least that's who he thinks they were. He's been getting increasingly jumpy, drinking plenty and putting a load up his nose. He relies more and more on Terry Gadd."

"And have you seen any of the Serbians in town?"

"I wouldn't know one if I saw one," I admitted. "I guess they look pretty similar to the Spanish. I've seen a few pictures of this war criminal, Dragomir, in circulation, but to me he looks just like an average Spanish bloke. Dark hair, moustache…"

"They seek him here, they seek him there." Baylis smiled. "Dragomir Radic is a bit of a Scarlet Pimpernel. Don't forget, he might well have changed his appearance, like you. He might have blond hair and no moustache by now. But if all the stuff that's blamed on him down here is true, he's become a very major player, very fast. He wants his share in the white stuff, and a man who's willing to torture and kill a whole village doesn't let much get in his way."

I looked out at the shore. Benalmádena was

approaching. The fiesta was still in full swing and fire-works lit up the sky. I looked at the dark hills that loomed over the town and began to feel some of the fear that was building up around this legendary criminal, this bogey man who was hiding somewhere, ready to pounce. My phone bleeped. Gadd.

Have you checked merch?

I hadn't, of course. We'd been busted as soon as we'd got the crates on board.

As if to answer his question, one of Baylis's men came on deck, looking for Ian. "Excuse me, sir," he said. "Something's not quite right here."

He spoke in a low voice, close to Baylis's ear. I saw the smug expression on my ex-case officer's face change to one of complete disbelief.

"So what the hell do you think it is?" Baylis asked.

"We haven't got the equipment out here to run proper tests, but my best guess is that we've just intercepted a large shipment of talcum powder."

FIFTY

The drumming grew louder and the mournful sound of bugle and trumpets accompanied our return into Benalmádena port. The fireworks continued to crackle overhead while Baylis looked like thunder. He made urgent calls on his phone, out of earshot.

One thing had been calculated correctly: this would have been the perfect night to slip in to port unnoticed. There was no one around, nobody saw us as we crept, shamefaced, back ashore.

I couldn't believe what had just happened. Who had been stitched up by whom? I found it hard to believe that anyone would try and turn over Patsy Kelly on a deal on that scale. It would have caused a third world war, and might still. Whichever way you looked at it, some shit was going to hit the fan.

And I hoped none of it would end up on me.

Nonetheless, I felt a little smug that my advice to Baylis had been vindicated, but it wasn't really the moment to say told you so.

As soon as we got ashore, Baylis hit the ground running. Adie and the Spanish seamen were released. Baylis already had enough egg on his face not to try and make stick a charge of smuggling talcum powder. I followed him up the pontoons as he continued to talk into his mobile. He was telling his plain-clothes operatives to head for the square now, to get ready to take Bodega Jubarry on his command. Then he turned to me.

"I'm going to send you in first to case the joint," he said. "You know the ins and outs and can give us the all-clear."

We wove through the back alleys, all the little short cuts I had become familiar with, until we came to the alley that ran along the back of Jubarry's. It was dark, lit by the occasional flash from the sky. Two plain-clothes men rolled up behind Baylis.

"Go!" he said in a stage whisper.

I ran past the wheelie bins and turned towards the rear entrance. Something was wrong.

The door was open. Not with Carlos or one of the part-timers smoking by it, but wide open, swinging on its hinges. I took a couple of steps further forwards. The lights were on, but there wasn't the usual hiss and clatter of a busy Saturday night. I sidled up to the door and looked through the gap at the hinges. There was no one there. I stuck my head around the door. Definitely empty. But then something worse: the door to the cellar was also open. There was no way I was going in to investigate.

I ran back along the alley where Baylis was waiting eagerly.

"I don't like it," I told him. "The cellar door's already open."

Baylis considered a moment. "We're going in," he said. The two plain-clothes officers followed him, running quietly, guns drawn and ready. I was unarmed and followed behind. They barged into the kitchen, pistols held out at arm's length. One of the men flung the cellar door back and threw himself against the wall. Silence. Tentatively, he began to edge his way down the steps, followed by the second man and Baylis.

I was waiting for gunshots, smoke or a grenade, but there was nothing.

I heard Baylis swear, and began to creep down the stairs after him. I heard him curse again as I emerged into the dull underground light. The plain-clothes guys stood, guns dangling at their sides. Baylis looked at me accusingly.

The cellar was completely empty.

"What do you know about this?" he hissed. I was speechless. The place had been secured and bolted with reinforced locks ever since Gav Taylor had helped himself. Terry Gadd had overseen it personally.

It was not looking good for Ian Baylis. Two major busts gone wrong in one night. Whoever had trusted him with this mission would not be pleased with him.

Whoever had trusted him with this mission would not be pleased with *me*, either. Neither would Terry Gadd nor Patsy Kelly. In fact no one would be thrilled: the difference being that Gadd would probably kill me.

"I've done my end of the job, Nimrod," I said. "Ysobel

promised me out once I'd delivered."

Baylis looked white with rage, his thin lips, normally pale, almost non-existent.

"You must be joking," he spat. "You have delivered nothing, you idiot. You've been stitched up, again, and in doing so you've made me look completely incompetent. Now get back out there and find out what's gone wrong."

"Out where?" I asked.

"Back to Kelly, Gadd, whoever."

"They'll kill me," I protested.

"Blame it on Dragomir Radic," he said.

We went back up into the kitchen. The door to the restaurant and bar had been blocked off. Planks of wood had been wedged against it and nailed in to prevent it from being opened from the bar side. Together with Baylis's men, I levered off the planks and reopened the door. The bar was empty too but looked as if a bomb had hit it. There were still people on the streets outside, but whatever had gone on here had clearly driven away the customers. I heard the sound of sobbing behind the bar and found Valerie, Juana's mother, curled up on the floor crying. I knelt down to speak to her, but when she looked up and saw who it was, she flew into a rage. She stood up and lashed out at me, digging sharp fingernails into my arms, slapping my face.

"What have you done to her?" she screamed.

"Where is she?" I asked. "Where's Juana?"

"They took her!" she shouted. "They will kill her, I know. It is your fault." She went to slap me again and I caught her hand.

"Who was in the kitchen?" I asked. "Who broke in?"

"I don't know," she said. "It was before. They locked the door and told us anyone who went in the kitchen would be shot. They took Carlos." Baylis and his men looked at one another.

"Let's go," he said. Then he looked at me. "You stay in town, get on it. Find out what you can, talk to bouncers, anyone who might have an inkling, any clue about what's happened here."

Baylis left and I remained alone with Valerie, who was still sobbing. I persuaded her that she must go home, that I would go looking for Juana and wouldn't stop until I found her.

I took two hundred euros from the till and gave them to her. A few million quid's worth had disappeared from the cellar, but the till was still full. I put Valerie into a cab outside and promised to phone, then I went back inside to lock up.

It felt strange as I looked around the empty bar. I realized, once again, how much my life had changed since I'd been here. Barry and Julie's reign already felt like ancient history. I walked through into the empty kitchen. The hinges would have to be replaced. I went to lock the back door, the scene of many stolen kisses with Juana, who I'd now failed to protect. Then back into the kitchen where I had fought Gav Taylor for my life, and killed him.

I stood staring at the wall. I felt shell-shocked and confused. I didn't know how much trouble I was in or with whom. What was certain was that I was in deep shit all round. I poured a vodka and knocked it back in short order. Then another. The burning liquid down the back of my throat shocked me back into reality and galvanized me into moving. I locked the front and went out across the square. I didn't know where to start looking for Juana. I'd tried her phone, of course, but it was going to voice-mail.

I'd reached the edge of the park when I heard the sound of breaking glass.

I turned and saw the shattered plate-glass window of Jubarry's in the distance. Inside, flames licked up the wall. I ran back across the square, but in that short time, wicker chairs and plastic tablecloths were going up and a vortex of heat blew out through the hole in the glass. It must have been a petrol bomb, thrown through the window. I looked around but could see no one. Whoever had done it must have waited for me to leave.

A few late stragglers started to come out of nearby bars and from the park and surrounding flats, gathering in front of the fire.

I was just about to pull out my phone and call the fire brigade when a car skidded round the corner into the square. It stopped right in front of me, a familiar white Porsche Cayenne. A Kelly henchman I knew as Stav Georgiou got out and grabbed me by the arm.

"Get in," he said.

"What about the fire...?" I wrestled against his meaty hand, looked in through the passenger door.

"Get in, you minge," Terry Gadd wheezed angrily. "You got a lot of questions to answer."

I got in.

FIFTY-ONE

It wasn't a comfortable ride.

Terry Gadd threw the Cayenne round the bends at breakneck speed as we headed up into the hills.

Headed, I imagined, on a one-way ticket.

"Where's Juana?" I asked. Stav Georgiou punched me in the ear.

"Stow it!" Gadd said.

I did. My legs were shaking with fear and I tried to stay calm by imagining myself somewhere nice. I imagined the beach, with Juana; our afternoons in the sun together, lying on the sand with waves lapping at our feet. I thought about other people I'd loved and was unlikely to see again.

My life had been short but eventful, I decided. And now I had someone else's life on my conscience, so maybe there was some rough justice involved. I'd packed more into the past eighteen months than most people did in a lifetime. Perhaps that's what happens when you live in the fast lane; you just burn it all up quicker.

The Cayenne slowed down. It was dark, but I could

see from the headlights that we were high up in the hills above Casa Pampas, where big, prickly pear cactuses lined the road and fleshy aloe plants towered above like giant asparagus. We pulled off the road down a short dirt track and into an area of waste ground.

Gadd stopped the car and Stav Georgiou threw me out of the door, where I fell onto the dusty earth. Then he followed me out and dragged me by the collar around to the front of the car. Across the wasteland a second car switched on its lights, blinding me. I was now caught between the crossed beams of the two cars. Spotlit – like a rabbit in the headlights.

"Kneel!" Terry Gadd shouted.

I knelt, facing the bonnet of the Cayenne. My hands were trembling like leaves, so I held them together in front of me, almost like I was praying.

Which I was.

I heard Gadd cock an automatic pistol behind me and I felt my mouth go dry. "You've got one fuckin' chance to tell me what went wrong."

"I don't know, Terry, honestly." My dry tongue stuck to the roof of my mouth and I could barely get my words out. "I did everything I was told. Turned up at the RV. We met the Moroccan boat, got the stuff and then we were busted by British customs and the Guardia."

"You texted me that the pickup was successful."

"It was, we just hadn't checked it yet."

Gadd walked round to stand in front of me. He swung his arm and backhanded me hard across the face. I felt a ring tear the flesh of my cheek.

315

"Bullshit," he spat. "They were there like clockwork. Tell me who you tipped off." This time he slapped me with a forehand stroke, his heavy palm stinging my face and knocking me sideways. He pulled me upright again.

"I didn't tip anyone off," I pleaded. "I don't *know* any- one."

"Who did you give the keys to the cellar to? You get them copied?"

"I didn't have any keys. You took them away after you changed the locks, remember?"

Gadd walked away for a moment, across to the other car. He stood in the headlights and I heard him speak to whoever was in the car.

"You heard him," he said. "He says he had nothing to do with it. It's up to you, but I don't like it. I want to bin him."

I heard low voices in discussion, then the crunch of feet as he came back up behind me. I felt the barrel of his pistol, cold and hard against the bone behind my ear. My heart was banging so hard in my chest I thought it might burst and release me from this moment. "Do you want to change your story?" Gadd whispered.

I shook my head.

"Well?" he asked. I shook my head again. "Nothing else you have to tell me before I blow your skull apart and spread your brains across the dirt for the birds to eat?"

I felt a sob rise in my chest. Tried to go elsewhere in my mind: beach, blue sky, New Cross, Stoke, anywhere but here. I heard a click as he took the safety catch off.

Through the fog of panic, I had a sudden thought.

316

"Just one thing," I said. My voice cracked and I breathed deeply, trying to steady it. "The big bloke. Calls himself Vic but it's not his real name. I think he's called Donnie Mulvaney. He might be the weak link. He gets drunk in that bar all the time and boasts to anyone who'll listen. He says he's connected with everyone – the Kellys, all the London crime firms, the Brink's-Mat, everything."

"So what?"

"He showed me a photo he had of a Serbian called Dragomir Radic. I just thought it might be connected."

There was a pause.

"Nothing I didn't already know," Gadd growled. "Not enough to get you off the hook, kid."

I heard the car behind me start up its engine. Felt the pressure of the pistol against my skull. Then a terrible bang and a flash of orange flame.

And then black.

FIFTY-TWO

When I came round I was sprawled across the back seat of the Cayenne. My Levi's were damp, my face was throbbing and my ears were ringing.

"He's alive," I heard Stav Georgiou say sarcastically from the front. His voice sounded muffled, as if he was talking though cotton wool. He let out a low chuckle. "What a faggot, fainting like a girl."

I said nothing but tentatively put a hand up to my head. My face was swollen and I could hear nothing through my right ear. I felt my skull; it all seemed intact. I half expected to find a hole like the one I'd seen in the head of the guy in Flanagan's car park.

So I'd fainted.

I lay back and watched the sky through the rear window of the car, my muddled mind trying to work out who must have taken the charlie from the cellar. It was a clear, black night, twinkling with stars, and I was alive. Not safe, by any means. But not dead. I thought about Juana, wondered where she was. Wondered who she was with, who had taken her. Whether she was still alive.

We arrived at Casa Pampas and Stav got out to unlock the gates.

"Still with us, sugarplums?" Gadd asked. "You wanna grow some."

"I thought you were going to kill me," I said.

"If it was down to me, I probably would have, but Patsy's superstitious, he wouldn't let me. He wanted me to test you out. He thinks you're on the level, that you're some kind of lucky charm for him. He protects you – because he thinks you protect him."

I couldn't think of anything to say to this.

"But I'm superstitious too," Gadd went on. "And I think you're a right Jonah. Nothing's gone right since Pat got you in the firm. I've never liked the look of you, as you know."

"Cheers," I said.

Terry Gadd turned in his seat, reached into the back and punched me, smack in the nose. Like a parent whacking an unruly child. It hurt, and I tasted blood. Before I could turn away, he punched me again, harder.

"Don't be cheeky, you bitch," he spat. "You're on last knockings as far as I'm concerned. I would as soon slice you up as look at you; gouge your eyes out with a spoon, then cut off your ears and make you eat them. And then I might think about disembowelling you and leaving you to bleed to death."

"Sorry." Apologizing seemed the sensible thing to do.

"No more lip," he said. "Last chance. Now get out the

319

car and do as you're told."

I stumbled out of the car and up the steps towards the house.

The lights were on throughout, but low. From the outside, the place seemed to glow red, and I could see flashes from TV screens in some of the windows. I looked across to the town where the odd stray firework still shot into the black sky, then faded, like the end of a battle. I had completely lost track of time, but I guessed it must have been four or five in the morning.

There were a lot of men assembled at Casa Pampas. Some – bald, bulky and tanned – were faces I recognized. Others – identikit versions, bald, bulky and pale – were new arrivals. Patsy had been bringing over reinforcements as his paranoia grew, like imperial bodyguards around a fading Roman emperor; all South London and Essex boys away on a busman's holiday. Some were sitting around, drinking and watching porn on a widescreen TV, while others snoozed or smoked. All of them gave off an atmosphere of surly malevolence, even the sleeping ones.

Patsy was sitting on the white leather sofa in the lounge, staring into space. He looked strained and lined. His hair was flattened and dark against his head and he looked as if he hadn't slept in a long time. Terry Gadd pushed me into the room.

"Here he is," he said.

Patsy looked up at me. Ignored my bloody nose. "What went wrong?" he asked flatly.

I spoke fast. "Like I told Terry, I really don't know. Honestly, I just followed instructions to the boat and they were on us as soon as we transferred the boxes. Some-one knew where the pickup was, and also that I wasn't at Jubarry's. You know I kept an eye on things."

Patsy looked across at Gadd. "What a cock-up." He slapped his hand against his forehead for what was clearly not the first time that night.

"Apparently Mulvaney has been in spouting about this and that," Gadd told him.

"About what?" Patsy demanded.

"About Tommy, Brink's ... about this Serbian."

Patsy took a long pull at his vodka and gestured for me to take a beer from the stack on the floor. It was almost warm, but welcome. He lit a cigarette.

"Do him tomorrow, Tel," Patsy said. "First job of the day, blow Mulvaney's ugly face off. I want him out of the way. That gorilla's been nothing but grief. Do him."

Gadd nodded. "You should think about getting some sleep, Pats." The light was coming up outside.

"I can't bleeding sleep!" Patsy shouted.

"You need to be in good shape tomorrow, it's a big day."

"I'm not going anywhere tomorrow, Tel," Patsy protested.

"You can't bottle this one, Pats," Gadd said. "We'll look like Frankie Howerds. We need a show of strength, need to show the mayor that he's still in our pocket. Let these Serbs see that and all. We need to act like nothing's happened. If this Dragonfly Radish, whatever he's called, sees us cave in over this, we might as well pack up and go home."

"Yeah, right," Patsy said. "And be in line for a twenty-year stretch if some people have their way."

"So…" Gadd said. "Not the time to throw in the towel. I've got some jellies if you want some kip."

"What sort?"

Gadd fished in his pocket and pulled out some sleeping pills. "Temazzies. Go on, have a couple. The rest will do you good."

Patsy held his hand out, took two pills and swigged some vodka. Gadd watched as Patsy swallowed them down. I wondered how long Terry Gadd had been administering drugs to Patsy Kelly. Patsy pulled himself to his feet and staggered out of the room. I heard his bedroom door slam.

Gadd looked at me, gestured for me to follow him. "Time for bo-bos, cocky-dick," he said, almost paternally. "You're in there." He pointed to a small room off the hall. There was a small sofa and a rowing machine. He opened a wardrobe and pulled out some tracky bottoms. "Get yourself a shower and put these on. You stink of piss." He threw the pants at me and I caught them. He put some sleeping pills on a side table. "Then take a couple of them and get some kip. You've still got a job to do."

"What job?" I asked.

"You've got to look after Patty-boy, hold his hand and make sure his nerve holds; make sure he don't run away. And stay where I can see you. After that we'll decide what to do about all these big mistakes you've made." He slapped my face lightly then made towards the door.

"Where's Juana?" I asked. I fully expected another slap.

322

"Who? Carmen Vagina? I dunno."

"You didn't take her?"

Gadd shook his head. "You should have taken more care of that bird. She's probably being screwed by a Serbian, like everyone else around here."

Then he shut the door and locked it behind him.

FIFTY-THREE

"Mr Taylor's got you off the hook," Terry Gadd said.

"What?" My head was still thick with sleep. I had taken the tamazepam: there was no way I would have slept without them.

"They've pulled Gav Taylor's body out the harbour."

A renewed sense of panic took hold of me and suddenly I was fully alert. I didn't know where Juana was and now Gav Taylor returned to haunt me again. I couldn't shake him off. My mind raced, wondering if there was anything to connect me to the body, how it had got there and what state it must be in by now.

I followed Gadd out of the room and onto the patio where Patsy Kelly, wrapped in a dressing gown, was pacing up and down after a swim. It was mid-afternoon and the sun was already on its way behind the hills.

"They identified him by his teeth and his false leg," Terry Gadd said. "He had plenty of gear on him. They found the package, but it had all dissolved."

Patsy lit a cigarette and swore under his breath.

"You ain't going to like this bit, Pats," Gadd said, "but he had papers and stuff relating to the Serbian on his body. Details of our drop in the Strait, floorplans of Jubarry's."

I kept quiet. As far as I knew, that was impossible. Gav was dead before even Gadd knew the details, I was certain. My brain was hurting, working overtime, trying to work out the real story behind Gav's reappearance. But one thing was for certain, it made me look better; less liable for the fake cargo and the Jubarry raid.

Bizarrely, Gav's dead body had probably saved my life.

Patsy was beyond swearing now. It seemed that he had been outwitted on every count. And there would be people, heavy people up and down the foodchain, who would want to know how millions of pounds of class A drugs had gone adrift on Patsy's account.

I felt pretty outwitted myself and almost felt sorry for him. He remained quiet, puffing on the cigarette. Then he turned to Gadd, resigned.

"What time is it?"

"Nearly five," Gadd said.

"We'd better get ready. Seven, it starts?"

Gadd nodded. "That's the ticket, Pat. Show them who's boss."

Patsy went inside.

"You're coming with," Gadd told me. "Keeping an eye out."

"To the bullfight?" I wondered why he wanted me there.

"No, round my nan's for egg and chips, you knob ... of course it's to the bullfight. You need some clothes. You're sweating like a pig and you look like a bag of shit."

An hour later I was showered and dressed in a tight white shirt, grey slacks and shiny black shoes that Gadd had pulled out of a cupboard for me. I looked like an Essex boy on a blind date.

The Kelly heavies gathered out on the patio, smoking and joking loudly, disguising hard-man nerves. They patted pistols under armpits and slid knives into pockets, comparing weapons.

I watched them through the window, acting out their bravado. The adrenalin was passing from one to another, growing and swelling with their pumped-up muscles.

Finally, Terry Gadd came out onto the terrace, freshly showered and shaved and swigging a beer. He was wearing probably the most disgusting shirt I had seen him in so far: canary yellow with palm trees and pink lotus flowers, totally at odds with the macho backslapping and hugging. There were shoulder squeezes and neck rubs dished out all round as Gadd galvanized them into action. Bull necks swelled with pride, cuffs shot from sleeves, and shoulders rolled under tight shirts as he gave each one his undivided attention.

Patsy joined me in the lounge, dressed for the occasion in true Patsy style. Cream silk shirt open at the neck, beige linen suit and two-tone shoes, like an old-school gangster.

"Look at them," he said. "They love Terry."

"Do they?" I found myself saying. "Or are they just scared of him?"

"His reputation means they respect him," he said. "They admire his fearlessness, his violence, his lack of remorse. He never weakens."

I glanced sideways at Patsy. I could have sworn I saw tears brim in his eyes as he looked out across the poolside. I looked away.

The afternoon sun washed everything with golden light. The spray from the water sprinklers on the lawn made rainbows in the light, and the men on the patio cast dark shadows; silhouettes as black as their hearts.

Patsy checked the chunky Panerai diver's watch on his wrist. "Here we go," he said.

I followed him onto the terrace and there was a respect-ful cheer and a small round of applause. Patsy waved his hand in the air, simultaneously accepting and quelling the applause.

"Right, gentlemen," he said. "Let's go."

Everyone made their way down the steps and through the gates. There were half a dozen cars lined up outside, Mercs and Beemers.

Gadd got into the front one and told me to go in the one behind, with Patsy. I sat in the back with Patsy, while Stav Georgiou and another monkey who was driving sat in the front. I felt uncomfortable being singled out in this way. It had happened before, and it wasn't necessarily a good place to be, so close to the boss.

We rumbled down the hill in a convoy. Patsy looked out of the window, across the dry valley, past dots of white houses, turquoise swimming pools and golf courses and on to the distant blocks of urban sprawl that lined the coast.

"Thirty years I've been here," he said. "Most of that down there was small fishing villages still. Just package tourists in Torremolinos, out the way. It was like the Wild West for a young bloke. No extradition treaty and a few Great Train Robbers setting up the blow business across the water. I was in at the start. Now it looks like the end. I can't go home now, no matter how bad it gets here."

He turned to me.

"I'm glad," he said. "I knew it wasn't you. Otherwise I'd have had to kill you."

I gulped and nodded.

"Terry had his suspicions, but my instincts are good about this kind of thing. I knew you were on the level."

Clearly Terry Gadd's instincts had been better. Which was worrying.

"You saved my boy," Patsy said.

"It was instinctive," I muttered, embarrassed.

"And you saved me." He looked straight at me and I was forced to hold eye contact. The anger had gone from his eyes. He patted me heavily on the leg.

"Thank you," he said.

FIFTY-FOUR

The Plaza de Toros was on the outskirts of town, up between Benalmádena Pueblo and the motorway, next to the football ground. It was not an old, traditional ring, but modern-built, hard-edged and concrete. This made it look less like a place of tradition and ritual and more like a place devoted to killing, which I guess it was.

I had never been to a bullfight before and I had picked my moment, arriving in a cavalcade of German cars driven by psychopaths. The Sunday bullfight after the fiesta was still a popular event with the locals, and the road up to the bullring was crowded with pedestrians. None of our drivers seemed embarrassed as they honked car horns, parting the sea of bodies in front of them. Spanish faces peered in through the car windows in curiosity and in annoyance at having been moved out of the way.

If Patsy was trying to make his presence felt, it was already working.

We parked right outside and watched as Patsy's assembled bodyguards got out of their cars and tugged again at jackets and shirt collars. Terry Gadd came over and opened our car door. I got out first, then Patsy. He was wearing sunglasses, which, with the suit, drew discreet glances from the passing Spaniards. We walked straight in through an ugly stone entrance, made only marginally prettier by a badly painted mural of bulls. Inside, I was instantly hit by the smell of animal, manure and straw. The bar was hot and crammed and full of excited Spanish chatter, but the people parted as Gadd pushed through and ordered beers.

There was a stuffed bull's head on the wall above our heads, and old bullfight posters. One proclaimed *El Inglés* – The Englishman – and was dated two years before.

"Frank Evans," Patsy said. He pointed at the poster. "I knew him. Ex-butcher from Salford. Been fighting bulls for forty-odd years. Still at it and he's nearly seventy with a knee replacement and a heart bypass. Bollocks the size of a house."

"Señor Kelly?"

I turned to see the mayor's driver and another man standing at Patsy's elbow.

"Señor Dominguez is here now and requests the pleasure of your company," he said, his English heavily accented. He gave a small bow and gestured towards the exit of the bar. Patsy glanced nervously at Terry Gadd, who winked confidently and assigned two bruisers to accompany us.

The mayor was sitting with other local dignitaries on a raised balcony on the shady side of the ring. He stood up when he saw Patsy and introduced him to some other stony-faced officials, then to his brother-in-law, Jesus Ybarra, the district commissioner from Mijas, who nodded without shaking hands.

Patsy sat down uneasily, his eyes darting here and there. I looked around the bullring. It was getting full, especially on the shady, *sombra* side. The cheaper seats were on the sunny side, which even in the evening was uncomfortably hot, but that too was filling up. I scanned the crowds for any sign of suspicious activity, suspicious faces … anything. The only obvious villains as far as I could see were our own, their shaven heads sweating and shiny.

A mournful trumpet squealed a fanfare. It was joined by a flute, drums and brass and had a settling effect on the crowd, the sorrowful sound that was bred in their bones. This was the *paseíllo* – the parade of all those taking part in the bullfight.

Horses entered the ring, mounted by weatherbeaten men in wide black sombreros. Behind them, younger men – *novilleros* – dressed in tight grey suits swaggered in on foot and raised their hats to the crowd, their bravado barely disguising their nerves. A polite rustle of applause spread around the arena, then grew louder as the *toreros* with their capes were followed by a procession of matadors in their sparkling *traje de luces*, "suits of light", which glinted in the late sun.

One, who stood at the centre dressed in a gold suit, appeared to be the star. He came to a halt in front of our box and saluted the mayor.

"Paco Barrera," the mayor said, clapping. "He is a big star from Madrid."

The crowd applauded loudly and the procession filed out of the ring for the *corrida* to start.

The first bullfighter out only looked about sixteen. He was whip-thin with a narrow, horse-like face and his suit fitted tightly, making him look small and frail.

"A *novillada*," the mayor told Patsy. "The bulls are less than four years old and it gives the young *novilleros* a chance to show their *cojones*." He glanced at me as if I was a waste of space by comparison. But then, I reminded myself, I probably didn't need to stab a few cows to prove myself.

I was proving myself daily.

Gates were flung open and a small bull hurtled into the ring, circling the arena, tossing its head in the air and snorting, finally coming to a standstill in the centre, where it stood, panting.

A couple of the older men ran around with pink capes, distracting it and getting it hot and bothered. Then a third, a *banderillero*, ran up and planted two long barbs into its shoulder. The bull bucked and stamped as the barbs lodged in its flesh and a streak of dark red blood ran sticky down its black hide.

Another fanfare, and then the young bullfighter approached the bull with his cape. He arched his back and goaded the animal until it made a run for him, then he swerved at the last minute with a flourish of the cape. The bull passed within centimetres of him. The crowd cheered and an old woman in front of me shouted "*Olé!*" in a deep, throaty voice that sounded like she gargled with gravel.

The bullfighter taunted the bull until it was panting heavily, its lips flecked with foam, then put it through a series of tighter turns and manoeuvres. By now it was confused and exhausted, and I could see the whites of its eyes, fearful and rolling, and strings of drool dangling from its mouth and dripping onto the sand. As this went on the sweat was pouring into the bullfighter's eyes, making him blink, his chest rising and falling with heavy breaths inside his tight jacket. One of the older men gave him a smaller cape and a sword, which he exchanged for the larger cape and concealed behind his back. He pulled faces at the tired beast and stamped his feet in front of it until the bull, summoning up its remaining energy, lowered its head and went for him.

Standing on tiptoes, the young bullfighter revealed the sword from behind the small red cape, then threw himself forwards and stabbed the sword between the bull's shoulders, behind the neck.

It was not a clean kill. In theory, the accurately placed sword finds a gap between the shoulders and slips in up to the hilt, penetrating the heart, and the bull dies quickly. In this case, the sword had hit something solid, taken a turn sideways and appeared again, sticking out between the bull's ribs. The animal bellowed in pain as it bucked around the ring. It was only a young bull and its eyes rolled wildly as it took in the last, tortured moments of its life.

The older men came out and distracted it again with bigger capes, while the young bullfighter ducked out of its way.

The young man had to prove his bravery once more. As the older men retreated, he tried to draw the bull to him again with the small cape. Then, as the exhausted animal passed, he withdrew the sword, holding it high, dripping with blood.

There were more triumphant *Olé*s from the crowd.

Although the animal was spent, it was still desperate, wild and dangerous, and the young bullfighter had to show his courage in finishing the job. He was handed another sword, long and sharp, but this time with a bar fixed across the blade a few centimetres down from the tip. He knelt in front of the bull and I could see him shaking as he tested himself, reaching out to touch its bloodied nose. The bull, trembling on its legs, lowered its head. The bullfighter stood, raising himself again on his toes, then with a sharp, stabbing motion, stuck the sword into the bull's neck just behind the skull. The sword went in a short way, and then stopped as the bar prevented deeper entry. But the first few centimetres of blade had severed the animal's spinal cord.

A tremor shot through its legs and it fell, stunned, onto its side, while one of the older men ran in and stabbed a short knife into the back of its neck, twisting it, making sure it was finished. The bull's legs twitched and jerked, then lay still as a pool of urine released itself from the animal's bladder, forming a dark pool on the ground.

The young man, pride restored, strutted around the ring, sword in the air, while the crowd waved handkerchiefs, shouted and applauded.

My feelings were mixed. I was not sure whether the

young bullfighter had done a good or a bad job. He had finished it, but not without pain, grief and mess. Whichever way I leant, my focus was fixed on the bull, which had a chain fixed around its neck and was dragged, limp and lifeless, from the ring behind a four-wheel drive, leaving a trail of blood in the yellow sand.

Señor Dominguez, the mayor, stood and applauded while the young bullfighter presented himself to the box, holding high a bloodied ear, which he had been granted in recognition of his efforts.

To my right, Patsy Kelly clapped absent-mindedly, looking out across the ring, his mind elsewhere. Jesus Ybarra, the mayor's brother-in-law, leant across to him.

"Señor Kelly," he said. "We must discuss business."

FIFTY-FIVE

Donnie began to feel jittery as he drove out of town.

It had taken him a while to get used to the idea, but in the end he had realized he had no choice in the matter. There was always the chance that he was walking into a trap, but that was a risk he would have to take. There were tripwires and pitfalls at every stage of this game. This time it was shit or bust. It hadn't shaped up so well down here in the long run, and if everything went OK, this might be his route out of the place.

He knew he'd blown his chances with Valerie, who had rung him this afternoon, screaming something about Juana and how it was all his fault. It was time to move on.

Donnie swung the BMW out onto the dual carriageway and drove towards the setting orange sun. He put on his sunglasses and considered the palm trees that lined the road. He wasn't given to artistic thoughts, but in this early evening light he thought everything looked beautiful. Like a painting; the pretty top layer giving no indication of the sketchy business lurking beneath the surface.

Donnie had to take the risk that one more dirty deal might be his way out. *Preferably on a Boeing 747, preferably alive.*

He lit a cigarette to calm his nerves and took the slip road to Benalmádena Pueblo. He could see the spotlight towers of the football ground and the bullring next to it. He parked in the car park and unhooked the crucifix and rosary beads that hung from the rear-view mirror, stuffing it into his pocket.

Donnie heard the roar of the crowd and the notes of a trumpet carried on the breeze. The fights had started; it was a good time to slip in. Donnie looked around. Entrance F, he'd said on the phone. He took a deep breath, stamped out his cigarette and went in.

The bull was huge.

They had got progressively bigger throughout the evening, but this one, brought out to face Paco Barrera, the main attraction, was a monster.

The gate flew open and I gasped, along with the crowd, as at least five hundred kilos of black-furred muscle pounded out into the arena.

Its head was almost prehistoric, with widely spaced, curved horns. The chest and front flanks were deep and defined with muscle, tapering away to a narrower waist and hindquarters, giving a suggestion of vast power combined with speed and manoeuvrability.

In spite of myself, I began to feel some of the sheer thrill that goes with these occasions, reaching out to something primitive in my make-up. I felt my pulse quicken as the bull thundered around the ring, men with pink and yellow capes diverting its attention this way and that.

Patsy had hardly noticed any of the life-and-death struggles being played out in front of us. He was deep in conversation with Señor Ybarra and the mayor. I strained to hear what they were saying, with little success, but I could see Patsy beginning to get heated, gesturing with his hands, his face reddening.

If Paco Barrera was losing his cool, he didn't show it. On the posters he was advertised as *"El Gallo"* – The Cockerel – for the arrogant way he strutted around the ring in his traditional pink socks, paying little attention to the beast that was beginning to fix him in its sights from the other side of the arena.

He waved and held his arms open to the crowd, showing off his glittering golden suit to the ladies, soaking up their adoration and applause.

Then Paco Barrera addressed the bull.

He stuck out his chest and stamped his foot, shuffling closer to the big black animal. Barrera looked very small as he approached, dwarfed by the bull's bulk.

The bull pawed the ground with its hoof, and Barrera dragged the pink and yellow cape across the sand in front of him. The bull dropped its head and with astonishing acceleration hurled itself at the matador. Barrera kept his cool and allowed the bull to thunder up to him, twirling the cape and neatly sidestepping as the deadly horns missed him by a whisper.

The crowd cheered. This was what they had come to see.

"No," I heard Patsy say, his voice raised. "No way. I've paid you lot for years. I'm not sharing it out with no one."

He looked around for support. "Where's Terry?"

I could see that the two Spanish dignitaries were getting quite angry too, their attention drifting away from the fight. I spotted Gadd down below in the crowd, walking back towards us, easily seen in his loud shirt.

As Barrera conducted two more passes, the bull coming closer each time, two *banderilleros* ran across the sand, jumped in the air and stabbed four barbs into the bull.

Far from wearing it down, the pain enraged the animal and it bucked and reared, trying to shake off the steel spikes. Barrera twisted and turned, making the bull run in circles and figure of eights.

"Where is this Serbian anyway?" I heard Patsy shout, not appearing to care who heard him any more. "Bring him here, show him to me. This is my turf. If he's the nuts, why isn't he here?"

Ybarra and the mayor exchanged a few words in rapid Spanish.

"We had a message," the mayor said. "Señor Radic is not coming. He said he doesn't want to deal with small-time crooks."

Barrera brought the massive bull to a standstill in the centre of the ring, where it regained its breath, panting, outwitted by this cocky man. Worn down but with nothing to lose, the bull was as dangerous as it had ever been.

Patsy Kelly had heard enough from his Spanish hosts. "Send a message back," he said. "Tell him to fuck himself." He stood up, his face pale with anger, ready to walk away.

And then I heard the gunshot, or if I didn't actually hear it, I felt the impact as flecks of Patsy Kelly's blood and brains sprayed across my face and shirt.

The women behind us jumped up and screamed, and people around us exclaimed in horror.

The commotion caught Paco Barrera's attention in the ring. It was only a momentary distraction, but it was a dangerous lapse of concentration. This time, as the bull rushed, it threw its head up at the last second, catching Barrera under the jaw with a razor-sharp horn. The crowd cried out as the bull lifted him off the ground, its horn piercing his neck and reappearing through his mouth. The bull tossed its head and Barrera was flung high into the air. He dropped, head first, onto the sand, where the bull rushed and trampled and stamped on him, then buried its horns into his ribs, tossing him around as if he was a rag doll. Men with capes distracted the bull while paramedics ran into the arena to pick up *El Gallo*'s limp body.

It was chaos.

The crowd became hysterical as fear and emotion spread like a virus. Near us, women were crying and screaming while their men, grey-faced, shouted for help. The two Kelly bodyguards drew pistols, waving them about after the event that they had clearly not prevented. I looked down at Patsy Kelly's body on the ground. His eyes were half open and looking up at the darkening sky, while a pool of thick blood spread behind his head and soaked into the linen of his suit.

The Guardia Civil bustled around the mayor and his brother-in-law, offering protection.

Terry Gadd finally made his way to us through the crowd, seemingly unaware of what had happened. He

340

saw Patsy's body on the ground, then looked at me, face hard and eyes cold.

"Oh dear," he said. "Didn't do a very good job of looking after him, did you, big balls?"

FIFTY-SIX

I ran.

I ducked between shell-shocked onlookers and jumped across families glued to their seats, protecting their children from the mayhem in the stand and the tragedy in the bullring. I saw a Kelly bodyguard lumber behind me, but I was light on my toes.

Without Patsy's protection, I was dead in the water. I hadn't had a chance to make head or tail of what Gadd was accusing me of, but it was clear he held me responsible in some way for the drugs bust, for Patsy ... for anything he didn't like the look of.

There were no tidy solutions here, it was just a real mess – sticky, bloody and unpredictable – and I knew the time had come for me to ship out. I weaved through the crowd, keeping my head down, apologizing on the way. When I reached the ground, I ducked into the *lavabos* to give myself a few seconds' breather.

I quickly washed blood spatters from my face in the toilets, so as not to draw extra attention to myself, then slipped out of the bullring. The place had gone mental, with Spaniards shouting and blocking every walkway. But it seemed that neither Gadd, nor any of the body-guards who had so spectacularly failed in their duty, had managed to follow me.

I hopped on a bus into town and got straight on the phone to Anna. The few people on the bus stared at the splashes of blood on my shirt. I was past caring. I sat at the back, out of earshot.

"He's been shot," I said. "PK's dead."

"Who was it?"

"Don't know. Everything seemed to be pointing at this Serbian gang, but I didn't see anyone."

"Where are you now?" she asked.

"On my way back into town. I need to find Juana and get out of here. Terry Gadd will be instantly on my case. He's on to me. I'm sure of it."

She went quiet.

"Can you get me a flight?" I asked. "I need to go to the flat and get some protection." I felt like I was going to be collared at any moment.

"I'll have to clear it with Baylis first," she said cautiously. I began to panic.

"I need to get out *now*. I've done my bit and I don't have time to hang around."

"All right," she said. "We'll pull you out. I'll text you some flight details."

"What about Juana?" I asked.

"What about her?" Anna's voice was clipped.

"Please, Anna," I said. "You promised. I'll find her. It's

too risky here. Patsy's dead, Jubarry's is wrecked, and all hell will break loose when Gadd comes looking. I couldn't have done any of this without her."

Anna sighed. "Listen, she'll be OK. We made sure someone was there to spirit her away. She'll be fine."

"No, she won't. She has to come with me. She's known here – if I disappear they'll track her down. It will compromise *me* as well as her. Please, Anna."

"OK. Two flights, nothing more," she said flatly. *"Hasta la vista."*

She rang off, and I jumped off the bus down towards the port and picked up a cab up to the apartment. I would need to put a few things in a bag: some clothes and a gun, which I could ditch at the airport once I was out of harm's way.

It was dark when I arrived back, and some instinct made me hesitate as I got to the door. I put my ear to it. I couldn't hear anything, but I could sense another human presence nearby. I thought for a moment. As far as I knew, only Barry had known where I lived.

I rang the buzzer. Nothing. I slid the key in the door and went in. It was dark; I pressed myself back against the wall and felt my way along to the living room, pushing the door open with my foot. I kept tight into the entrance before switching on the light.

There was no one there.

I crept through to the bedroom and found nobody there either. I needed to get the gun, money and stuff from under the bath, so I felt my way into the bathroom and pulled the string to the little shaving light above the mirror. I saw in the mirror that the shower curtain was pulled across behind me.

Not right.

I swung round, ready to pull it back when an arm stuck out, pointing a pistol at my head. The other Baikal I had hidden under the bath. The hand was shaking. It was attached to a thin, brown wrist. I reached out and pulled back the curtain.

"Don't shoot!" I shouted.

It was Juana.

It took her a second to register that it was me, and then she lowered the gun. She climbed out of the bath and hugged me. She was shaking. Despite my panic, a wave of relief washed over me. I realized how worried about her I'd been, but I'd pushed it to the back of my mind, not wanting to think the worst. I couldn't believe I had her in my arms again. I covered her face with kisses.

"I thought you were dead," she sobbed.

"So did I for a minute." I laughed shakily, beginning to sob myself. "It was a close call. Where have you been?"

"A guy grabbed me from the bar late last night," she said. "One of yours English. He said it was too dangerous and brought me here. I've been waiting ever since."

I was grateful that Baylis's lot had finally listened and kept her safe for me. I hugged her tight and felt her body give against mine. Felt her crying subside and become calmer.

"Kelly's dead," I said. "Shot in the head. It's going to get really ugly – I can't stay here. I'm going back to London."

I felt Juana flinch in my arms.

"And you're coming with me," I said. "It's too dangerous for you, too. Pack a bag. We're going as soon as I can
get a flight."

I was completely exhausted. My nerves were jangling
and I needed sleep. But of course I couldn't sleep. Every
minute I stayed in the flat increased the risk of my being
tracked down. I lay on the bed next to Juana, my arm
around her shoulders and her head on my chest. I checked
my phone again and again for incoming messages. My
other hand gripped a pistol at my side. My mind was racing, imagining a knock at the door at any moment.

We couldn't get away quick enough.

*Donnie sat in the VIP bar of El Elefante in a backstreet off
24-Hour Square. It was still in full swing at 4 a.m. and Donnie
was wide awake: a combination of adrenalin and several lines of
the very pure cocaine that had just come on to the market.*

*He'd dropped into a few places, picking up gossip and
rumour from bouncers, bodyguards and club owners. News
of Patsy's killing had spread in minutes, making everyone an
instant expert in gangland politics.*

"He was losing his touch…"

"Terry Gadd was shagging his wife…"

"It was a Colombian…"

"This Serbian warlord…"

"The SAS."

*The rumours grew louder and wilder as the night went on,
followed by reports of new gang-on-gang violence. There had*

been two stabbings and a shooting in 24-Hour Square alone. If you took one key player out of the game, another would be ready to step in. The turf wars would go on, whoever was in charge.

Donnie took in all the theories and kept his own counsel. He'd come unstuck before by opening his gob.

His day had gone as well as could be expected. Now he might be able to take a bit of a holiday. He looked at his watch. It was creeping towards 4.30 a.m.

Just a few things to tidy up and he'd be offski. Donnie swallowed the last of his beer and headed out into the dawn.

FIFTY-SEVEN

My phone buzzed with an incoming text at 6 a.m.

I was glad. I must have drifted off eventually, but my dreams had been full of images of Patsy Kelly's blown-apart head: bull's horns emerging and blood gushing from his mouth, eyes, nose, ears. Images of his broken body being tossed around and trampled by a monstrous bull.

There had been no interruptions during the last few hours of the night but my hand was still sweatily gripping the gun.

Juana rolled over and yawned. *"Que hora?"*

"Seis," I said. I read the text.

Flight EasyJet 8602, Malaga-Gatwick dep. today,
Mon. 10.05, arr 11.55. Tickets x 2 one way.
£60. Bargain.

"We've got flights," I told her. "Leaving at ten. We'll need to go around eight." I had a strange feeling, a mixture of exhilaration and apprehension. Excited to be getting out; apprehensive because I knew I couldn't relax until I touched down at Gatwick. I let out a sigh. Once we were away from here, it would all be fine.

"I'll make coffee," Juana said.

I packed up any remaining surveillance kit and left it behind the bath. Whoever set this place up in the first place would probably clean up after. I stashed the Baikal in my holdall.

We drank strong coffee and dunked stale croissants. The coffee helped bring me round and I suddenly felt more optimistic. Juana sensed my change of mood and put her arm around my shoulders, kissing my neck.

"I've never been to England," she said. "I'm excited."

Although I felt a little excited myself, I couldn't quite overcome my paranoia about being hunted down at any moment. I tried to stay cool for her sake.

"You'll love it," I said with a smile.

I wanted to talk to her about everything we were going to do, about the places I was going to take her. But in truth I didn't know what I was going back to, how things would pan out after this job. I didn't have a picture of the future.

I didn't even know if I would be able to tell Juana more about myself. I would want to be ditching Pedro Garcia as soon as possible. She might not even like the real me, I considered.

At eight-fifteen, we grabbed our bags and locked the empty apartment, then made our way down to the street. I unhooked the keys to the apartment and threw the car keys to Juana while I posted the door keys through the letter box. Juana walked towards the Alfa.

"I've got lots to tell you," I said. "Stuff you don't know about me."

"Mystery man." She smiled. "And I have a lot to tell you."

"You first."

She laughed flirtatiously. "I'll save it for the plane. Come on. We'll be late."

The morning was already getting hot and I fancied my last drive in the Alfa with the roof down.

"Put the roof down, *guapa*," I said. "I'll bring the bags."

I picked up the bags and walked towards the car. I watched as Juana unlocked the door and got into the driver's seat to lower the automatic roof.

And then I saw a figure dart into an alley at the end of the street and I had a terrible thought.

Gadd knew the car, even if he didn't know where I lived. With a couple of bent coppers on board, a red Alfa convertible wouldn't have been that hard to find.

"No!" I shouted, still ten metres away. "Wait. NO!"

I saw Juana turn round and look at me from the open car door, smiling, white teeth, beautiful face frozen, caught in the moment.

Then watched as she turned the key in the ignition and blew herself to bits.

FIFTY-EIGHT

Donnie was no fan of sailing boats. He'd not actually been on the water since he'd been here. The sea was for paddling hot feet in and for diving in as a temporary hangover cure.

Or for dumping bodies in.

He even felt a little nauseous just walking along the pontoon, feeling it bounce underneath his heavy step. It was still early, after all. As much as he dreaded the boat, he knew that flying was out of the question. Too many questions. It would only be a couple of days of misery and then he could put his feet up and spend a few quid on a proper beano.

He found the boat at the end of the furthest pontoon. Dave Slaughter was on deck.

"Don," he said. He held out his hand.

"Dave," said Don. He took the hand, shook it, then used it to step daintily over the taffrail onto the deck. Dave patted his back and gave Donnie a look he'd not seen for a long time.

Respect.

There was no doubt about it. In the last day or two, among those in the know, his rep had gone sky-high. But Donnie knew that really it was a case of either him or the other bloke. If Donnie hadn't accepted the job, there would have been a bullet in his own head. His audacity had paid off. It was both payback and a show of loyalty to the real guv'nor.

And now he finally felt like he was properly back in the game.

Half an hour later, Donnie stowed the gun below, underneath the bunks with the rest of the gear: five hundred keys of blow, give or take a gram or two. Donnie didn't need to know the details of how, where or who had managed to cop the biggest shipment of cocaine he had ever seen. The logistics were left to cleverer minds than his. He had been given a simple but high-risk task, and had pulled it off old-style.

He changed into shorts and sat back out on deck. Shirt off. They motored out of Benalmádena in the quiet of the morning, and not without a pang of regret, Donnie watched the sun shimmering over the place that had been his home for the past year.

But at least he was alive.

The sea was calm enough not to make him feel Moby Dick and he and Dave enthusiastically accepted the large vodka and tonics that Carlos, late of Jubarry's, brought up on deck.

Carlos had turned out to be very useful all round: free with his tongue, easily bought and the mixer of a mean drink.

An hour later, they turned into the coast again, towards a town called Nerja. They dropped the anchor and drifted for a while.

"Why we stopping, Dave?"

"We're picking him up," Dave said.

"Oh no," Donnie said. "I didn't know that was part of the deal."

"Nor did I," Dave admitted. "Only got the order last night. From the top."

Donnie started to feel a bit gippy, bobbing on the waves. He looked to the coastline to try and fix his eye on the horizon to even things up. He caught sight of an inflatable dinghy with an outboard motor, buzzing through the waves towards them. As it came closer, he could see the familiar blond mullet and colourful shirt.

Minutes later, he was catching a rope thrown by Terry Gadd and hitching the dinghy to the back of their boat.

"Good morning, ladies," said Gadd, hauling himself aboard.

He seemed in good spirits, Donnie thought – as might any villain who'd pulled off a twelve million quid coke sting under his boss's nose.

"Good morning so far, anyway. Everything going like clockwork, just got a ding." He mimed an explosion with his hand, then looked at his Rolex. "With the wind behind us, we should be in Majorca in time for a beer tonight."

"Be nice," Dave said. "The trip over was pretty easy."

Carlos put his head above the hatch. "Mallorca?" he asked.

"It's pronounced Merjorker," Gadd said.

Carlos came out on deck and looked around him. "No, it's not that," he said. "I thought you said I would go to Tangier."

Gadd pretended to look puzzled. Tutted. "If I said we were going to Tenerife, you'd want to go to Elevenerife, Carlos. Joining the awkward squad, are you?"

"I just need to go to Tangier. I have arranged it all."

"Have you? Oh dear. Well, you'll have to change your plans."

"But this is not the deal. I have done so much for you, Señor

Gadd." A pleading note crept into Carlos's voice. "Please just give me my money and drop me off."

Donnie watched Gadd's face as a familiar expression crept over it; a tightening around the mouth, nostrils flaring.

"Drop you off?" Gadd repeated. "OK, OK, I'll get your money and drop you off. Tell you what, you take that dinghy and you can go ashore from here – or motor all the way to Tan-friggin-gier if you want."

"It's a long way," Carlos protested.

"Get in the dinghy," Gadd ordered.

Donnie nodded and helped Carlos climb over the steps in the stern and down into the dinghy where he wobbled, trying to get his balance. Gadd reappeared with a plastic holdall.

"Here's your pay-off, you sad shit," he shouted down to Carlos, and pulled a long automatic pistol from the bag. He threw the empty holdall at Carlos.

Carlos could see what was happening and Donnie watched as he hopelessly tried to catch the bag, then protect himself with his bare arms. It was like shooting fish in a barrel.

"No!" Carlos screamed as Gadd put the first shot into his belly. Carlos doubled up as blood spread across his white vest. He screamed again as a second bullet pierced his leg and again as a third went into his flailing arm. The dinghy began to deflate as the stray bullets burst it. Donnie turned away, saw the pleasure on Gadd's face as he shot more bullets into a screaming Carlos, finally putting one into his head that threw him backwards into the sea.

Donnie had seen and done some bad things in his career, but this time he knew he really had done a deal with the devil.

Gadd unhitched the deflating dinghy, then grinned at Dave

and Donnie as Carlos's body floated in their wake.

"Buenas noches, *señorita*," Gadd sang tunelessly. "Now, are you just going to sit there or are you going to get me a drink, Don?" he asked. He held out his hand.

"You done a good 'un. No hard feelings?"

FIFTY-NINE

"Juana Carmel Ruiz Ortega," Tony Morris said.

He pushed the photograph across the table for me to see. It was Juana all right. A few years earlier, hair a little shorter. Every bit as pretty.

I felt my throat constrict and another lurch of emotion heave through my chest. I wasn't going to cry. My crying had been done.

I'd howled while chunks of windscreen had been pulled from my chest and face with tweezers. I'd cried as, sedated, I'd been put on a flight from Málaga, where Anna and two armed security men had picked me up at the other end and taken me to a safe house. I'd cried as the image of the red door of the Alfa spinning across the street replayed in my mind, along with the other images burned in my brain; of Juana's dismembered hand, landing palm up at my feet.

I made myself look at the passport-sized photo again, paperclipped to a formal certificate from a dossier. Tried to take in the words that were printed in English and Spanish alongside.

Dead. *Muerto.*

Tony rubbed his hand over his cropped head, uncomfortable in the face of my grief.

"I'm sorry, I really am. She was an innocent bystander, mate. We checked her background as soon as you looked at her. Her old man was inside, for drugs-related stuff, but she and her mum had moved on. Starting again, trying to make a life for themselves. She just got caught in the crossfire; another casualty in the drug wars down there."

I knew the implication: Juana had got involved in it all because of me.

Me. I'd pursued her, gained her confidence. Duped her.

I looked up. Tony was watching me, his eyes full of that paternal sympathy that only he seemed able to generate. Anna, sitting next to him, was staring at the table.

"Her death was accidental, Eddie. She wouldn't have known you were a plant, and of course you would have said nothing to make her think you were. You played it well."

A hot flush of guilt overrode my already fragile state. Of course, I *had* admitted, once I'd got comfortable with Juana, that I was gathering intel, although I'd only told her half the truth. Her involvement, and her death, were down to me. My own need for emotional support, for love, had resulted in the death of a beautiful girl. The car bomb, whoever had planted it, had been meant for me. I wished it *had* been me.

I said nothing.

"I think she really liked you, Eddie," Anna said. She cocked her head to one side, the kind of mechanical sympathy only Anna could summon up.

"Trouble is," Tony added, "the more people you get involved, the more leaky the whole barrel of biscuits gets."

Despite myself, I almost laughed.

"You just don't know who's talking to whom. The gossip goes around the bars, the clubs, it all gets back."

I felt sweat pouring down my back as it began to dawn on me that maybe, despite all my hard work, I'd been the weak link, the leak that had messed up the operation. I'd got comfortable talking to Juana, to her mum, to Carlos, to Donnie even. God knows what I'd let slip. Maybe I was shit at the job I'd been given.

Shit at keeping it all to myself and keeping it in my pants.

"The car bomb was meant for me, right?" I asked.

"Don't know," Tony said. He glanced at Anna. "Probably."

They looked at one another. Then, as if to let me off the hook, Tony said, "This doesn't go outside this room. But Napier has suspended Ian Baylis."

"He didn't manage to find his Serbian warlord?" I offered.

"The Serbian was Ian's big idea," Tony said. "Do you know what I mean by disinformation?"

I shook my head.

"It means planting material to make people think that something is going on when it isn't ... to divert them, to rattle them, to make them change their plans – and ulti-mately slip up."

"How?" I asked.

"For instance," Anna put in, "we got a team in dressed as binmen to pick up Gav Taylor's body."

I winced at the memory. Remembered Juana saying there had been a commotion out back.

"We had to do a post-mortem for your protection. You didn't need a manslaughter rap against your name as well. For your information," Tony went on, "his skull was so thin around his head injury, a well-placed punch could have killed him."

It didn't make me feel a great deal better.

"But we kept the body on ice," he went on. "So when it looked like it was getting sticky for you, we were able to ditch the body in the harbour with information about the drop to make it look like he was the one who'd grassed them up. They used to do it in the war. Drop bodies in the Channel with fake invasion plans, which the Ger-mans would get when the body washed up."

I was sometimes really impressed by the lengths this organization went to, this time on my behalf.

"Thanks," I said. I meant it. "So where does the Ser-bian fit in? No one ever saw him."

"That takes us back to the disinformation," Tony said. "It's Ian's area of expertise. He had this idea of creating a fictitious villain who would scare the shit out of every-one, mostly because they couldn't see him. Ian has spent two years putting out text messages and emails from this Dragomir Radic, issuing false newspaper reports about his war crimes, spreading rumours in the bars, handing out pictures of the bloke, his legend getting bigger as the rumours spread."

"And it worked." I was amazed by Baylis's cunning. "It certainly rattled Patsy Kelly."

"Up to a point," Tony said. "But Ian's a very logical guy. He thought everything would fit into place like clockwork. He doesn't really understand how criminal minds work when they're fuelled by twenty-four-hour drinking and enough cocaine to sink Colombia. They get paranoid, violent, jumpy and schizo. Unpredictable."

I knew the type.

"Plus, Ian wasn't sharing his intel with everyone. He's an ambitious bloke and wanted the big collar for himself – and, as you know, he jumped in too early with the information you fed him. He got overexcited and cocked up."

I felt guilty all over again. Who would have known that I would be feeding duff information back to Baylis?

"I'm sorry if any of this is my fault," I said.

"That's the trouble with this stuff, mate," Tony said. "It's not easy to place the blame. Once one phase is over, it raises a whole new set of questions. It doesn't stop. Most of these cases are a mixture of successes and failures. So, on the positive, you're still with us and there's one less Kelly knocking around – but there's still a massive haul of cocaine entering the market that we didn't manage to nab."

"I'm sorry about Juana, Eddie," Anna said.

I felt my nose fizz and I tried to speak, but my voice came out as a strangled sob.

Tony looked away, embarrassed. "Operation cock-up

closed, until the enquiry," he said. He rubbed a hand over his forehead and scratched the back of his neck. "I need a drink. And you, mate, need a rest."

Anna slid the box of tissues back across the table.

I did need a rest, a long one, and although Anna and Tony had tried to make me feel like I had done my best, I still felt like I'd failed. I'd been sloppy. I'd got involved again, and allowed myself to get hurt. I grabbed a tissue and dabbed at the tears that were running down my face.

I looked up again at Tony, scratching his armpit, and Anna, chewing her lip, putting her papers together and heading off for another lonely night, and thought to myself that all of us have our weaknesses.

Nobody's perfect.

EPILOGUE

I've had very few callers at the new flat. I'm not even allowed to say where it is for the moment, but it's safe to say I'm back in London, pretty central.

It's a good spot. I can get out at night or get a Tube to another part of the city, where I can disappear among the crowds in a club or a pub.

Anonymous.

I might talk to someone, chat to girl, but I keep it light. I'm not ready to make friends with anyone. Let alone get involved.

I've had some more counselling, for what it was worth. Spent a little time back at the old girl's, but that depressed me even more. So when they asked me where I wanted to live, I asked to be in the thick of things. You can really be hidden away in London.

Like I say, I've had few visitors, so when Tony turned up at eleven one morning I was surprised. I'd only just got up. If I can't sleep at night, I go out and walk the streets, across the parks. Sometimes I don't get back until it's light.

"You look rough, mate," he said. Then he stepped inside and hugged me. It felt strange and welcome at the same time. I don't think anyone had touched me since I'd last kissed my mother goodbye.

I made us a cup of tea while Tony mooched around the flat, picking up books I was reading and flicking through them aimlessly.

"I worried about you when you didn't answer your phone," he said.

"I switch it off most days," I admitted. "So?" I prompted. I handed him a mug and he sat down at my small kitchen table.

"So," he said. "I needed to contact you."

"Why?"

He looked down at the table and wiped up sugar granules with his finger. "For your own safety."

I felt a familiar sensation in my gut. Uncomfortable; fearful. "What do you mean?"

"He knows you're alive."

"Who does?"

"Tommy Kelly."

"How?"

"We're working on that. We sent someone to see him in Belmarsh. He requested it. He knows you're alive and back over here."

The information jolted me out of myself. "So do I have to move again?"

"No, he doesn't know where you're living. It's weirder than that. He wants to see you."

"What?"

"He's asked our contact to find you and he wants to see you."

My guts tightened further. I suddenly felt small and afraid.

"What do you think I should do?" I asked after a pause.

"I think you should go and see Tommy Kelly."

ACKNOWLEDGEMENTS

With thanks to Mark Billingham for continuing to be a sounding board for wobbly plot points, and for his continued friendship and support in all areas. We both enjoyed *pulpo a fiera* outside a bar in Benalmádena and both used it in books. Thanks to the chef.

To Sarah Lutyens for wise words, to Gill Evans for her faith in Eddie and me, to Emma Lidbury for making me look as if I can write…

And to secret policeman "Special Branch Paul" for his undercover stories, anecdotes and insights, all delivered with beer and the utmost discretion.

UNDER COVER

READ BETWEEN THE LINES

READ
- Sneak previews
- Author interviews

DISCOVER
- Trailers
- Behind the scenes footage

WIN
- Review copies
- Signed books

COMMENT

Have your say on the books that you want to read

Scan the code to watch our book trailers*

Discover more at
WWW.UNDERCOVERREADS.COM

Peter Cocks was born on the banks of the Thames in Gravesend. As a boy he boxed, sang in a church choir and won a Chopper bike. As an adult he's worked as a silk screen printer, shop assistant, manager, salesman, actor, cook, performance artist, TV presenter, antique dealer and interior designer in London, New York, Paris, Tokyo and Australia. He has also performed in and written many BAFTA-nominated shows, such as *Globo Loco*, *Basil Brush*, *Ministry of Mayhem* and *The Legend of Dick and Dom*, and he co-wrote the Triskellion trilogy with bestselling crime author Mark Billingham under their pseudonym, Will Peterson.

Body Blow is Peter's second Eddie Savage thriller, sequel to the hugely popular *Long Reach*.